HUNTED
BY
FIRELIGHT

BOOKS BY KRISTA STREET
SUPERNATURAL WORLD NOVELS

Fae of Snow & Ice

Court of Winter
Thorns of Frost
Wings of Snow
Crowns of Ice

Supernatural Curse

Wolf of Fire
Bound of Blood
Cursed of Moon
Forged of Bone

Supernatural Institute

Fated by Starlight
Born by Moonlight
Hunted by Firelight
Kissed by Shadowlight

Supernatural Community

Magic in Light
Power in Darkness
Dragons in Fire
Angel in Embers

Supernatural Standalone Novels

Beast of Shadows

HUNTED
BY
FIRELIGHT

paranormal shifter romance

SUPERNATURAL INSTITUTE
BOOK THREE

KRISTA STREET

PREFACE

Hunted by Firelight is a paranormal shifter romance and is the third book in the four-book *Supernatural Institute* series. The recommended reading age is 18+.

CHAPTER ONE

WYATT

"Avery, I just want to talk to you. That's all." I crept toward the crackling dome she'd erected around herself, the hairs on my arms standing on end the closer I got to the electrical magical apparatus. "I'm not going to hurt you. I promise."

Wariness entered her brown-flecked-with-gold irises, and the scent of fear wafted from her, the sour fragrance permeating the domed shield which rose from the field like a glittering purple star.

A growl rumbled in my throat, coming from my wolf, before I could stop it.

Her eyes flashed wide.

Shit. Damn wolf. "My love, I—"

A huge crack came from the dome, and a punch of potent magic zapped me squarely in the chest.

The force of it made me fly back, my body shooting through the air as Avery's gasp followed.

I landed fifteen feet away, my head whacking against the dirt. For a moment, I couldn't breathe.

Fuuuuuuuuck. That one hurt. Grimacing, I brought a hand to my chest, right to my heart.

One thing I'd learned since midnight? The dome responded to my mate's emotions. Whatever it was she'd created around herself, it was as though it were a part of her.

And she didn't like when I approached it.

Nicholas let out a low whistle. The vamp sat in the grass. Sweat dripped profusely from him as the midday sun burned directly overhead. "That one looked particularly nasty, commander."

With a groan, I sat up, still rubbing my chest as Avery followed my every move from beneath her shield.

"Are you sure she's your mate?" Nicholas drawled.

"Yes," I snapped and massaged my chest.

"It's just that most mates don't try to kill each other when—"

"And most mates don't die and are then reborn with some unknown power in them!"

He raised his hands in surrender. "My, my, so testy. I

was simply pointing out the obvious. No need to bite my head off."

Another growl threatened to rumble in my chest, but I suppressed it. I didn't need another jolt to my heart from the dome. Because as much as I hated it, Nicholas was right. Avery wasn't acting like my mate. She was acting like I was a complete stranger who was out to harm her, and the only way she could stay safe was if she protected herself through any means necessary.

Even if that meant harming me in the process. Not exactly typical mate behavior.

She eyed me again, her expression still wary, but I thought I caught a glimmer of remorse in her gaze.

I scowled. She *should* be remorseful. The shock I'd just taken to the heart would have killed a human.

I straightened my shirt, then stood and prowled back to where I'd been sitting earlier.

With a low snarl, I plopped back down on the grass, my wolf no happier as he paced inside me.

The tall stalks bent beneath me, my heavy weight breaking the delicate plant life when I stretched my legs out. The movement sent a waft of pollen into the air. Wildflowers danced in the breeze as the pale-green sky in the fae lands stretched overhead.

Nicholas and I had been sitting in this field for

nearly twelve hours and had managed to create a large area of wilted foliage.

But it was either that or I created a perimeter of dead flowers as I prowled relentlessly around the magical dome that my mate had encased herself in. Given that my pacing had only heightened the anxious scent coming from her, I'd forced myself to stay sitting.

Well, most of the time.

"I don't know how much more of this I can take." Nicholas fanned his face, grimacing under the sun. Beads of sweat coated his alabaster skin, although streaks of red now scored his cheeks. It was almost noon, so the sun was nearly at its peak.

"You don't need to stay," I told him, keeping my voice quiet so as not to startle Avery again.

"That's what you said three hours ago."

"And I meant it. You're what, five hundred years old? The sun's gotta be hurting."

"I'm five hundred and ninety-three, if you want to be precise."

"Exactly. You're beginning to look partially cooked. Just go, old man. Why don't you head to SF headquarters and report to Wes. I'll stay here. There's no way I'm leaving her."

"Old man." He sneered. "How long have you been waiting to use that one?"

4

I sighed. "Believe it or not, I haven't been. I've been a bit more preoccupied with Avery instead of thinking up ways to bait you." I dragged a hand through my hair, irritation coating my stomach like acid. "Although that hasn't stopped *you* from trying to bait me."

"In my opinion, you deserve it, and as for your first point, I would gladly leave this insufferable heat, but that doesn't end our predicament. What are we going to do about her?" Nicholas pointed at Avery. "She hasn't shown any signs of releasing that . . . whatever *that* is."

That happened to be the impenetrable dome of magic that my mate had built around herself during the night.

Once again, a rare celestial event in the fae lands had done something to Avery.

Only two weeks ago, the Safrinite comet had struck, infecting her with a power that leeched her magic and life source. And last night, it had finally killed her, only to have another celestial event—the fae lands' solar system alignment—resurrect her from the dead.

But she'd come back changed. That event had not only brought her back to life but it had also robbed her of her memories and changed her in ways we didn't understand. New potent power filled her slender body, and it was power none of us could comprehend.

One thing I knew, though, it was immense. Avery

had created the dome after the alignment. She'd never had enough magic to do something like that before.

The magic will erupt in the heir destined to forge our path, creating the path for the gods to be born.

The line from the text in the ancient tome again flashed through my mind. When Avery had awoken, violet light had flashed in her eyes, and colossal power had radiated from her soul.

My stomach turned over as my jaw worked.

A month ago, Avery would have never possessed enough magic to create a protective dome so powerful. Now, she'd created it in a blink.

"The texts Masters Ambrose, Godric, and Romanus found predicted this." Nicholas wiped at the perspiration above his lip. "And only when the Safrinite comet returns will the true prophecy occur. The magic will erupt in the heir destined to forge our path, creating the path for the gods to be born. Only then will we rise."

"I was just thinking about that." I leaned back on my elbows more. "That and the picture Master Ambrose showed us last night."

"The drawing of the fae lands' solar system, the Safrinite comet, and the alignment?"

"Yes, all of it is linked, and she's tied to it. She has to be the heir."

"*She* has a name, you know," Avery called from under her magical dome.

Dammit. Guilt bit me that my mate thought me so callous to speak about her as if she wasn't here, but she was right to be annoyed. I *had* been speaking about her on and off with Nicholas since, for the most part, she'd refused to engage with us.

"You're right." I inched forward on the grass unconsciously, then stopped when I realized what I was doing. "Do you remember what your name is?"

Instead of replying, my mate's forehead puckered. Another troubled look descended over her features like a veil. The annoyed expression she'd worn after hearing Nicholas and I talking about her vanished.

"My name . . . it's, um . . ." She shook her head, then glared at us.

The hopeful feeling in my chest faded, my body withering back into a hunched position. I ripped out a handful of thick grass and threw it. "Shit," I muttered under my breath. "Why can't she remember who she is?"

"That's the million-dollar question, commander," Nicholas replied. "If we knew the answer to that, I doubt we'd be sitting here in this sweltering heat."

My stomach growled for what had to be the twentieth time. None of us had eaten or drunk since the alignment, but I couldn't leave Avery for food and water.

If she bolted, there was a good chance we wouldn't be able to find her given the power she now held.

"I can't handle this anymore. My sincerest apologies, Major Jamison. I'm going to headquarters." Nicholas blurred to a stand, then in a blink he was standing in the forest at its edge. Shade covered him, the thick grove of trees shielding him from the sun's harshest rays. He could walk partly through the forest to the nearest portal.

"You should have done that hours ago," I called to him.

He extended his middle finger.

My lips curved up despite the steady thrum of anxiety that pulsed through me. I still hated the bastard, but he'd proven useful in the past twenty-four hours despite his annoying jabs. Without his help at the Bulgarian libraries, we might not have returned to the fae lands in time to save my mate.

I ripped out another handful of grass, my mood darkening again when I remembered what had happened twelve hours ago.

The haunting message in the ancient tome again blazed its way to the front of my mind.

"Creating the path for the gods to be born," I whispered, then glanced at Avery.

She quickly averted her gaze when we made eye

contact, then drew her knees tighter to her chest before wrapping her arms around them. Her beautiful mahogany hair draped down her back as her full lips thinned into a line. She rocked back and forth, her gaze occasionally darting to me and then to where Nicholas had been, but the vamp had already departed.

She'd been like this for twelve hours, but at least the terrible power she'd initially unleashed when she'd woken—which had created the strangest pausing sensations as if the world had stopped turning—had ceased. Whatever had been birthed inside her following the alignment was either gone or . . . it was dormant and she wasn't using it.

I studied my mate as she watched me warily. She still looked like Avery, like *my* mate. The beautiful curve of her neck, the winged arches of her eyebrows, and the slender legs she cradled to her chest all screamed that she was the woman I loved.

And thankfully, her brown-and-gold eyes looked like hers again, that flashing violet light no longer present. But she still didn't remember me, and more importantly, she didn't appear to remember herself.

I inhaled, taking in her rich lilac scent. That fragrance solidified my belief that she was still *Avery* and not some demon born of a sacrifice who was merely impersonating my mate.

"Avery? I swear, I'm not going to hurt you." I wanted so desperately to touch her, but right now, she didn't want that. But dammit, I had to try to get through to her. "Please, you have to believe me. I would never hurt you. You mean too much to me to even consider that."

She shot me another distrustful glare, and magic sparked in the dome, a charged particle leaping from it.

I winced when it hit me, but at least, that was a small one.

I resumed plucking blades of grass, and tried to act like I didn't have a care in the world. "Your parents are probably wondering how you're doing. You were going to see them again today." I waited, to see if she'd respond, but all she did was press her chin to the tips of her knees and rock more. "Danielle and Bryce Meyers are in Bulgaria right now. They're your parents. They came yesterday from their posts in India. Do you remember? You met with them, reminisced about your childhood, then promised to see them again today. I could bring them to you if you want. Or we could go back to Bulgaria, see them, and get you something to eat."

She bit her lip and darted another glance at me, her gaze fierce.

"All you have to do is release the dome around you, then we can go see them."

Her gaze narrowed. "And what if I do and you hurt me? I've seen how strong you are."

Her question was so quiet, so lacking in trust, that my inner wolf's hackles rose. A protective instinct surged within me, threatening to release a growl from my throat. I swallowed it down, knowing that would only worsen the situation.

"I would never hurt you," I said again.

Her brow furrowed, and even though she looked away, she still whispered, "How do I know I can believe that?"

My nostrils flared, and I resisted the urge to slam my fist into the dirt. My wolf's response was similar.

He snarled and paced in my belly. He'd been as agitated as me once we'd seen how our mate shunned us, and his heightened responses weren't helping.

"Avery—"

"Stop calling me that!" she seethed.

"But it's your name."

"So you say."

I gritted my teeth and tore a hand through my hair. "It's true. Your name is Avery Meyers, and you're twenty-three years old. You just completed three months of new recruit training at the Supernatural Forces. You were supposed to be on your way to the Supernatural Ambassador Institute to begin your new career. You'd be there right now if it hadn't been for the Safrinite comet and what it did to you."

"The Safrinite comet?"

"Yes." I sighed. "It's what started all of this. Two weeks ago, its magic changed you. Your body had a response to it that we don't fully understand. All we know is that it began eating your magic and stealing your life force. It—" I sucked in a breath. "It killed you last night, but the alignment brought you back—"

"Killed me?" A look of horror washed over her face. "Last night? I died?"

"Yes. That's right." I hung my head. *Dammit.* None of this was easy. Even though Avery remembered the English language and was able to converse, she didn't remember anything else.

"Why don't I know who you are?" she asked.

"I honestly don't know. The alignment took something from you." *Or birthed something inside you.* I thought again about that power she'd unleashed and the violet color in her eyes. "But, Avery, *please*, just give me a chance to prove to you that I won't hurt you. Remove the dome, and let me help you."

She glanced up at the buzzing magical dome. "You promise? You promise to the depths of your soul that I can trust you?"

"I promise on my life."

She bit her lip, a frown tightening her features.

The dome shimmered, the translucent purple magic sparkling. It thinned for the merest second, then strengthened. Her eyebrows drew together more, a look of absolute concentration on her face.

The magic glimmered a second time.

A small hole appeared in it.

Then another.

A buzz emitted from my tablet.

Avery's head whipped toward me, and a crackle of power burst across the dome, thickening it to twice the width it was previously.

"What was that?" Her eyes grew wide.

Dammit. Why did I have to get a message right at this moment?

"It's just my tablet." With slow movements, I extracted it and showed her the electronic device. "This is how I communicate with my job. And right now, my boss just sent me a message."

She glowered, then moved as far away from me as the dome allowed.

My nostrils flared. "Shit," I whispered under my breath. It was the closest she'd come to dismantling the barrier, but now she looked like an angry kitten. I was surprised she wasn't hissing again.

"This better be worth it." I tapped the screen on my

tablet, and a message from my boss, Wes McCloy, appeared.

> Any progress?

I scoffed at the irony. *There was.*

If he'd waited another ten minutes perhaps I'd actually have good news to report.

Sighing, I typed in a response.

> No. Magical dome still intact. Her memories are still gone. She's still convinced that I'll hurt her.

His response came readily.

> I'm sending reinforcements. Return to headquarters for a proper debrief when they arrive.

My jaw locked, my finger hovering over my tablet. I nearly typed in, *No.*

But Wes was my boss.

I took a deep breath. *Fucking duty.* I had to follow orders, which meant I had to leave Avery. *Dammit all to hell.*

Wes knew that Avery was my mate. He knew how hard it would be for me to leave her.

Fuming, I closed my eyes and tried to slow my breathing. I pictured Avery as she'd been last night.

An image formed in my mind of her lying on her back, in our bed, back in our chambers in the Bulgarian libraries. She writhed beneath me as I plunged my length inside her, then she screamed when I brought her to climax, right at the moment I claimed her.

My heart ached at the memory. Only last night I'd claimed Avery as my mate in every sense of the word. When I'd been battling my wolf over the need to mark her as ours, in the midst of fucking her, she'd curled her hand around my nape and brought my mouth to her neck.

She'd coaxed me to do it, wanted it, begged me to.

So I had.

I'd bitten into the tender skin on her neck, my wolf coming to the surface just enough to elongate my teeth and fuse my magic with hers. My magic swirled inside her, twining around her limbs, infiltrating her cells, and forever tingeing her scent with mine. All male wolves would have known that she belonged to me.

For two brief hours, she'd been *my* mate—the other half to my soul, the bonded piece to my inner puzzle— and she'd welcomed my magic inside her.

Because of our bond, I felt it when she'd died. The tether that linked us had been severed. And the trauma of it would haunt me forever. I would never forget the feeling of that tiny, delicate thread being cut. It'd felt as if someone had snipped a ribbon. It'd been that fast, that smooth, yet the effects of it had barreled through my veins and torn out my heart.

So last night had not only been the very first time I'd made love to Avery, but it had been the night I lost her, too, and the experience shattered me.

I hung my head. *I want you back, Little Flower. I'll do whatever it takes to get you back.*

A cracking sound in the forest had me lifting my gaze. A second later came the very faint sound of footsteps.

In a blink, I was standing, my hands fisted as heat pulsed under my skin. I scanned the trees. Golden leaves fluttered in the wind. Some of the foliage shimmered a deep-blue and magenta, hinting that the life in this realm was so alien to earth's.

I inhaled, scenting the breeze, but the forest was downwind. A quick assessment of my mate showed Avery as she'd been—still curled into a ball and none the wiser that someone was in the forest watching us.

"Major Jamison?" a woman called.

My tensed shoulders relaxed just as Avery's head snapped up.

"Corporal Morris?" I used Charlotte's new title since

she was now officially a member of Squad Three, having passed her final test.

Avery's former new recruit squad mate emerged from the trees, donned in Squad Three's uniform. Behind her stood a very anxious-looking couple—Avery's parents, Bryce and Danielle Meyers.

Charlotte gave a small smile. "I believe you were told reinforcements were being sent, sir?"

CHAPTER TWO
AVERY

The woman continued to crouch on the other side of the dome, her energy excited and awed. "Babe, this dome is the shit, seriously, even I couldn't penetrate this with an arrow soaked in *kuraia*. But it's been more than twelve hours. Don't you need to eat, drink, and you know, pee or something?"

Pee?

The woman, who called herself Charlotte, stayed hunkered down and was careful not to touch the side of the dome as she chatted with me. Behind her, a middle-aged man and woman sat in the grass, anxiously watching us.

I squirmed again. Was that what was causing this very uncomfortable feeling low in my belly? That I had to pee? Or was having to pee what was causing the rumbling sound in my abdomen?

If one of those sensations meant I had to pee, then she was right. I did need to, quite desperately actually, but when that man—Major Jamison—had been here, even these unusual feelings inside me couldn't have persuaded me to leave the dome.

My breath sucked in when I remembered him. He'd sat in the grass with me after I'd woken up, never leaving, never faltering, and insistent that I knew him. I could tell that he felt things for me. His gaze had been so intense, his eyes glowing at times, and the growls that had come from him let me know that he wasn't fully . . .

I scrunched my eyebrows together. What was that word?

Oh, yes, *human*. I knew that he wasn't fully human, and for some reason, that scared the shit out of me. Not because I feared *him*, but because every time he grew near an unsettling somersaulting feeling began in my stomach.

I didn't understand that feeling either.

And I didn't like it.

It felt too . . . unnerving.

Thankfully, he'd departed when Charlotte and the older couple had shown up, although the displeasure written all over his face had let me know he hadn't wanted to leave.

"So even though your memory is gone, it can't all be gone, right?" Charlotte drawled. "If it was, you wouldn't be able to talk with us since, you know, English is a learned language."

Language. Right. That was the words we were making.

"Will this electrocute me if I touch it?" Charlotte brought a finger closer to the dome, forcing my attention back to her. Buzzing filled my ears as the magic in the curved shield responded.

"Um, I don't know if you should do that. I don't have full control over—"

A loud *zap* hit my ears when an electrically charged particle jumped out and zinged her.

Charlotte's hand whipped back. "Motherfucker! It tried to fry me." She waved her hand, shaking it.

I gave her an apologetic smile. I still didn't entirely understand how this magical dome worked, but I did feel safe under it.

"And to think you made this." She laughed, still waving her hand. "You've got serious game now, girl. Major Jamison wasn't kidding when he said your new magic packed a punch."

My smile faltered. Seriously, who was he? My

uneasiness grew when his image readily appeared in my mind—his incredibly broad shoulders, his strongly cut jaw, his dark hair, and the weeks' worth of beard that graced his cheeks.

He was very easy to look at, but his attractiveness was the deadly sort. He'd had predator written all over him even though he'd promised not to hurt me.

Predator. I cocked my head. What a strange word, but it had popped in my mind when I thought of him. Because somehow I knew that's exactly what he was.

And as a predator, how did I know that I could trust him? Especially when his mere presence did something to my insides.

Ugh. His presence made me feel . . . I grumbled. I didn't know exactly how he made me feel, but everything about him put me on edge in a squirmy sort of way. And not in the I-have-to-pee sort of way.

My fingers curled into my palms again as Charlotte continued talking.

I knew she was trying to put me at ease, and if I were being fully honest with myself, it was kinda working, but *why* couldn't I remember who I was or how I got here?

Charlotte leaned back on the grass, tilting her head to bask in the sun as the couple waited a few yards behind her. "Hey, did I tell you that Eliza's in the

Processing Bay now? She just started her new job there, just like I'm now officially a member of Squad Three. She's loving it so far but has a lot to learn. I think she's secretly sad that she won't see Major Fieldstone anymore. Oh! Speaking of my new commander and squad, whatcha think of my new get-up?" She jumped to standing and pivoted, giving me a clear view of her tall, strong body clad in a full-body black and dark-gray jumpsuit. The jumpsuit was strapped with weapons.

A bow was slung around one of her shoulders along with a quiver of arrows. The deadly weapon rested between her shoulder blades. Various knives and throwing stars were securely fastened into the multiple pockets that graced her legs, and she wore a belt that held one of those tablet thingies that Wyatt had carried too.

"Pretty fancy, eh?" Charlotte grinned, and her auburn hair flashed red in the sunlight. "It sure as hell beats the green cargos and T's we had to wear during training, don't ya think? And do I look badass or what? I especially like all the deadly shit I get to carry now." She waved to the weapons on her legs, then crouched down again and went back to lounging in the grass.

She flashed me another smile. "Now, just between you and me—definitely don't tell Major Fieldstone this

—but half the reason I wanted to join the SF was for this very outfit. It's killer, right?"

I laughed, momentarily forgetting about the power that strummed through my veins. "It's pretty awesome looking," I agreed.

She winked, her eyes twinkling. "I know, right?" She sat up again, all pent-up energy. Even though I didn't remember her, I could tell that she wasn't someone used to sitting still. "I wonder what you'd be doing right now if you'd gone to the Institute."

"The Institute?" I rearranged how I was sitting again. *Damn.* This I-had-to-pee sensation was only getting worse, and the power inside me wasn't helping. It continually coursed through my blood like lightning on water. It was so strong and my urge to urinate was only making it worse.

"Yeah, the Supernatural Ambassador Institute. That's where you would be right now if all this crazy celestial shit hadn't happened to you. You would have been starting your new job."

I frowned, pulling my bottom lip into my mouth to nibble. Major Jamison had said the same thing. "I don't remember that."

Her gaze dimmed, some of her cheer faltering. "I know. It's absolutely crazy what's gone down. Eliza and I had no idea this would happen after you left for

Bulgaria, but what do you say? Do you wanna finally come out of there and hang with me? I've missed you, and I have so much to fill you in about. Namely, the party you missed after our final tests, in which I may have gotten a bit intoxicated since they were serving fairy wine, and I may have hooked up with one of the recruits from our new recruit squad. Surprisingly, he was an absolute animal in bed. In the best way," she added in a rush.

She glanced over her shoulder at the middle-aged man and woman still sitting in the grass behind her. They'd stayed quiet, watching raptly as Charlotte and I talked.

Turning back to me, Charlotte lowered her voice. "Although I don't think the details of that conversation are something your parents want to hear."

Nerves prickled my skin. *My parents. Right. That's who they supposedly are.*

I craned my neck to see around Charlotte. The couple wore worried expressions. But even though I didn't recognize them, I saw myself in their features.

The woman had the same dark hair as me. The man's mouth of a similar shape to mine.

None of it made sense, because even though I didn't know my name, I knew what I looked like, and I knew that I could be their daughter. Yet, I didn't know them.

I abruptly glanced down, my breath coming too fast again.

What the hell happened to me?

"Fuck," I whispered. I wrapped my arms around my legs and began rocking again.

My chest rose unsteadily as the anger, fear, and frustration grew strength inside me. The dome crackled, sending sparks skating along its surface.

Charlotte backed up an inch, her easygoing smile dimming.

I closed my eyes, willing myself to calm down, to not feel so freaked out, but the immense power that burned inside me—it was nearly overwhelming, and I didn't know what to do with it.

Ever since I'd woken up and seen the dark-haired commander and the man he said was a vampire hovering over me . . .

Shit.

I squeezed my eyes tighter, blocking out the sunlight entirely. The force of the energy that hummed in my core, danced through my organs, and rushed through my veins—it was so consuming. So incredibly charged.

I took another deep breath, then another. Whatever this power was, it wanted out, yet I didn't know how to let it escape.

"Avery?" Charlotte said quietly. "Girl, I know you're

scared. I know all of this is so fucking terrifying and confusing, but I'm here to help. I want to help you. You just have to let me."

I opened my eyes to see her pleading expression and the concern on her face.

"We were friends, weren't we?" The energy continued to hum inside me, boiling in my veins and crackling near my skin.

"We were. We still *are*. You, me, and Eliza have been the best of friends for the past three months, but just because you can't remember me right now, that doesn't mean I'm not your friend any longer."

I swallowed, then squirmed again. Seriously, I was going to pee my pants. This feeling was so strong, and this power so overwhelming, that I'd probably urinate lightning.

"Can you remove the dome?" Charlotte tucked a strand of auburn hair behind her ear. "Let's get you out of this heat and somewhere more comfortable."

I squinted at the sun. It wasn't hot under the dome, which apparently meant my magic also regulated the temperature in here, but my lower stomach was now cramping painfully.

I licked my lips. "Okay. I'll try."

Closing my eyes again, I concentrated on the magic vibrating inside me. It hummed through me, as if a part of me. I pictured happy, calming thoughts, or at least, what I thought might calm me.

Hot tea. A slice of cake. Flour dusted on my hands.

Some of the magical humming lessened, as if the tuning fork vibrating inside me didn't thrum quite so loudly.

"That's it," Charlotte whispered.

I scrunched my eyes together more. *Laughter and smiles. The smell of cookies. Sunshine on my face.*

"You're almost there," Charlotte said encouragingly.

The scent of baking bread. Dancing till dawn. Silky flower petals between my fingers.

My breathing deepened, growing even. The vibrations lessened even more, not gone, just . . . less.

"Avery?" Charlotte said.

I opened my eyes, not because I knew that was my name, but because I'd learned that was what everyone called me.

She smiled. "Look."

I glanced around me as warmth from the sun hit my skin. My jaw dropped. The dome was gone. Entirely gone. "It worked," I exclaimed.

"Damn straight it did."

"But how?"

"You tell me."

I pushed to a stand, my legs protesting after sitting

for so long just as the couple behind Charlotte burst into grins.

"Well done, Avery," the woman called out.

I managed a placating smile, but my internal power still coursed through me, racing along my electrical synapses in bursts. At least right now, it didn't feel quite so daunting.

"What made you release it?" the man asked.

I shrugged. "I thought about . . . happy things." I frowned. "But how did I know about all of those things? How did I know those things made me happy and would calm me when I don't actually remember any of them?"

Charlotte shrugged. "No idea, but one step at a time, eh? In time you may remember." She held out her hand to me. "Come on. You've gotta be busting if that little dance you're doing is any indication."

My cheeks flushed because my legs were crossed, and I kept bouncing up and down.

Charlotte leaned down and whispered, "There are trees right over there. Nobody will think twice if you pop a squat."

I muffled a laugh, somehow understanding what she meant, as the man and woman behind Charlotte took a step toward us. Their relief was so evident at my escape from under the dome that it nearly eclipsed my need to pee.

Nearly.

"I'll be back in a minute," I told them, then dashed toward the trees.

THANKFULLY, I didn't pee lightning. But the relief I felt when the liquid rushed from my body . . .

I needed to remember that the next time my lower stomach ached it was probably due to needing to pee.

Wind whistled softly through the trees as I stood and arranged my clothing. While thinking about my predicament still freaked me out, the fact that I no longer felt physically uncomfortable helped, if only a little.

Charlotte's and the middle-aged couple's voices carried to me on the breeze. I couldn't see them since I'd stepped far into the trees to have privacy, but I knew they were waiting for me.

I placed my hand on a tree. Its bark felt like rough fibers under my skin. I ran my finger up and down it, marveling at its texture, when a branch cracked behind me.

I whipped around, my eyes wide, as images of Major Jamison returning flooded my mind.

But nobody was there.

Shaking my head at my reaction, I began walking toward where I'd entered the forest when another crack sounded.

I swirled around again only to see . . .

Nothing.

"Seriously, calm yourself," I whispered under my breath.

Still, a sense of uneasiness filled me. I knew I was alone in the forest, yet I didn't feel alone.

Twirling back around, I picked up my pace. Vibrations from the magic inside me hummed through my veins, skating along my skin, and electrifying my nerves.

By the time I reached the forest's edge, I was running.

"Whoa, girl," Charlotte said when I emerged from the trees and raced toward them. "You look like you saw a ghost."

I stopped at her side, heaving. A ghost? An image of a translucent shape took form in my mind. *Ah, someone that has died but has not left the world. That's what a ghost is.*

But then I knitted my eyebrows together. How come I remembered things like a ghost but not who I was or these strange sensations inside me?

The people who called themselves my parents took a step toward me.

"Everything okay?" the woman asked. "Charlotte's right. You look scared."

Some of my harsh breaths slowed. I still didn't recognize her face or her voice, but she seemed genuinely concerned. I shook my head. This was all so confusing. "I'm fine. I just heard some snapping branches in the trees, like someone was walking in the woods or something."

Charlotte tensed, one hand going for her bow, the other for an arrow.

I waved a hand. "It's nothing. Really. Nobody was there. I think I'm just stressed and hyped up after everything that's happened."

Charlotte released her grip, but the tense lines around her eyes didn't lessen. "We should head toward the capital. We have a room waiting in one of their inns. General McCloy has decided he wants us to stay here in the fae lands. He and Major Jamison think whatever happened to you is directly related to this realm and are hopeful that something here will fix your memory."

Bryce—or rather, my father—nodded in agreement. "I'm just so thankful that Wyatt got you here in time to save you."

"You were so weak yesterday," Danielle agreed. "But today . . ." She looked me up and down. "You look so strong and healthy, and Wyatt said the healing witches think your memory may return in time."

"You've spoken with . . . *him?*" I couldn't bring myself to say Wyatt's name. I was more comfortable calling him Major Jamison since calling him *Wyatt* made that damned fluttery feeling begin in my stomach again.

Danielle nodded. "He called us this morning with an update."

Charlotte checked her device. "We should get a move on. I've been instructed to take you to the Hog's Head Inn once I got you out of the dome." She scanned the field. "Now, there should be an enchanted carpet arriving any second."

I scanned the horizon. A mile away, the capital gleamed. Tall golden gates surrounded the city that was built on a naturally rising mound. I squinted. Thatched-roofed houses, gleaming walkways, and shops seemed to fill the city, and at the top of the steep hill, an imposing castle soared.

My shoulders slumped. I didn't recognize anything about the capital either.

"Here it comes!" Charlotte said.

My eyes widened when a large carpet flew toward us, hovering just above the grass. It glided to a halt a foot away from us, and bobbed up and down, as if waiting.

"After you." When I just stood there, Charlotte laughed. "Just hop on it. It won't bite. I promise."

My stomach let out another growl, so I slapped a hand over it. "Sorry. I don't know why it keeps doing that."

"It's because you're hungry. We'll get something to eat at the inn. Now, onboard you go." She herded me toward the carpet.

I tentatively raised my foot and placed my weight on the carpet. It dipped slightly when I stood but not much. I marveled at the feel of the carpet fibers sliding under my shoes. It didn't feel solid, more like what one would feel if walking on a waterbed.

I frowned and plopped down. *How do I know what a waterbed is?*

Before I could contemplate my patchy memories, my parents and Charlotte were seated cross-legged beside me, and then we took off.

I yelped when the carpet flew over the grass, picking up speed with each second. Wind blew around us, and the scent of wildflowers filled my nose.

Unable to help it, I laughed.

My parents and Charlotte joined in.

"These are a delightful way to travel," my mother said above the wind. "We used to come here when you were a kid, just to commission a carpet ride."

My laughter faded at the hopeful look on her face. I gave her an apologetic shrug. "I'm sorry. I don't remember."

Her smile remained but looked forced. "No matter. In time you probably will." She patted my hand, then laughed when we shot over a small mound in the land only to dip down on the other side.

"I fell off one of these a few years ago," Bryce said good-naturedly from behind me. "I was fumbling with my phone, trying to get it out of my pocket. I wasn't paying attention to where I was sitting. We shot around a curve, and I tumbled right off."

My lips parted as I pulled my hair into one hand to keep it from blowing into my eyes. "Were you hurt?"

Danielle rolled her eyes. "Yes, he was, and hopefully he learned his lesson from it."

"What happened?" Charlotte asked.

Bryce laughed. "I broke my arm, but it was easily healed within a week since I got straight to a healing center in the capital. That was when you were in your first year of university in the UK, Avery. You'd wanted to come visit me, but I'd insisted it wasn't a big deal, so you stayed at school."

His eyes dimmed, and my stomach clenched, although the sensation wasn't from needing to pee. Since my stomach didn't make a sound, I was guessing it wasn't hunger either. Whatever this new sensation was, it was caused by Bryce and Danielle wanting me so desperately to remember them.

"Almost there," Charlotte called out.

The tall gates to the capital appeared. Two large men with golden skin and wicked-looking spears stood on either side of the gate. As we sailed closer to them on the carpet, they stepped toward one another and extended their spears to make an X. A loud clang reverberated through the air as the carpet drifted to a stop.

"This will just take a moment." Charlotte hopped off the carpet and sauntered toward the sentries. They said something to her, and she responded.

Their eyes turned silver, but whatever she'd said seemed to make them happy.

A second later, Charlotte was back on the carpet and we were flying at a more controlled speed through the now open gates.

"Only a couple minutes from here." She grinned. "Then we can get settled and have something to eat until everyone else arrives."

I tensed as we flew over the golden walkways. "Everyone else?"

Charlotte nodded. "Major Jamison's coming back at some point today, and he's probably bringing other SF members too."

CHAPTER THREE
WYATT

Nicholas stood in the corner of Wes's office, while my boss sat behind his large desk. Bright sunlight shone through the tall windows behind him. Bare trees were scattered along the Idaho hills, reminding me of skeletons and bones.

Wes steepled his fingers. "So it's agreed. We'll keep Avery in the fae lands until we learn more. Again, are you sure she's not a danger to others?" he asked me.

"I don't believe she is, sir." I leaned forward, resting my forearms on my knees. "She seems more intent on protecting herself than harming anyone."

Wes knew that the dome had magically shocked me, but it'd been in response to something I'd done. Avery hadn't shown aggression for no reason. She'd been in pure defense mode.

36

Wes nodded. "That's reassuring, but I still want you to take Farrah back with you. She can assess Avery and get a better understanding of the new power inside her. If she detects any instability, Avery will need to be moved to a safe house. We can't risk any supernatural's safety."

"Understood, sir." My palms itched as I sat on the edge of my seat. My wolf prowled in my belly. He'd been on edge ever since I'd left my mate. "Is there anything else?"

Wes angled himself toward Nicholas. "Have the gargoyles found anything new?"

"I believe they found a few more references to the comet, but I won't know the details until I return to the libraries." The vampire lounged against the wall, one foot crossed over the other as he occupied the small shaded area in the room that the sun didn't touch. His blond hair brushed his shoulders, artfully tousled.

"Keep me posted. I'd like a full write-up by tomorrow."

Nicholas inclined his head. "Of course, sir."

Wes nodded toward the holographs glowing around us. The central large globe depicted earth, but the sphere next to it showed the fae lands' planet. "Looks like Charlotte's made progress."

The holograph automatically zoomed in, showing

the glowing dot on the sphere, indicating my former new recruit's coordinates. She inched steadily toward the capital. Charlotte was on the move, which only meant one thing—she'd coaxed Avery out from under the dome.

"I noticed the same thing, sir." I stood from my chair, no longer able to sit still. If Charlotte was moving toward the capital, she was taking my mate to the inn as her orders directed.

Wes dipped his head. "You're dismissed, Major."

I was already at the door, opening it before the last word left his mouth. I felt Nicholas's gaze follow me. I'd barely spoken to the vampire since arriving back at headquarters. I knew that would soon change. If the gargoyles had indeed found new information, an imminent meeting with the vamp was in my near future.

"Safe travels, commander," Nicholas called good-naturedly.

I dipped my head curtly. With any luck, I'd arrive in the fae lands shortly after my mate reached the Hogs' Head Inn—a popular establishment in the capital for weary travelers. The SF often used it for business purposes—it was where I'd stayed during my recent month in the fae lands while on assignment. We also used the inn when moving prisoners or had to conduct short meetings with local fae and needed a private room to do so.

I texted Farrah, the SF's healing center's most prestigious healing witch, telling her to meet me at the SF garage. I didn't give her much time to ready herself. I knew I should, but being so far from my mate was beginning to take its toll.

I needed to see Avery.

And I *needed* her to remember me.

IT WAS midafternoon by the time Farrah, and I stood at the capital's gates. The sentries scanned us, then watched us pass, their humanoid faces blank and devoid of emotion.

Farrah carried her monitoring equipment in a large duffel bag. I'd offered to carry it, multiple times, but she'd declined.

We passed a vendor on the street just inside the capital. Kebabs of spicy meat hung from his stand. The heavy fragrance clung to the air like a perfume.

"Tell me more about Avery's symptoms, Major," Farrah said in a shrewd voice when we hopped onto the sidewalk. "Can she truly not remember anything?"

I shook my head. "She remembers language, but beyond that—no, I don't think so. Although, she mostly refuses to speak to me. Maybe she remembers more than I realize."

"But she doesn't even know who she is? Not even her name?"

"No, not even her name as far as I'm aware."

"Then your initial suspicion that she can't remember anything is probably accurate. Knowledge of self is usually the last to go when someone's mind is jeopardized."

The street angled upward, and Farrah's breathing increased. She began panting, and I held my hand out again for her bag, but she shook her head.

"And you say that she physically *died* last night right before the alignment?" she asked between breaths. "But when the alignment occurred, she was abruptly brought back to life?"

My steps paused. Remembering that moment made my heart squeeze. Because seeing Avery pass away, right in front of me . . . I would never forget that.

"Major?"

I jerked upright and resumed my pace. "That's right. She died right beforehand. I'm sure of it."

I didn't tell Farrah how I knew that. The mating bond Avery and I'd briefly shared had been snipped when she'd died, as though an entity had cut the thread which connected us. The only time that happened naturally was at the moment of a mate's death, so I *knew* to the depth of my bones that Avery had physically died. I hadn't mistaken that.

"But she's different now. Not only did the alignment rob her of her memories, but she has a new power inside her too." I described the tremendous power that had initially erupted in her, how her eyes had flashed violet, and how she'd created the dome to protect herself.

"And she maintained that dome for over twelve hours?" When I nodded, Farrah hoisted her bag higher up her shoulder. A light sheen of sweat now coated her brow, drawing attention to the graying hair on her head. "Interesting. I've never heard of such a thing."

"That makes two of us." I waved ahead. "The inn's just up there. Not much longer." I signaled for her to follow me around the corner to the inn's street.

Farrah let out a grateful sigh.

A fae couple passed us on the sidewalk, their hands joined. They were all smiles and had eyes only for each other, but when they felt the energy radiating off me—alpha energy I was having a hard time controlling—they adjusted their path and crossed the street.

I was too tired to feel guilty even though my magic

was affecting supernaturals around me. At least Farrah wasn't complaining, although, given her job in which she commonly worked with male werewolves, she was probably used to it. That and something told me Farrah was not one prone to complaining.

She gritted her teeth when the sidewalk again angled upward, but at least the inn came into view in the distance.

Three blocks down, the small establishment rose two stories from street level but sat back from the road as a small fenced yard graced its front. Its typical fae thatched roof shone in the sun. Old boards that were painted a dark blue graced its outer walls, and a wooden sign hung suspended over the main door. A hog's head emblem was carved into the siding, typical of establishments created around five hundred years ago.

Considering the capital had been around since ancient Egyptian times on earth, this establishment wasn't considered a historical relic, but still, it had stood the test of time. More than a few wars in the past few hundred years could have destroyed it, but it was still standing.

"And what's the plan regarding Ms. Meyers after I assess her?" Farrah asked after wiping the sweat from her brow.

"With any luck, the gargoyles will have more answers soon. Hopefully they'll find a clue that will help rid Avery of her new magic and will help us find a way to restore her memories. Until then, we need to keep her safe."

Farrah gave me a confused look. "Safe from whom? Herself? Or is she being threatened?"

I stiffened. It was a valid question. As far as I was aware, nobody was threatening my mate, but we also didn't fully know what role Avery played in all that had happened to her.

Words from the ancient texts again filtered through my thoughts. *For on the night of the heir's conception, the great prophecy will begin. The stars will amass to twice their size, and the magic will be born in the fated starlight couple. And only when the Safrinite comet returns will the true prophecy occur. The magic will erupt in the heir destined to forge our path, creating the path for the gods to be born. Only then will we rise.*

My hands curled into fists.

But who will rise? The new power inside her? Is that what it meant?

My thoughts drifted to the drawing of the alignment. A group of robed men had been depicted beneath it. We still hadn't identified them.

We'd only become aware of the ancient tomes and scrolls in the past two days. All of that information was still so new, and we didn't understand what all of it meant.

Nicholas and I had figured out that Avery's parents were the starlight couple, and Avery was the heir, but beyond that, the only thing I knew was that the ancient promise was ominous.

"Right now, we don't know," I finally replied. "So our job is to keep her safe."

"What about the new magic she possesses?" Farrah asked when we crossed the second block. "Do you believe others are safe to be around her?"

I sighed. It was the same concern Wes had voiced and was the entire reason Farrah accompanied me to the inn. "To be completely honest, I don't know that either. I have a feeling we haven't seen the half of what she's capable of."

That thought had been toying in the back of my mind all day. If Avery was capable of making the dome, she had incredibly strong power inside her, especially since she'd constructed that magical shield uncon-sciously. *Imagine what she would be capable of if she actually tried to use her magic and controlled it.*

"But she's never purposefully tried to hurt anybody since she woke up," I added, thinking of the remorse I'd seen on her face when she hurt me. "And the Gods know, she now has the power to."

Farrah nodded solemnly. "She was never an aggressive person before the Safrinite comet and planetary alignment from what I saw. Perhaps her good nature has stayed with her."

Hearing that helped ease some of the tension coiling inside me. It wasn't just the lilac scent around Avery that confirmed she was still the woman I knew. Her actions also supported that. Farrah was right. When Avery had felt threatened, she'd gone on the defense—creating the dome. She hadn't lashed out at anyone. And the few times her dome's magic had zapped me, she'd looked genuinely horrified, another reaction I would expect to see in my mate.

Because the Avery I knew would never willingly hurt somebody else unless she was threatened, and the fact that she *hadn't*, despite all that had happened to her in the past twenty-four hours, only proved that she was still my mate. Still *my* Avery.

She just didn't remember herself.

"You seem tense," Farrah commented as our feet tapped along the golden walkway. We hopped off the sidewalk, crossing the final intersection to the inn.

"What makes you say that?"

"Other than the alpha power coming off you?" Farrah gave a pointed look to my hands.

My breath sucked in when I saw the dark hairs sprouting through my skin. *Damn.* I was losing it. Not only was my internal magic radiating off me like a poorly controlled furnace, but I'd also physically allowed my wolf to emerge without realizing it.

"I take it my eyes are glowing too?"

"Yep," Farrah said as we approached the inn's door. "They're bright gold and have been since the SF garage."

I curled my fingers into my palms, digging my nails into the skin. I took a few deep breaths until my wolf finally submitted to my suppression. "My wolf's been a bit on edge."

I didn't mention that this was because I was away from my mate when she needed me most. Any male wolf would have a hard time controlling himself in a similar situation.

Farrah cocked her head, breathing heavily as we stopped at the inn's front stoop in the shade. She studied my features. "Is this all because you've developed feelings for Ms. Meyers? Which I know you have, given what I've witnessed, so don't even try to deny it."

"I wasn't going to." Mostly because I no longer needed to. Avery wasn't an SF member anymore. Her position had ended the day after her final test, right after we'd left for the Bulgarian libraries. I could freely date her with no consequences. "And yes, these reactions are because I've been away from her. It's been hard to control my wolf."

The healing witch plopped her hands on her hips. "You're probably also having a hard time because you're tired. Anyone with eyes can see that you haven't been sleeping. When was the last time you slept, Major?"

My lip curled. "I don't see how that is any of your concern."

She cocked an eyebrow. "My orders were to ensure the health of all involved on this assignment. *You* fall under this assignment."

I sighed since I knew she wasn't going to let this go.

"Well?" she demanded. "How long has it been since you slept?"

"Two days."

She muttered something under her breath, then awkwardly pulled her tablet out from one of her robe's deep pockets. She began tapping on it.

I suppressed a growl. "What are you writing?"

"Just a reminder to give you a sleeping draught tonight. You won't be helpful to anybody if you run yourself ragged."

"I'm fine," I snapped, but a rough growl erupted from me despite trying to stop it.

She rolled her eyes. "Clearly."

A snarl again rose in my chest, but I managed to suppress that one. As much as I hated to admit it, Farrah was right. I did need to sleep, but sleep deprivation had never stopped me from doing my job in the past and it sure as hell wouldn't stop me now. Besides, during commander training we were required to go a full week without sleep while still fully functioning. Two days compared to that was nothing.

Farrah rearranged her bag again and placed her hand on the inn's golden metal door handle.

I pushed the door open for her, the hinges creaking, so she wouldn't have to struggle with the door and her bag.

She grumbled a thanks, and I inclined my head, but as soon as the door opened further, a distant, subtle lilac scent hit me.

My head whipped up, my pulse racing. My wolf whined eagerly in my belly. My mate had been in this room recently, probably in the past hour.

Nostrils flaring, I pushed the door completely open and followed Farrah inside.

The sting of potent magic pummeled my skin when I stepped over the threshold. It felt as if I'd pushed through a heavy drape. Like most business establishments in the fae lands, a magical ward encircled the property, keeping out individuals with nefarious endeavors.

Inside, the low ceiling nearly brushed the top of my head. A cold, ancient-looking fireplace took up the far wall. Several old stuffed chairs, of various sizes to accommodate different supernatural and fairy species, sat in a semi-circle in front of it. And the carpet beneath our feet was so thin and threadbare that, not for the first time, I wondered if it was as old as the tilting, uneven walls of this half-millennium-old building.

A couple was in front of us, checking in, so Farrah and I hung back.

"May I help you?" the fairy working at the counter asked the couple. He stood no taller than four feet. Horns sprouted from the top of his head, curling like a ram's, and hooves peeked out of the bottom of his navy trousers.

Farrah drifted closer to me, then said under her breath, "Is he a Silten fairy?"

"He is," I replied quietly. "His name's Filestaira. He's been working here for a few years now."

A smile curved her lips. "I've never seen one before since they usually avoid this continent. In fact, I've only ever met Nolus fairies. Have you met any of the other fae races?"

"A few, but like you, I've worked mostly with the Nolus."

Farrah continued to watch in delight as the Silten fairy went through his routine while checking in the couple. He ran a gnarled finger down his open ledger, searching for the reservation. I studied him, inhaling his damp, earthy scent and subtle musk.

Farrah was right that it was unusual to see a Silten fairy in the capital—a species that normally only resided on the continent across the Adriastic sea. And since all of the fairies who worked for the SF were Nolus fae, I wasn't surprised she hadn't met a Silten before.

"I always wished that a Silten, Solis, or Lochen fairy would come work for the SF. I'd love to get to know those species."

"Don't hold your breath," I whispered back.

She sighed. "Yes, yes, I know. If they never apply for any positions, it's not like we can hire any."

I chuckled. She had a point. None of those species worked for the SF, not because the SF was biased, but because the Silten fae—like the other fairy species in this realm—wanted nothing to do with earth.

It also didn't help that most of the fae species kept to themselves and their corners of this realm. The fae races looked vastly different from one another, and they didn't like to mix.

Unlike the Nolus fairies that resided in the capital and this continent, the Silten fae didn't have various shades of hair color, pointy teeth, glowing skin, or otherworldly strength. Tails, hooves, scales, and horns were the common features of Silten fae.

Silten fae also lived differently and preferred more natural accommodations. They were often found in underground dens, hollow logs, and wooded forests. As far as I knew, none of them owned houses or had any interest in cities.

Unfortunately, it was those inherent differences that made Nolus fairies believe that the Silten fae were lower class, so I wasn't surprised that few wanted to live here.

The couple finished checking in, so Farrah and I stepped forward.

Filestaira's mouth twisted in a smile when he saw me. "Major Jamison. Checking in?"

"Yes, although the rest of my party should already be here."

"Ah yes, they are." The fairy checked his ledger, his strange accent lilting his words. "The other guests in your reservation checked in an hour ago. Now, if you'll kindly place your hand here."

He waved at the opaque sphere that looked like a glass ball at the end of the counter, and I placed my hand on it.

Magic enveloped my palm, its glittering bands holding me in place. The sphere glowed brightly. A second passed, and the magic released me just as luminescent words erupted across the ledger, as if being written out of thin air.

Once my name, address, and identifying information were fully written, the words dimmed until they resembled the other ink-spewed words written across the page.

"You're all checked in, Major Jamison." He turned to Farrah, then waved at the opaque ball. "Please do the same."

Farrah also complied until her details magically appeared beneath mine on the ledger.

When finished, the fairy slid two keys across the wooden counter. "Is there anything else you need?" He smiled again, his square teeth like blocks in his slightly protruding mouth.

"No, thanks, Filestaira." I pocketed my key. "Are the others in our party in their rooms?"

He cocked his head, his large eyes blinking. "I wouldn't know, Major Jamison. We don't keep tabs on our guests. All I know is that they checked in an hour ago."

I grunted just as Farrah picked up her bag.

"Second floor, end of the hall!" Filestaira called as Farrah and I headed toward the stairs.

I waved a thanks and pushed open the door to the stairwell.

I didn't try to help Farrah with her bag again, since I knew she would deny my assistance, and despite telling myself to wait for her, my pace picked up.

Avery's scent grew stronger with every step I took. I bounded up the stairs three at a time, the wood beneath my soles creaking in protest.

When I reached the second floor, I hurried to the end of the hall, knocked once on the door, before inserting the key and opening it.

Avery startled when I stepped over the threshold, a soft yelp escaping her.

A shimmer of magic erupted around her, not forming into the dome again, but electric sparks abruptly sizzled in the air, and her eyes flashed violet for the merest second.

For a moment, I couldn't move. I soaked up her presence, inhaling her surprise, which smelled like rainwater, and then trailed my gaze over every inch of her.

She wore the same clothes from last night, the ones I had dressed her in after we'd made love and she'd fallen into a deathly sleep. Dark shadows rimmed the bottoms of her eyes. Disheveled hair fluttered down her back, which wasn't surprising since Charlotte had them travel here on an enchanted carpet. The wind on those could be brutal.

But it was the immediate guarded look in her features that stopped all excitement from racing through me.

As before, an apprehensive scent crept into the lilacs, replacing the brief rainwater one.

Charlotte pushed away from the wall, the picture of SF perfection in her military getup. "Major Jamison, it's good to see you again, sir." She stood straighter, coming to attention.

I dipped my head. "Corporal Morris."

Panting came from the hallway, then Farrah appeared at the door a second later. Her chest heaved, and she dropped her heavy bag the second she stepped into the room. "Well, I have to say, I've never attempted to run up two flights of stairs while carrying equipment. I can't say I'll do it again."

"I did offer to carry it," I reminded her.

Avery's wide eyes turned to Farrah, but upon seeing the healing witch, some of the apprehension in her scent dimmed. So she didn't feel skittish around Farrah.

I smothered the scowl that wanted to etch onto my face. Considering Avery's parents sat on the bed just behind her, she wasn't afraid of Bryce or Danielle either.

In other words, so far, she was only afraid of *me*.

My fingers again curled into my palms. I resisted the urge to punch a hole through the wall, because something told me *that* wouldn't put my mate at ease.

"Avery." Farrah dipped her head toward my mate. "It's nice to see you again, although, I'm guessing you don't remember me."

Avery shook her head, making her dark hair sway. "No, I don't."

"This is Farrah Cumberland," I said more gruffly than I intended. "She's one of the healing witches that works for the Supernatural Forces. She's been meeting with you daily for nearly two weeks." I searched my mate's face for a flicker of recognition or a flare of awareness, but . . . nothing. A dash of ice filled my belly. "Do you recognize anything about her?"

Avery frowned, her gaze sweeping over the healing witch. Lines appeared around Avery's mouth when her lips pursed.

She shook her head. "No, I don't remember any of you."

Bryce and Danielle shifted on the bed behind her. They shared an anxious look, then her mother reached forward, placing a comforting hand on Avery's shoulder.

Surprisingly, Avery didn't jump. A swell of envy

rushed through me. So other people could touch my mate, but I couldn't.

But then that worried look returned to Avery's face. "Why can't I remember anything?"

She abruptly stood and moved to the corner of the room. Magic zapped in the air around her. She hadn't erected the domed barrier . . . yet.

Shit.

But just when I lifted my foot to rush toward her, intent on calming the panic coating her scent, Charlotte whistled, a grin spreading across her face as she sauntered toward her.

"Babe, seriously, your magic is the shit. But as much as I love it, I also think you need to cool it. Your memories will probably return in time, and everybody in this room is someone you already know, and is only here to help you. Promise." Without a moment's hesitation, Charlotte reached for Avery's hand. She threaded her fingers through Avery's, then squeezed.

Silence descended over the room as everyone held their breath.

When a small, embarrassed smile tilted Avery's lips up, a collective release of breaths followed. Score one for Corporal Morris, the newest member to the SF who just proved how worthy she was of being a numbered squad member.

Charlotte laughed and pulled Avery into a hug. Avery tentatively returned it.

My chest heaved as I took in the obvious affection between the two women. For whatever reason, Charlotte's blasé, down-to-earth attitude resonated with my mate; it comforted her in a way I hadn't been able to in the sixteen hours since the alignment.

And while I was happy that somebody had connected with Avery since her life had been turned upside down, I would also be lying to myself if I said I wasn't jealous as fuck.

Because in only a few short hours, Charlotte had earned Avery's trust—something I hadn't been able to do in sixteen hours despite coveting it more than anything.

My wolf snarled, his hackles rising. He didn't like it any more than I did.

Granted, Charlotte was a woman, the same age as my mate, and a friend, so it wasn't overly surprising that the two had connected, but I wanted my mate to turn to *me* for help and comfort.

Even though most humans would have cringed at my possessive nature, amongst wolves, it was considered normal. Everybody in the supernatural world knew that a mated werewolf male would do anything to protect his mate. Whether that be to shelter her, comfort her, or be whoever she needed him to be in whatever moment—a male considered it *his* job to do so. Satiating that need soothed our instincts. It was in our nature to be the missing piece to our mate's puzzle.

Yet I couldn't even manage the simplest provisions that my mate needed right now. I plowed a hand through my hair.

The movement seemed to catch Avery's attention. She darted a glance my way, her tongue slipping out to lick her lips uneasily.

My hand fell. *Fucking hell.* I couldn't even show my displeasure right.

A subtle push of alpha magic escaped me. Charlotte grimaced when it hit her. Avery, however, showed no outward reaction to it, and her parents were so consumed with watching their daughter that I doubted they even noticed that I'd once again lost control.

Farrah, however, gave me a pointed look. I could practically read her unspoken message—that I needed to take a step back, get some decent sleep, and get my head back in the game.

If only it were that easy.

Farrah hoisted her bag onto the bed, then unzipped it. "I brought several of my scanners along, Avery. I'd like to run a few tests right now, if that's all right?"

"Tests?" Avery's hands twisted. She shot a worried look toward Charlotte.

Her friend merely shrugged. "She's not gonna hurt you if that's what you're worried about. I think you should let her run the tests. The sooner we figure out what happened to you, the sooner we can fix your memory."

Avery nodded, and her twisting fingers loosened. "You're sure?"

Charlotte crossed her arms and leaned against the wall. "Girl, I'll never steer you wrong."

Some of the frown lines puckering Avery's forehead smoothed.

"Okay, that's fine." Avery's gaze darted to me again. "What do you need me to do?" she asked Farrah.

"Lie down on the bed so I can apply some probes."

"Do I need to undress?"

Farrah eyed Avery's loose T-shirt. "No, I can slip everything on under your clothing."

Avery's attention slid my way again, her scent so potent it took on a bitter taste, like dandelion greens. Her hands fiddled at her sides, before she locked them together in front of her. She shuffled her feet, the anxiety pouring off her in waves so strong I could've smelled the emotion two blocks away.

My wolf began pacing inside me, and I was two seconds away from doing the same in this room.

"Does he need to be here for this?" Avery asked Charlotte under her breath.

I stilled. My mate's whispered comment was like a punch to my gut.

Charlotte cast me a veiled look of pity.

"I can step out if you prefer," I told Avery.

She nodded quickly, then shuffled her feet again.

I walked stiffly to the door, my footsteps silent. I wrenched it open and was just about to leave when a loud growl came from Avery's stomach.

Spinning around, I scowled. "Has she not eaten?" I snapped at Charlotte.

My former new recruit shrugged apologetically. "I ordered food an hour ago, sir. It's still not here."

I stormed back to the door. "I'll get it. Just get the damned tests done," I barked at Farrah.

The door slammed behind me before any of them could respond, the sting of my mate's rejection biting me like a venomous snake. It wasn't lost on me that Avery had allowed everybody else to stay in that room except me.

I knew I was losing it again. Letting my temper get the best of me was no way for a commander to be acting, so I stopped halfway down the hall and forced myself to take deep steadying breaths until I reined in my anger.

But dammit, apparently the only thing I was good for anymore was fetching food for my mate. Fuck knew I'd failed at everything else that I'd tried.

Grumbling, I headed toward the stairs again, cursing the Safrinite comet and whatever sick joke the universe was playing on me and my mate. But if she wanted food, then dammit, I was bringing her food.

CHAPTER FOUR
AVERY

"This won't take long. Please lie down." Farrah, the woman in the long robe with a no-nonsense attitude, gestured toward the bed closest to the wall.

I lay on it, the soft comforter sliding against my back. Even though I didn't have to undress for her to apply the probes, Bryce still turned to face the window until she was done.

When finished, I breathed a little easier that attaching the probes had been painless and quick, even though the lingering magic from *him* still shimmered in the air.

Magic hummed around me when the probes activated, yet my attention still focused on the feel of Major Jamison. I couldn't see his magic, but I'd felt when it'd hit me right before he left, the powerful wave like an ocean tsunami. It hadn't bothered me, but I'd felt it so strongly. The man was *powerful*.

That fluttering started in my stomach again when I remembered his stormy eyes as he'd stalked out of the room.

"This will only take a minute," Farrah said, pulling my attention back to her.

She picked up some kind of handheld scanner. One thing I was quickly coming to learn about these people was that they relied heavily on technology. Most of them carried those weird tablet things. Farrah was no different. She positioned her device directly over me, all of her attention on it.

"Here we go."

She tapped a button, and a colorful display of lasers erupted from the machine. Like the probes, I didn't feel anything other than a vibration of magic as the lasers bathed me in their light.

Once finished, she tapped a button on her machine and its quiet whirring noise vanished. She gave me a brief smile. "All done."

Before I could reply, she was removing the probes from my skin, peeling them off like Band-Aids.

"That was fast," I managed.

She flashed me a smile. "Told you it wouldn't take long."

"So what does the report say?" Charlotte asked, looking over Farrah's shoulder.

Charlotte's jumpsuit glimmered when she placed her hands on her hips. I had no idea what material it was made of, but it appeared thick and moved like a second skin.

"The report is calculating now." Farrah's focus remained on the device.

Curiosity got the better of me, so I swung my legs over the bed to stand and join them. Bryce and Danielle did, too, and all five of us hovered over the machine like we were peering into an aquarium full of exotic fish.

Numbers began to appear. Then graphs.

Farrah's eyebrows shot to her hairline.

I cocked my head. "Is something wrong?"

She cleared her throat. "Um, no, it's just . . . surprising." She waited until all of the data populated, her eyes growing wider with each new calculation.

"Well?" I said.

She worked a swallow, then tapped the screen. It went blank. "Do you mind if I run the scan again?"

"Seriously?" Charlotte's eyebrows shot up. "Is this one inaccurate?"

"Not necessarily." Farrah waved toward the bed. "If

you don't mind, Avery, I want to ensure the second set of data matches the first one."

I did as she asked and waited quietly for the second scan to finish. When complete, we all crowded around the device for a second time.

"Well?" Charlotte placed her hands on her hips. "Is the data the same?"

Farrah took a deep breath, fascination filling her eyes. "Indeed it is. I've never seen anything like it." She sat on the bed, patting for me to join her.

As soon as I sat, she proceeded to show me all of the graphs, miniature scans, and lines. Her voice grew more animated with every second that passed.

"Your power is truly off the charts. I've never seen any supernatural on earth with power this strong. I would love to run these scans again at headquarters—if Major Jamison decides to bring you to earth—to get a better understanding of what it all means."

"So when you say you've never seen any supernaturals on *earth* with power like this, does that mean you've seen power like that in other realms?" Charlotte asked. "AKA, here?"

Farrah shook her head. "No, sorry, I didn't mean that literally. What I meant was, I've never assessed any supernatural anywhere with power this strong."

The power she spoke of still hummed through my

veins. It felt as though rivers of lightning zapped around inside me. As strange as that was, it didn't hurt.

"Is it bad that I'm like this?"

Farrah smiled. "Not at all. Just surprising. And the scans show your power isn't unstable, so that's good news." She cocked her head. "You truly are a little mystery, but I'd much rather have you like this than how you were a few days ago."

"How was I then?"

Her smile faltered. "Not good. You were very weak."

"That's why you died, remember?" Charlotte's wry comment stopped the tension pooling inside me.

"I need to tell General McCloy about this." Farrah began to pack up her equipment. "Since you're stable, there's no need for me to stay here."

"General McCloy?" I said. "Who's he?"

"The head of the Supernatural Forces," Bryce replied before Farrah or Charlotte could. "He's Charlotte's boss's boss. Isn't that right?"

"That's the one!" Charlotte grinned.

"Why does he need to know?" Energy began to crackle around me. The power inside me sparkled, like shimmering lights just waiting to strike. I took a deep breath. The same feeling had happened before I'd unintentionally created the dome.

"He's in charge of my assignment since he directed

me here. I have to tell him." Farrah collected another piece of machinery, carefully packing it.

"Hey." Charlotte nudged me. "It's nothing to be worried about. General McCloy has known everything regarding your little death and rebirth from the get-go. Just another normal day at the office." She snickered, playfully bumping into me again.

Some of the sparking electrical synapses inside me lessened. As before, I couldn't stop the smile that spread across my face. There was something about Charlotte that felt . . . safe. I didn't know why, but I felt like I could trust her. And she'd truly been nothing but blunt and to-the-point since we'd met. I had a feeling if something was up, she would tell me.

And that was exactly what I needed right now.

I nudged Charlotte back. "Okay, well, then you better report to your boss's boss, too, before you get fired."

Charlotte laughed. "He can't fire me. It's my first week on the job. Well, actually . . ." She scratched her chin. "Come to think of it, that's a great reason to fire me. I better not fuck this up." But instead of looking worried, she just laughed again.

I joined her, a giggle bubbling out of me like a spring sprouting from a meadow.

And that was how Major Jamison found us when the door opened and he crossed the threshold.

As soon as he entered the room, all laughter died on my lips. The energy in me hummed wildly again, but then I inhaled.

Food.

He held two large trays filled with various dishes, drinks, and desserts.

Stalking to the small table by the wall, he set them down, then turned to face me with his hands on his hips.

My eyes widened, and I didn't move.

His rigid jaw looked forged from steel, his green eyes a stormy torrent. Energy radiated from him in simmering waves, and the rounded muscles in his shoulders bunched when he placed his hands on his hips.

"It's good to hear you laughing. Are you still hungry?" A veil descended over his eyes, all emotion cutting off. He stayed like that, watching me. Waiting.

My heart picked up again in a staccato beat. But before I could respond, my stomach growled loudly.

"I take it that's a yes." He picked up a plate off the tray and began dishing food onto it.

He piled it high with succulent meats, breads, cheeses, and vegetables. There was even a pot of what looked to be sweet fruit.

"Oh, she doesn't like carrots!" my mother said from where she perched on the other bed.

Major Jamison's hand stilled, his jaw clenching. The energy from him increased tenfold, and Bryce gave Danielle a look.

What? she mouthed. "She doesn't," she said under her breath.

But I was pretty sure Major Jamison heard her.

After scraping the carrots off, he finished dishing everything else on the large plate. I didn't know what to make of him serving me, since I was completely capable of standing and portioning food onto the plate myself, but given the brewing storm in his features, I opted to stay on the bed.

Damn. The man just made me . . . Fuck, I didn't even *know* what this feeling was in my stomach, but it suddenly felt as if I couldn't eat a thing even though I was ravenous.

After the plate was heaped to the point of spilling over, Major Jamison brought it over.

He stared down at me, his face completely blank. "I gave you a little of everything." He glanced at Danielle, then back at me. "Except for the carrots."

I took the plate from him, one of his fingers brushing mine in the process. A hundred watts of electricity zinged up my arm, shocking my nerves and making me yank the plate away from him. Some kind of vegetable tumbled off onto the floor.

Before I could retrieve it, Major Jamison had picked it up and was striding toward the trash. He dumped it in the bin, then looked over his shoulder. "I'll let you eat . . . in peace."

In a blink, he was at the door and out the room, the door closing with a strong *thud*.

Silence fell. Everyone just stood there as the tornado that was Major Jamison had come and gone.

Charlotte was the first to break the quiet as the tantalizing aromas from the generous meal wafted up to greet me. I tentatively picked up my fork as she cocked her head. "You really don't like carrots?"

I shrugged, a huff of a laugh raising my shoulders. "I don't know. Maybe I should try one."

And now that Major Jamison was gone, I had no problems doing so. My appetite returned, and I began inhaling the food.

However, when it came to the orange vegetable that my mother insisted I'd never cared for, I took one bite and wrinkled my nose.

She was right.

I didn't like carrots.

MAJOR JAMISON DIDN'T RETURN for another hour. I managed to polish off most of the food in the time he was gone, everyone else digging in, too, since we were all hungry.

But while the food was delicious, I still found that it wasn't enough to completely hold my attention.

I kept thinking about Major Jamison and the obvious agitation he was feeling. That and I felt a bit guilty that all of us had eaten but he hadn't.

"Do you know why, um, Major Jamison is so—" I didn't know what the right word was as Charlotte licked her fingers after eating the last little cake that'd been coated in a sweet honey glaze.

She raised an eyebrow. "Pissy?"

I snorted. "I guess that's the word."

She rubbed her hands together, dispelling the crumbs from them. "That's a good question. And if I didn't know better, I'd say that he wants to claim you but can't."

"Huh?" I replied just as my parents' heads whipped toward Charlotte.

Farrah had finished packing up and was getting ready to head back to earth, so she wasn't paying much attention to us.

"He wants to claim her?" Bryce's eyebrows rose.

Charlotte took a deep breath. "Shit. Not exactly the best conversation to have with your dad around."

Danielle elbowed Bryce, then pulled him to his feet. "Come on, hun. Let's go for a walk."

"But, she just said that Avery's commander—"

"I know what she said, but right now is probably not the best time to have us around, like Charlotte said. Let's let the girls talk."

Before Bryce could protest further, Danielle had him on his feet and out the door. Farrah looked up when they passed her.

"Everything okay?" the healing witch asked me and Charlotte.

"Just peachy." Charlotte grinned, then lounged back on the bed, her bent elbows propping her up.

"In that case, I'll be heading back." Farrah heaved her bag onto her shoulder. "Avery, if anything changes or you begin to feel differently in any way, please tell Major Jamison so that I may return and assess you again."

I managed a nod before she departed. When it was just me and Charlotte in the room, I crossed my legs underneath me and faced her.

"Okay, so what the heck are you talking about? Claiming me? What's that?"

Charlotte fingered a lock of auburn hair behind her

ear. "It's a werewolf thing. Since I'm a female wolf, I've seen plenty of male wolves acting like Major Jamison throughout the years." She shook her head, her lips tilting up. "Something tells me that you were keeping things from me during the past three months. Have you two hooked up?" But then she shook her head. "No, you wouldn't remember. Dammit! What I wouldn't give for all the juicy details that you probably kept from me."

That roiling feeling began in my stomach again. "Hooked up? With Major Jamison?"

She shrugged. "I wouldn't be surprised if you did. You were kinda all googly eyes for him when we were new recruits, but I didn't think you'd ever act on it, so maybe you didn't. But damn, I'm pretty sure what I just witnessed was a male wolf who wants to claim a female."

I crossed my legs more tightly underneath me. "What makes you say that?"

"Well, for one, it explains why he showed up at our apartment *three times* before he left for an assignment the other week. Two, it explains why you two went alone to Bulgaria together, and why he's being so moody when the man's never been moody in all the time I've known him. And three, it explains why he's been so protective of you ever since shit went down after our final tests. And let's not forget that he just brought an entire restaurant of food on two trays for you to eat.

Wolves who want to claim a woman will do anything for her, and considering the only thing you've let him do is feed you, well, he kinda went overboard."

I swallowed the thick lump in my throat, my heart pattering wildly. "So you're saying that he *likes* me?"

She laughed, her head tilting back. "That's the understatement of the year." She straightened, then tapped her chin. "I mean, I don't know for sure that Major Jamison's taken an interest in you, so I don't want to make shit all awkward between you two by bringing this up, but I wouldn't be surprised if he's developed feelings for you."

My chest heaved. "Feelings. For me. Okay." I leaned forward and took a deep breath. I was breathing so fast now that it seriously felt like I was going to pass out.

Charlotte patted my back. "Hey, sorry. I didn't mean to freak you out or anything."

Electricity crackled inside me, a light hum skating across my skin.

"Ouch!" Charlotte whipped her hand back. A spark rose around me, close to where she'd been touching me.

"I'm sorry." I made a sour face. "I didn't mean to do that."

"S'okay. Deep breaths, girl. We don't want you going all electrical and burning this place down."

I laughed, and some of the energy inside me calmed.

I seriously loved how easygoing she was, not in the least bit fazed by the chaos inside me. Still, I closed my eyes and did as she suggested.

The electrical storm that'd been building inside me returned to quiet zapping.

"Shit, girl. This power in you is seriously wicked. I wonder if you could power a city."

I groaned. "If my life wasn't such a mess right now, I'd be game to find out."

She gave me a sympathetic look. "Yeah, it's kinda crazy right now, isn't it? But no matter, I've been assigned to you until this is all sorted out, so I'll keep you from burning any shit down."

I laughed again, rolling onto my side as she joined me. But in the back of my mind, what she'd said still lingered.

Did Major Jamison seriously have feelings for me?

CHAPTER FIVE

WYATT

My wolf prowled in my belly as I stood outside under a setting fae sun. Stars appeared in the sky, even though hanging lanterns illuminated the busy street in the capital's business district where I waited outside, unseen, while Charlotte and Avery shopped.

I'd stayed away from Avery for the rest of the day, but had been keeping a close eye on her through messages with Charlotte and my silent stalking. And since Avery didn't want to be anywhere near me, I'd booked a second room at the inn for the night.

Even though my new room was adjacent to Avery and Charlotte's, I didn't like it.

I didn't want to be away from my mate. I wanted her

at my side, within eyesight, at all times. But since she wasn't actually in any danger that we knew of—crazy prophecies notwithstanding—it didn't make sense to smother her like that.

Especially when she didn't want it.

I eyed the boutique again that Avery and Charlotte were perusing. Since the SF had given me a generous budget to use while researching the strange illness that plagued Avery, I'd insisted that Charlotte take my mate shopping. Avery didn't have any clothes here. What she'd packed for our trip to the Bulgarian libraries— before the alignment—was still back in our bed chambers there, so I'd told Charlotte to let Avery purchase whatever she wanted.

Scents from a nearby café carried to me on the warm breeze. A sweet spice and a fragrant herb sparked my senses. I didn't recognize either, which meant they were fae ingredients.

My stomach growled, but I ignored the appetizing aromas and kept my focus on Avery. She and Charlotte were currently inside a dress shop. The female fae working with them gushed over Avery's measurements. I gritted my teeth when the shopkeeper brought out a dress with a low-cut top and fitted waist, but of course, Charlotte wholeheartedly approved.

When my mate stepped out of the changing room donned in it, with her breasts straining over the top as the colorful blend of fabrics cinched in at her waist then flared gently over her hips, I nearly came in my pants.

She was so fucking beautiful.

But then two supernatural males strolled by on the street—one a wolf and the other a fairy—and stopped to give Avery a double take. I nearly lost it right then and there.

They whispered to one another under their breaths. Thankfully, they were downwind so I didn't catch their exact words, but I was pretty sure they were sexual comments which would have made me attack even though I was on duty.

A growl rose in my throat when they nudged each other and snickered, but then they carried on, Avery none the wiser to their apparent lewd conversation.

I slammed a hand through my hair and dipped deeper into the shadows of an alleyway. I stayed like that, hidden from view, as Avery continued trying on new clothes. I watched her, knowing I was stalking her but unable to help it.

But then the hairs on the back of my neck abruptly stood on end. Again.

I crouched and whipped around, my hand going for my concealed weapon, but—

Nobody was there.

It was the third time I'd felt that way today.

Years of training and hand-to-hand combat prickled my senses. Someone had been directly behind me, sneaking up on me even though the empty alleyway was the only thing staring back at me, the air eerily still.

The same thing had happened an hour ago, and two hours before that. My senses had tingled, alerting me to *something*. Yet as had just happened, nothing was there.

I inhaled, my nostrils flaring as I scented for a supernatural, an animal, or another presence, but—

Nothing.

The air was devoid of anything other than the smells coming from the shops and the supernaturals walking by on the street.

In fact, the air was *too* empty.

There should have been scents from the nearby garbage. A rotting fruit, similar to a plum on earth, sat on the ground next to the bin. I should have been able to detect that withering flesh, yet . . .

Nothing came from it.

I tensed, keeping my back against the building, and my hand firmly on my particle gun. Its comforting whir registered against my palm.

My wolf whined, also on edge. He'd been pacing all day, mostly about Avery, but now . . .

He agreed. Something didn't feel right.

I inched closer to the street but kept my attention on the empty alleyway behind me.

The first time I'd detected someone, I could have said it was a fluke. The second time, maybe an unusual coincidence. But three times? No. Three times meant something was at play here, and I wasn't one to ignore my instincts.

The ancient tome's dire warning came back to me. *Only then will we rise.*

My wolf's magic heated my skin, urging me to shift, but I didn't. I needed fingers right now—not paws—because I needed to contact Wes.

I blurred closer to the front of the alleyway, so if an invisible assailant attacked me, he or she would have to do it in public for all of the fae and supernaturals walking by on the street to see. That would of course attract attention and get frantic calls to the Fae Guard here in the capital.

Avery had no idea about this chilling development. She still twirled in front of the shop's mirror, exclaiming her delight at the new fitted pants and shimmery sweater she'd tried on.

I pulled out my tablet, placing a call to Wes.

It took a moment to connect, since it required intricate magic to connect to earth from the fae realm.

"McCloy," he said by way of greeting.

"It's Jamison. I need backup. Now."

For a heartbeat, silence followed, then came a rapid, "What happened? Are you, Charlotte, Avery, and her parents somewhere safe?"

"We're still okay. Charlotte, Avery, and I are in public. I don't know where her parents are." I kept my attention focused on every slight movement. My eyes felt gritty. The lack of sleep was catching up with me, but now wasn't the time to grow complacent. "I've been feeling strange things all afternoon. I think someone's following me."

"Any idea who?"

"No. None. Whoever it is, I think they're using cloaking spells. No scents. I can't see anything, hear anything, smell anything, but something's off. My instinct's telling me someone's following us."

"We can bring you all back to headquarters. I can send portal keys."

My jaw tightened. That meant leaving the fae realm.

An image filled my mind of Avery weak and dying. She'd weakened after spending two weeks on earth, and it was only when we'd returned to this realm that she'd been reborn. I didn't know if returning here was what saved her, but I couldn't risk her health again.

Who was to say transferring realms wouldn't trigger

something new. What if she weakened again? Except this time, what if we couldn't save her? There were no imminent celestial events. I couldn't risk that.

"No. We'll stay here. I don't want to risk Avery's health. A realm transfer could trigger another downfall."

"Copy that." Another pause, and I knew he was sending rapid-fire messages. Whirring sounded in the background, then tapping. "I'll send Squad Three. I'd send your squad, but we've had a little skirmish break out. Squad Three is my only free squad until tomorrow morning, but they won't be able to mobilize for a few hours as they're currently returning from a short assignment in Canada."

"And my squad?"

"In Jakarta."

"Shit." I would have preferred working directly with my own squad. Having Dee Armund at my back would have been preferable, but Squad Three would have to do. And no doubt Charlotte would be happy to see them since that was her squad.

"You know the drill," Wes said. "Keep low until they get there. I'll send an expedited message to the king's advisor asking for clearance for Squad Three to enter."

I growled. "Hopefully no issues from them." The king and queen could prove problematic when Supernatural

Forces' assignments spilled into their realm. It wouldn't be the first time they'd denied our requests.

"Hopefully not. Considering Bavar Fieldstone is Squad Three's commander, the king and queen may be lenient, but if they're not you may need to contact the Fae Guard. They're better than nothing."

"I will if it comes to that." But I hoped Wes was right about the king and queen allowing a quick entry since Bavar was their nephew. "I'll need Avery's parents out of here too. I can't guard them if Avery's in danger."

"I'll take care of it. Anything else you need?"

"No. I'll be in touch."

As soon as we hung up, I sent Charlotte a message. I made sure to keep out of sight, but I still kept a constant eye on Avery.

Her laugh rang out, carrying into the streets. Another dress adorned her. This one was longer but had thin straps, which highlighted her lean arms. After training with Dee for three months, her body was toned beneath her natural curves.

She was so strong now, so *alive*. So different from the weak shell she'd been just yesterday.

And even though Avery didn't remember anything, her lilac scent clung to her, the fragrance as ripe as a freshly bloomed flower. And her mannerisms were the same. She still dipped her eyelashes when she was unsure, and fiddled with her hands when she was nervous.

She was still my Avery. *Mine.* Which meant I needed to keep her safe.

I paced on the street, no longer trying to conceal myself. Avery's attention was on the mirror anyway, and if she saw me out here? I sighed. She may not be happy, but circumstances had changed. Staying away to please her was no longer an option.

Charlotte's head dipped when my message finally reached her. The damn messages always took longer to reach devices in this realm.

The smile on her face disappeared. She glanced out the window, in the direction in which I'd told her I was waiting.

Her slight nod followed before she said something to Avery and then took their items to the counter.

I pushed away from the building I was leaning against when Avery and Charlotte emerged from the shop. Several bags dangled from their hands. Even though Avery was still smiling and laughing, Charlotte's emotions now looked forced.

She did as I'd trained her to do, constantly checking her six and never letting her guard down. Still, it made me uneasy that Charlotte and I were the only SF members currently in this realm protecting Avery.

While I knew Charlotte was capable, she was also green. What was supposed to have been a low-risk assignment for a brand-new corporal had just flipped.

I stabbed a hand through my hair. Because that inexperience was something that could not only get Charlotte killed but my mate too.

At least Charlotte was taking my warning seriously. The young corporal had said something to Avery about it getting late and needing to head back. They left the shop promptly and began walking to the inn as I'd ordered Charlotte to do.

In the evening light, shadows rimmed Avery's lower eyelids. I knew she was tired, but she still seemed sad that their shopping trip had been cut short.

My tablet buzzed in my pocket. Relief poured through me when I read Wes's message. He'd spoken with Avery's parents, letting them know that their daughter was retiring for the night, and that the SF needed them to return to earth's realm.

Good. They were going back to earth.

I needed to keep Avery's parents out of the picture. Guarding Avery with only Charlotte at my back was bad enough, but to also have Bryce and Danielle under my protection? Out of the question. I needed all of my attention on protecting my mate and protecting her only.

Despite not having slept for two days, my mind stayed sharp. I let my wolf out more, just enough to heighten my senses. My eyes glowed as they allowed me to see in the dark, and my nostrils continually flared as I searched for threatening scents.

But so far, none. And my sixth sense was no longer tingling. The other three times it had warned me that something imminent was about to happen, but now, it was calm. In other words, whatever, or whomever, I'd detected back in the alleyway had retreated.

The only scents around us now were the common aromas in the capital—spicy foods, magical metallic wards, and the hundreds of individual identifying scents of the fae and supernaturals I passed.

My chest rose when I took a deep breath and craned my neck to better assess the coming intersection. Avery and Charlotte walked ahead of me. Avery still didn't know that I was tailing them.

My fingers tapped against my thigh as I checked my six again. Still nothing.

Even though I hated Nicholas Fitzpatrick with a passion, I was eager to get an update from him. With any luck, the gargoyles would have found more in their search to explain what had happened to my mate, and possibly to explain *why* we were now being followed. And with any luck, we would know if leaving this realm again was wise. If it was, I'd have Avery back at SF headquarters in a heartbeat.

It was dark by the time Charlotte and Avery returned to the inn. I'd loped silently ahead of them to first scope out the inn's perimeter before their arrival.

It was clear.

Still, tension continued to slide along my limbs even when they both stepped over the inn's threshold unharmed. The magical wards around the old building flared, their metallic scents of copper and iron firing before settling once again. I could only hope those wards would be strong enough to keep out whomever'd been tailing me.

"Major Jamison." Charlotte dipped her head respectfully when we all met in the small entryway. She stood ramrod straight, her eyes sharp.

"Corporal Morris. Avery." I greeted them, then glanced around the empty room.

All looked normal.

Avery's cheeks flushed, and as before, she looked anywhere but at me.

My stomach tightened. "How was the shopping

trip?" I asked, hoping my light question would put Avery more at ease.

"It was fine." Her brows pinched together. "Are Bryce and Dan—I mean, my parents—back yet?"

I placed my hands on my hips. "I'm afraid not." I paused. If Avery were a normal protectee, I would have made up a white lie as to why her parents were no longer here, but she was my mate. I couldn't lie to her. "They're no longer in this realm."

Her eyes widened. "They aren't? Why not?"

"Because I asked them to leave."

Her lips parted. "Why would you do that?"

"My job is to guard you and you alone. It's harder to do that if I also have to guard your parents." Before she could ask for specific details, I nodded toward the numerous bags she and Charlotte held. "Did you get everything you needed?"

Energy crackled around Avery when we briefly made eye contact, but as she had previously, she quickly looked away. "I did. Please thank your, err, boss for me. That was very nice of him to supply me with so many clothes."

"It wasn't General McCloy who gave the order to take you shopping." Charlotte arched an eyebrow. "It was Major Jamison. He said to let you get whatever you wanted."

A flush danced up Avery's cheeks. "Oh, um, in that case, thank you." She took a deep breath. "Anyway, should we head upstairs?"

"This way." I ushered Avery and Charlotte down the hall. Before I realized what I was doing, I placed my palm on Avery's lower back, gently guiding her toward the stairs.

Her entire body stiffened, and electricity buzzed under my hand. I snatched my hand back, gritting my teeth that I could no longer touch her as my instincts screamed at me to do.

Avery gave me a side-eye, her breathing fast, then she side-stepped to put Charlotte in between us.

I locked my jaw tighter.

When we reached the end of the hall, we trudged up the stairs, me leading the way, Charlotte bringing up the rear. I tried to be subtle, but I scoped out the hall before allowing Avery to step out of the stairwell.

"It's getting late," I said, when we approached our doors. "Probably best to turn in."

Avery gave me a funny look, then glanced between Charlotte and me. "Okay, I guess that makes sense since we didn't sleep last night, but it's kind of early, isn't it?"

Charlotte yawned, the gesture sounding entirely genuine. She slung an arm around Avery's shoulders. "Girl, come on. It's been a long day."

As before, Avery's shoulders relaxed under Charlotte's easygoing nature. My mate peeked over at me, her gaze lingering on my face when she thought I wasn't looking, but as soon as I faced her, she bolted into the room.

CHAPTER SIX
AVERY

Wyatt was pacing. I couldn't hear him, smell him, or see him . . . yet, a very subtle vibration shook the floorboards, and I *knew* that he was pacing in his room adjacent to ours.

Ever since Charlotte and I had returned from our shopping trip, he'd been tense.

Initially, he'd disappeared after Charlotte and I retreated to our room, then he'd returned carrying a tray of food for supper saying I should eat before going to bed.

As I'd dutifully eaten, despite the fluttering in my stomach which he always provoked, he'd been on high alert. When he wasn't standing at the window constantly looking out of it, he was waiting by the door as if trying to sense something on the other side, or sending messages on his tablet as he communicated with someone in the SF.

And if that wasn't worrying enough, his body had oozed tension as his surly mood flooded the room. An extra day's worth of beard also coated his cheeks, and his eyes had taken on a gritty, bloodshot look that only came from lack of sleep. He needed rest more than I did, yet despite that, his energy had been strong, his alpha power vibrating around him.

Which meant something was definitely up that I wasn't privy to.

Before crawling into bed, I'd finally asked Charlotte what the hell was going on.

"He sensed something this afternoon," she explained. "It's probably nothing, but just to be safe, we're going to stay awake tonight." She winked. "Get some shut-eye, eh? We'll keep ya safe."

So Wyatt had sensed something. But what?

I turned over in my bed, the room dark around me. My damp hair splayed out, leaving the pillowcase cool. I'd showered and changed into fresh clothes maybe thirty minutes ago, then climbed into bed after Wyatt left and Charlotte again insisted I sleep.

Yet despite fatigue pulling at my eyelids, begging me to drift into oblivion, that strange dipping feeling again filled my stomach. I was pretty sure it wasn't because I needed to pee or was hungry. I'd come to learn what those sensations were, so this new feeling had to be caused by some other emotion I had yet to identify.

Charlotte still sat on her bed. Her back was to me, her attention on the window. She was fully dressed in her SF uniform with her weapons strapped to her.

"Are you really not going to sleep at all?" I asked quietly.

She glanced over her shoulder, the moonlight illuminating her profile. "No. My orders are to stay alert, but that doesn't mean you can't sleep. You've got to be tired since you've been awake for over a day. You should try to get some rest."

I sighed heavily. "You sound like my mother."

Charlotte tilted her head. "You remember your mom saying stuff like that?"

I frowned. Did I? The retort had rolled right off my tongue without a thought, so did that mean that was something I would have heard her say? Or did my confused brain have me say that because it seemed like a natural response?

I groaned. "Honestly, I don't know. I can't actually remember my mom saying that to me."

And I couldn't. My mind was one big foggy mess right now. Whenever I concentrated and tried to remember anything past language or the everyday info about random stuff, there was just a large blank cobweb of nothingness. No memories of myself. No recognition of those I once knew. No understanding of emotions or bodily sensations. *Nada.*

But I did know what a waterbed was, thinking back to when I'd first stepped on the magical carpet. I grumbled. How useful.

Charlotte turned to face me more. "It's okay, girl. It may come back in time so don't sweat it too much. Now go to sleep. We'll keep you safe, and you need to rest."

I opened my mouth to talk more. It didn't seem fair that they would stay awake while I slept, but then a yawn escaped me. I stifled the sound with the back of my hand, then tried to think of something Charlotte and I could talk about, but nothing came, and I knew I couldn't blame my lack of stimulating conversational topics on my memory loss.

Charlotte was right. I was tired.

"Fine. I'll try and get some sleep."

She laughed softly. "Sweet dreams."

FIRE ROARED *from a pit in the earth. Its dancing light crackled and snapped. A dark night sky loomed above, punctuated with*

glistening stars, yet the world here felt empty and vacant. *Except for* them.

Robed figures stood in a circle around the pit. They chanted, their hands joined as their low humming filled the air.

I hovered above them, my body weightless. Terror slid through my veins as my ethereal form lifted and dipped, ensnared in their rhythmic song.

Their chanting grew, words flowing from their lips in a language long dead. The power of the words buzzed through me, rising in my chest higher and higher.

Pain abruptly blazed along my limbs.

I screamed, clutching at my chest, my stomach, my throat, but the electrical fire roaring inside me burned hotter.

Their song grew stronger, their magic lassoing me.

I cried out as their binding snapped me tight. A geyser of power roiled inside me. No! They were trying to take it!

I gasped, my body writhing in pain as I fought their control of my spectral form.

But my body wasn't mine. I didn't control it. I didn't own it.

It was theirs.

One of the figures stepped over something, and I saw that it was me *he'd maneuvered around. My pale body lay on the ground, eyes closed. A sheet covered me from the chin down.*

The figure peered up at me. His face was a mask of

shadows and light, there but gone, present yet past. Something about him was off. I couldn't see his features. I couldn't identify anything at all about him. But he felt wrong.

"You will give it to me." His voiced chilled me to the marrow of my bones. "I will control the power in your veins, oh Goddess of—"

A whisper had me bolting upright in bed, a scream trapped in my throat.

Darkness surrounded me. My heavy pants filled the air as I clutched the sheets, my fingers curling into them.

Where am I? What's happening?

"Avery?" a deep voice said urgently.

Wyatt.

I reached for him, instinct begging me to grasp his shoulders and bury my head against his frame. *Wyatt.* I needed him. I needed to be with him.

He was there in an instant, his warm body enveloping me, his oak and pine scent everywhere.

"I'm here," he whispered. His arm encircled my waist, pulling me close.

My fingers wrapped around his shoulders, my heart pounding wildly as I tried to figure out where I was and what was happening.

"A dream . . . I had a dream, I think. These men—"

"Avery listen to me," Wyatt said interrupting. "We need to leave. Someone is after you. I felt it earlier, and I feel it again now. The wards around this inn have flared twice. They're keeping out whoever's trying to get in, but they're weakening. And if whoever is after you breaches them, we need to move."

"What? Someone's after me? You mean, that's why you and Charlotte stayed up—"

His pocket buzzed, and he pulled back just enough to whip out his tablet. A message glowed on its screen, but it flashed so quickly that I couldn't see it.

"Dammit!" he seethed.

"ETA?" Charlotte asked briskly.

I blinked. My friend's silhouette appeared by the window, pulling the curtain back.

Shit. This was serious.

"Too long," Wyatt growled. "They're another hour out."

"What's happened? Who's out there?" The aftereffects of the dream, or whatever had terrorized me to wake up in the middle of the night, still fogged my mind, but already the details were slipping.

Instead of answering me, Wyatt gently swung my legs to the side of the bed. "Avery, I need you to put your shoes on." His voice sounded so gravelly and deep, and his wolf shone in his eyes.

I slipped my shoes on. "Okay. Does that mean we're going somewhere?"

A blast suddenly rocked the building, jolting me from the mattress to slide off its side.

I yelped, just as Wyatt yanked me to the floor, then placed his heavy body over mine.

"Get down!" he yelled to Charlotte.

My friend crouched to the floor just as the window shattered. Glass flew everywhere. Huge deadly shards embedded in the walls, the headboard, the carpet. It was only because Wyatt and I were nestled between the two beds that we missed their blows.

"Stay covered!" he yelled.

Charlotte crouched, her arms covering her head and protecting her face when another huge vibration strummed through the building. The scent of blood and iron filled the air.

"Shit!" Wyatt's hold on me tightened. "The wards are down! Remember your training, Morris!"

Before I could process what was happening, Wyatt had raised himself just enough to crouch over me. A humming weapon was in his hand. He aimed it at the shattered window. Magical bullets erupted from it, shooting from the end like blazing meteors moving at light speed.

Charlotte bolted up onto one knee, her bow in hand. She shot an arrow through the window. A loud groan came from outside.

Elsewhere in the building, screams erupted as the other guests woke from sound sleeps. Another rumble shook the floor, except this time the *entire* floor shifted, tilting beneath us.

"We need to move!" Wyatt yelled to Charlotte.

She tucked and rolled, executing a perfect backward somersault. The maneuver put her right at the end of my bed, and her eyes flashed my way.

In her luminescent irises I saw a touch of fear but also excitement. She was enjoying this.

"Cover us," Wyatt snarled.

My breath rushed out of me as Wyatt's arm clamped around my waist, and then I was flying.

The wall shattered to my side when he catapulted us toward the door. Plaster shards flew everywhere. Someone was firing at us. Firing at *him*.

I wrapped my arms around my head, bracing myself as the electrical power inside me began to sparkle and sizzle, growing and swelling, begging me to let it out. But what did I do with it?

Just as we reached the door, a shadowy figure floated in front of the window, then entered the room.

"Charlotte!" I screamed.

Her back was to the intruder. She leapt toward us, but a spell shot from the shadowy figure and hit her square in the shoulder.

Wyatt exploded through the door into the hallway, and then we were racing down it. I pummeled his back as I dangled over his shoulder like a sack of potatoes. "Stop! Charlotte fell!"

But he didn't pause.

"We need to go back and get her!"

His jaw clamped shut so hard, his teeth snapped. "No! I need to keep *you* safe!"

"Wyatt, please! We can't leave her!"

Another groan shook the building, and dust from the walls puffed around us.

The lights went out.

Screams rose from the first floor.

The floorboards shook again.

A terrible roar came from the end of the building.

"Wyatt!" I pleaded.

"My orders are to keep you safe!"

Another explosion rocked the building, and Wyatt stumbled toward the wall.

Electricity zapped along my skin, my hair standing on end. The volcano of power inside me was begging to erupt.

"Please! We can't leave her."

Gritting his teeth, he didn't let go and instead swept open the door to the stairwell just as a glow burst in the hall behind us, emanating from the room

I'd been sleeping in. The room that Charlotte was still in.

A black mist formed outside the doorway, slinking along the floorboards toward us. It rose and swelled, growing in size.

My eyes widened as we disappeared down the stairwell, and the terrifying mist disappeared from view.

I didn't manage to see anything else since Wyatt's movements turned into a blur. He moved so fast. So unbelievably fast.

But we'd left Charlotte.

"We have to go back!" I screamed.

We burst through the bottom door onto the main floor. Other guests in the inn were frantically running about. It was dark everywhere, and the walls kept vibrating as ancient magic sparked around us.

"What's happening?" a fairy yelled to a woman as they raced down the hall.

"Are we under attack?" somebody else wailed as a child began crying.

"Does the king know?" a man bellowed as he clutched a suitcase to his chest.

It was chaos. Everywhere.

Wyatt grunted when a man shot out of his door and barreled into us, before steadying himself and sprinting again. The world turned into a blur once more. The next thing I knew we were bursting through the front door out into the cool night.

"Wyatt, no! Stop! Please!" Choked sobs worked up my throat.

But he refused to slow.

"Wyatt. Let. Me. Go!" A huge rush of energy shot from me of its own accord, zapping him in the chest. *Damn.* I hadn't meant to do that.

He came to a careening halt, and I scrambled from his arms.

I stood on the lawn, the inn behind us emitting terrible creaks and groans. Wyatt rubbed his chest, his face twisted in a grimace.

A moment of guilt clouded me. I had no idea how badly I'd hurt him, but I guessed it hadn't been a simple shock given the expression on his face. But I needed to focus on Charlotte, not Wyatt.

I crossed the two feet of distance between us and grabbed his shirt. "We have to go back and get Charlotte."

"My orders are to protect you, and Charlotte knows—"

"I don't give a fuck what your orders are! We're not leaving her!" I shoved away from him, intent on getting Charlotte myself, when his large hand shot out and gripped my upper arm.

A snarl tore from me, and the power inside me swelled, but before another surge of energy could break away from me of its own volition, Wyatt released his grip.

"Avery," he pleaded, his eyes glowing as brightly as the moon. "I need to keep you safe. I can't risk any harm coming to you."

And that's when I saw it and heard it. The desperation in his eyes. The raw fear in his words. His actions weren't because of orders. They were because of his feelings for me. His feelings were why he'd left my friend—his *squad mate*—behind.

I remembered what Charlotte had said. *Wolves who want to claim a woman will do anything for her.*

But I couldn't leave my friend.

"I'm going back inside for her if you won't."

"NO!" His bellow made me pause as a terrified inn resident streaked past us, clad only in nightclothes. Another rumble came from the building, and the west side fell an alarming foot.

"Wyatt, the building is going down! We don't have much time. If we don't get her now, she'll die."

His gaze whipped to the building. Tension roiled around him, energy waxing and waning.

"Look! It's coming down!"

He blinked, then staggered back. As if coming out of

a trance, his face paled. "Shit! What have I done?" he whispered.

"Please, if you ever cared for me, please go back and get her. Do it for *me*."

His jaw clenched, and in a blur of action, he whisked me off the lawn and stopped near the street, the inn even farther away.

His glowing eyes met mine. "Stay here and create the protective dome around you. I can't believe I fucking left her, and I can't believe I'm now fucking leaving you!" His mouth slammed into mine, his kiss quick and violent.

Before I could utter a sound of surprise, he disappeared in a blur.

My lips parted as understanding dawned. It'd taken him two seconds to move me, *kiss* me, and be back inside the building.

I fingered my mouth. *Good Gods.* Wyatt had feelings for me. Charlotte had been right.

Wrapping my arms around myself, I shook those thoughts off and watched in horror as smoke rose from one side of the building. More screams followed as a tingling sense of fear crept up my spine. A part of my mind knew that I needed to create the dome again—even though I wasn't entirely sure how I'd done it in the first place—but before I could try, the hairs on the back of my neck stood on end.

"I didn't think it would be this easy," a man said calmly from behind me. "With that wolf guarding you non-stop, I didn't think he would leave an opening."

My breath stopped as I spun around. That voice. Something about that voice . . .

My heart beat harder as I came face to face with a tall robed figure standing just on the other side of the short fence that lined the inn's property. His face was hidden, only his mouth revealed.

An ache coiled around my gut. Something about his mouth looked familiar.

"Do you know how long I've been waiting for you?" He glided closer to the fence as the screams continued behind me. "For thousands of years, that's how long I've been waiting, and finally, here you are."

Icy dread slid through my veins, and I stumbled backward just as Wyatt burst through the door with an unconscious Charlotte draped over his shoulder. "Avery!" he roared.

The building collapsed, the entire western side suddenly giving out as movement from the other side of the property drew my attention.

A group of figures appeared from around the corner, their bodies also adorned in long robes.

All of the blood drained from my face.

It was *them*. The figures from my dream.

The fuzzy dream came roaring back.

The fire.

The chanting.

The robes.

The otherworldly spells.

They were here for *me*. Wyatt's instincts had been right.

I spun back to the tall one, gasping in shock when I found him standing right in front of me. He'd moved so fast and so silently.

Terror clawed up my throat as I tripped over my feet to get away from him. The power inside me roiled, but fuck me if I knew how to use it on command.

I bumped into something, and a cloud of oak and pine scents wafted around me.

Before I could respond or try again to form the dome, Wyatt was in front of me, his body blocking me from view, as Charlotte lay unconscious on the ground.

"You're not taking her," he snarled.

The man, or supernatural, or whoever the hell he was, laughed. The fucker actually *laughed*. "Is that what you think, wolf? She's not yours. She's *mine*."

Granted, I didn't know Wyatt at all, or know much about this claiming business, but I had a feeling that was the absolute worst thing this dude could have said to the commander.

An enraged growl tore from Wyatt just as the rest of the building crumbled, the old, teetering walls snapping like matchsticks. More screams came, one cut off by a gut-wrenching crunch.

Before I could process what that meant, magic shimmered around Wyatt, and I knew he was about to shift into his wolf.

But then the other robed figures were around us. They'd moved so fast, one second on the side of the property, and the next encircling us.

They began chanting under their breath as a spell shot toward me.

I shrieked and tried to dodge out of the way, but I wasn't fast enough.

Wyatt stopped from shifting and grabbed me, hurtling me out of the spell's path at the last second.

The wind was knocked out of me from the abrupt movement, and the power inside my body hummed all the more. *Use it! Use the power to stop this!*

But I didn't know how. Even though adrenaline pumped through my veins, and the terrible power inside me bubbled and roiled, I didn't know how to command it.

You still need to try.

Electricity sped along my skin, zapping Wyatt. He hissed but didn't let go.

Fuck, that wasn't what I'd meant to do.

"Take him out," the tall man said, his eerily calm voice never wavering.

The rest of the robed figures raised their hands in unison. A blast of spells shot from them. With them encircling us, Wyatt had nowhere to go but up.

He leapt, his feet leaving the ground at an impossibly fast speed, but the spells followed.

They hit him simultaneously. All of them.

A scream trapped in my throat. Wyatt landed with a sickening thump next to Charlotte.

Disbelief coursed through me as the figures moved in closer. All I could do was gape at Wyatt and Charlotte on the ground.

They were both silent.

Unmoving.

Blood trickled from Charlotte's shoulder.

Wyatt's head lolled to the side.

Oh Gods!

Terror bloomed inside me that was so potent and raw that it ensnared my senses, flooded my mind, and became a living entity within me which consumed everything I saw and felt.

Were both Wyatt and Charlotte dead?

"Take her." The tall man's command sliced through me.

Hands reached for me, ripping, shoving, and pinning. The robed men formed a solid wall around me.

But I couldn't tear my eyes away from Wyatt and Charlotte. *This can't be happening! This isn't real. I'm in a dream. None of this is real! They're fine.*

Despite my internal denial, the wails and moans continued coming from the ruined building that now lay in a pile of smoke and cracked wood. Supernaturals were trapped beneath the rubble, dying and terrified, their cries being snuffed out like candles.

Oh my God, they're dying. The other guests are dying. This isn't a dream.

The robed men's hands continued to paw me, before lifting me. My feet were no longer on the ground. And Charlotte and Wyatt still hadn't moved. Because they were probably dead.

The world turned into a sea, as if everything moved through thick black water. Sounds, sights, and smells all blended into one. An echoing void opened within me, as the electrical energy in my chest charged and grew.

Wyatt and Charlotte. No. No. They can't be dead. Please, no.

I lashed my arms out in pain as an insufferable grief consumed me. *Please don't let them be dead. Please!*

An agonizing chasm of torment split my sternum. The hands slipped, their hold loosening until I fell to the ground.

And then they were reaching for me again. Groping. Tugging. Pulling. *Owning* me.

But I crouched to the ground, curling into a ball, my arms covering my head as anguish erupted in my chest.

The crack inside me opened further, fissuring like the earth splitting wide open during an earthquake. Images of Wyatt and Charlotte immobile on the ground flooded my mind again and again.

The crack widened, and then—it *exploded*.

Burning, surging energy skated up my chest and through my arms. The force of it knocked my head back. I shot to standing, arms flying out.

The robed figures flew through the air, as if a nuclear explosion had ripped through them, sending the men careening in a blast outward, and then—

Everything went still.

The world stopped.

Time froze.

The crashing, burning, and screams—they just . . . *stopped*.

Around me, everything had ceased. Frozen in time.

The robed figures were suspended in mid-air. Wyatt and Charlotte were unconscious on the ground. The blood flowing from Charlotte's shoulder didn't move; a drop of it hovered immobile in the air. And the tall robed figure by the fence waited vacant-looking and unmoving.

I slowly turned in a circle, taking in the paralyzed world.

What just happened?

But I didn't have time to process it. Whatever power had been unleashed inside me was buzzing through my system, and pouring out of me in vengeful waves. Electricity fired along my nerves, heating my blood. Sparks flew everywhere.

And I had no idea how long it would last.

A flicker of awareness shuddered through me, drawing my attention back to the robed figure by the fence. He didn't move, yet I *felt* him watching me. His gaze was glued to mine as I reached for Wyatt and Charlotte.

The man knew what was happening. He understood it, but he still couldn't move, although his eyes did. They followed me.

Fear crawled up my chest in icy tentacles as the immense power flowed through my limbs. I picked up Wyatt and Charlotte, one under each arm, as if they were cotton-stuffed rag dolls. But they were both tall. Their legs dragged on the ground. Still, their weight and

KRISTA STREET

long forms didn't stop me. The power coursing through me was so great.

I began to run.

The crystalized world flew past me in a blur. I ran and ran and ran. I passed silent houses, fae standing frozen in the streets, fields of immobile tall grass, walls sheathed in gold . . .

I left it all behind. I ran until the city faded and the view of a great sea spread out before me.

Burning pain raged through me at the sheer magnitude of energy it took to keep the power activated while carrying hundreds of pounds of weight.

Even though the world stayed immobile, I was anything but. Ragged breaths cleaved my lungs. Sweat trailed down my temples. Lactic acid built in my muscles.

Regardless, I kept going, pushing my body and mind to its absolute breaking point.

I ran until the colossal power in me grew small and misty, mere vapors of the mighty explosion that had rocked time and space.

I ran until the world jolted to a start, the air moving, the insects chirping, the stars twinkling.

I ran until I couldn't run anymore.

I collapsed in a field, the sound of waves crashing in

the distance. The world faded to nothingness as my body finally broke.

Wyatt and Charlotte fell to the ground beside me, still unconscious and unmoving. Then my eyes closed as exhaustion overtook me.

CHAPTER SEVEN
WYATT

Muffled sounds drummed through my head. Cotton filled my mouth. And it seriously felt like my chest had been cracked open.

"Major Jamison?" a man said.

The foggy voice tugged at me. Then I was moving and vibrating. No, not vibrating, someone was shaking me.

"Major Jamison?" the same voice spoke again.

"If you would kindly step aside, Lex," a second man said, his voice as smooth as velvet. "You may return to Charlotte. She's still unconscious from the enchantment."

A rustling sound came next, as if whoever'd been shaking me had moved back.

"Wyatt?" the second man said. "Please be a good chap and *wake up!"*

Ringing sounded in my ears at his loud tone, then my eyelids cracked open. A figure hovered above me, a nighttime sky behind him.

I blinked. "Bavar?" I croaked.

"That's correct, my friend, Major Bavar Fieldstone at your service." A flash of orange hair registered in my senses, but I groaned when pain split through my skull. Then a memory pummeled my mind.

Avery.

Robed men.

A spell.

Burning pain.

Then nothing.

"Avery!" I roared. I bolted right up to sitting, but Bavar's hands shot out, gripping my shoulders.

"She's okay. She's here and safe."

I inhaled. Pounding filled my chest. My heart. It was thundering against my ribs like a galloping beast. I rubbed my breastbone. The touch elicited an ache that hadn't been there previously, but I didn't relax until I caught her lilac scent.

It flowed to me in the night, like mist from a moor. My frantic heart slowed, my breathing returning to normal. "Where is she?" I rasped.

"With Charlotte. You both took some nasty hits." Bavar gave a pointed look to where I was rubbing. "You took a spell directly to the chest. If you weren't such a stubborn bastard who's proven quite difficult to kill, I'd say you're lucky to be alive."

Some of the tension filling my shoulders lessened, but then I took in our surroundings. "Wait a minute, where the hell are we?" I'd expected to see the smoldering inn at my back and the street up ahead, but instead we sat in a field that stretched over gentle rolling hills. I swung around.

The capital's lanterns burned brightly in the distance at least twenty miles away.

I faced my friend again, relief filling me. "Your squad got to the inn in time and saved us. Thank the Gods."

Bavar settled back on his haunches, his hair disheveled and wild, as if he'd run his hands through it multiple times before I'd woken up. "Well, that's not exactly what transpired, but we shall get to that in a minute. As for where we are, we are currently west of the capital near the Adriastic sea." He pointed over a mound. "The wharf is just over that hill, and the capital's storage warehouses reside over yonder." He pointed north.

I winced when another slash of pain ripped through me. "What about Morris, how badly is she hurt?"

The fairy's lips thinned. "She's still unconscious and has a nasty wound to her shoulder, but we found her in time. Lex is tending to her. She needed a blood transfusion."

"A blood transfusion . . ." It all came back then—the attack and my innate need to protect Avery, which meant I'd left Charlotte behind. Left her to *die*.

"Fucking hell," I whispered. "I left Morris after she went down." I threaded both hands through my hair even though the movement hurt. "I actually left her, Bavar."

Bavar frowned, silent for a moment before replying, "What are you talking about?"

Shame flooded me, heating my skin. "When we were attacked at the inn, I panicked and lost it. Avery was in danger, and my wolf was urging me to save her—" I squeezed my hair between my fingers. "And Morris is a brand-new corporal who was in completely over her head. And what did I do? I abandoned her, all to save my mate." That contradicted every code the SF stood for. We never left anyone behind.

The fairy commander's frown deepened as his orange hair glowed in the moonlight. "That's certainly something we shall need to discuss, but Corporal Morris will be fine so we have avoided a tragedy." He paused, his brow furrowing. "I'm obviously missing something here, because I thought this assignment was not anticipated to be violent. If it was, Wes never would have assigned Charlotte to it."

"No, we didn't anticipate danger. We thought the threat to Avery came from the stars, not the ground, although it's now become glaringly obvious the threat is from both places. And you're right, Wes wouldn't have assigned Charlotte if we'd known that. The only reason she's even here is because of the history she shares with Avery."

"So you're saying this new threat came from within this realm and was directed at *you?*"

"Not me. Avery." I worked my jaw. Just thinking about it made my stomach twist. "The attack was orchestrated to abduct her. There were about a dozen men working together. They all wore robes with hoods which covered their faces."

He cocked his head. "Robed figures working in unison. Hmm, sounds rather cloak-and-dagger with a flair for the dramatic. Any idea who they were?"

"No, I didn't get a good look at any of them, but I'm assuming they were sorcerers."

"Did you catch any of their scents?"

I growled. "No. They're using advanced cloaking spells. It was only my sixth sense that detected some-thing amiss this afternoon, and I can tell you that if I hadn't been on so many assignments and wasn't so in-tune with listening to that sense, I never would've known they were there." I described the sensations. "At least one of them was tailing me throughout the afternoon."

"And Corporal Morris never detected them?"

"No, hence why she's too green for this assignment."

Bavar clapped me on the shoulder. "Well, it's no longer just the two of you, and at least she's fared all right. She may have taken a debilitating spell, which went right through her suit, but she shall live and make a full recovery."

"It went through her suit? That's why I smelled blood on her." I frowned. "But only powerful sorcerer magic can penetrate our suits. We'll need to check the data-base, see what sorcerers in the community are capable of that."

Bavar stroked his chin. "Only thing, I don't believe it was sorcerer magic that punctured her suit. It has a bizarre scent to it, and there are strange markings around the perimeter of the hole created by the spell, not to mention it singed the material green."

My frown deepened. "But if it's not sorcerer magic, then what is it?"

"That's another very good question, my friend."

I shook my head, thinking of the scrolls again. "Only

then will we rise," I murmured, then my eyes widened when I remembered the tiny circle of robed men in the drawing—the one Master Ambrose had shown us of the alignment right before Nicholas and I had whisked Avery back to the fae lands. "Shit! The scrolls hinted at this group."

I told Bavar about the picture. "The tomes and scrolls also gave us cryptic warnings, but nothing specific enough for us to prepare or know who those supernaturals were." I relayed the text about the starlight couple, the heir, and the gods being born, but my brain grew fuzzy as I tried to connect the dots.

Bavar patted me on the shoulder. "I'll have Wes and Nicholas fill me in on the rest. I have to say, you look quite tired. When was the last time you slept?"

I sighed warily. "It's going on three days."

"And you were in the fae lands for a month before returning from your last assignment. How much did you sleep during that period?"

"Not enough. I know it's affecting me."

He made a noise in his throat, a mix between discontent and understanding. "She's your mate, Wyatt. Don't be too hard on yourself, although, you're right. You fucked up. You shouldn't have left Charlotte. But I also know that you only did that because of two things: your instincts to protect your mate at all costs, and how you're currently so sleep deprived that your judgment is getting impaired. You've been able to control your instincts previously. I have no doubt the reason you weren't able to tonight was because of your ragged state."

"But we're trained to be sleep deprived," I growled.

"Yes, to an extent. But we're not invincible. You can't go weeks with little to no sleep and expect to be unaffected, so that's why I'm ordering you to rest for the next few days. We're going to a safe house until we can get a better handle on what we're dealing with. Once we're on our way, I'll have Lex give you a sleeping draught so you can rest during the journey, and once we're there, I'm taking over and you're taking a much needed break."

I opened my mouth to protest, but he beat me to it.

"Wyatt, your mate will be with you. She'll be safe. My squad is fully functioning. Well, almost." He glanced toward where Lex still tended to Charlotte. "Which means there's no excuse for you to continue running yourself into the ground." He paused, studying me. "Are we in agreeance?"

I remembered what Farrah had said. She'd seen the signs, too, and had tried to warn me, but I'd been too hell-bent on guarding Avery to listen, and because of that, Charlotte had almost died.

"Agreed." I ran my hands roughly over my cheeks. *Jesus, when did I grow a full beard?*

I sat up straighter, searching for my mate again. Avery sat near Charlotte who was lying on the ground about a dozen yards away. Moonlight bathed them in white light. Several Squad Three members stood around them.

As if sensing my stare, Avery glanced at me. When we made eye contact, her lips parted, and my heart crashed against my ribs. Fear still coated her face, her eyes were wild with it, but something else wafted from her too.

I inhaled.

She abruptly turned, giving me her back as she picked up Charlotte's limp hand. However, she subtly glanced at me a second time. She tried to hide behind her curtain of hair, but I felt her watching me, assessing me.

Despite trying to act as if she'd snubbed me, I caught the relief pouring from her in steady waves—relief that had only registered once she saw me awake and sitting upright.

That fragrance made my nostrils flare more. My wolf rumbled in pleasure. On the outside, Avery may be pretending that she didn't care about me, but emotional scents didn't lie.

I remembered the kiss I'd plastered on her mouth before I'd entered the collapsing building. And the things I'd said to her while she'd been under the dome. She had to know that she wasn't a simple protectee to me.

So now the question was, what would she do with that information? At least she was relieved to see that I was okay, and not indifferent. It was a far cry from the fearful scent she'd carried after waking in the dome.

I finally dragged my attention back to Bavar. My head still pounded, but it had lessened since waking. Thanks to my enhanced healing abilities, I was already well on my way to recovery despite my body's sleep-deprived state.

"So what's the status of this assignment now?" I asked Bavar.

"Squad Three is officially on this case. Once Charlotte's able to walk on her own, we'll be moving to a safe house. My orders are to keep us in the fae lands and not to leave your side until this assignment is solved and closed."

"And what about how we ended up here? You said we'd get to that later. It's later."

Bavar tipped his chin up. "Well, that's where it gets rather interesting. According to Avery, she carried you both here."

Despite my rapidly healing body, I was still certain I'd misheard Bavar, which indicated my brain was potentially suffering from a concussion. Because it'd sounded like he'd said *Avery* had carried me and Charlotte here, that Squad Three hadn't brought us here like I'd originally assumed.

"Your squad isn't the reason we're here?"

Bavar shook his head. "No. We only found you all via the tracking hex woven into Morris's suit. And given that both you and Charlotte were unconscious when we arrived, I don't believe Avery's lying. She must have carried you both here."

"She didn't have a portal key hidden away somewhere?"

"That was my first thought, too, but she's insistent she's never owned one, let alone used one."

"But the inn is *miles* away."

"Indeed."

I inhaled, my heart thudding again. A tang of salt coated the breeze. "But how did she do that? That would require incredible strength and speed." Even *I* would have struggled to do that as an alpha wolf.

But then I thought of the dome she'd encased herself in after the alignment, of the immense magic that had taken.

Bavar cocked his head. "She said she stopped time."

"I definitely have a concussion. It sounds like you said she stopped time."

"You don't have a concussion, and that's what I said."

I shook my head. "What do you mean?"

He threaded a hand through his hair and recounted what Avery had told him.

I sputtered, words refusing to form on my lips.

"I know. It's a lot to take in, but I've heard her new power is quite strong. Perhaps she's telling the truth and she really did stop time, and perhaps that power is why those robed men are after her."

I cradled my cheeks again. "What in all the realms has happened to her? How is this possible?"

"That I cannot answer, my friend, but the sooner we get to the safe house, the better." Bavar stood and offered me a hand up. "We're moving this operation to north of the capital, to the Shroud Forest. The magic there is particularly vexing. It makes it harder for others to track, which means we'll most likely remain hidden for a few days from whoever tried to abduct Avery, but the journey will take a while. I wasn't able to procure portal keys on such short notice, so Heidi will cloak us as we travel. We move after Charlotte wakes."

"Right." I stood and dusted the dirt from my pants, my mind still reeling from what I'd learned, then I approached my mate. *Stopped time. Carried us here. But how?*

I inhaled again, needing to scent her lilac fragrance. She may command otherworldly power now, but she was still my Avery, and I needed to be near her.

Her shoulders tightened when I approached.

I crouched at her side. "Are you hurt?" I asked gently.

My gaze skimmed over her features, taking in her wide eyes and soot-smudged cheeks. Charlotte still lay unconscious on the ground. The wound near her neck had a thick bandage over it, but no new blood seeped through it.

"No," Avery replied. "Just . . . tired."

"Bavar said you carried us here."

"I did."

"How? Charlotte and I are bigger than you. And how did you get us away from them?"

"Didn't he tell you?"

"He did, but I want to hear it from you."

Her hands trembled, and she clasped them together. "When I saw you and Charlotte on the ground, I thought you were both dead, and then the power inside me—it unleashed." A fearful scent oozed from her pores. "And then time stopped, so I picked you both up and ran us away."

I rocked back on my haunches, remembering the

violet light in her eyes, the brilliance of her power, and how I'd experienced that strange feeling of time stopping and restarting when she'd first woken up.

Good Gods. What in the actual fuck?

"There's something else. That tall robed one, he said he's been waiting for me for thousands of years."

I jolted, then glanced at Bavar.

"We're already on it," Bavar said. "I've sent this new information to Nicholas. The gargoyles are searching for answers as we speak."

Satisfied, I rocked closer to Avery. "Are you okay?" I forced my fear down, but fuck, this was nearly out of the SF's league. We'd never had an assignment like this before.

She nodded quickly but glanced down, twisting her fingers.

Heidi, Lex, and Bishop—several Squad Three members—were standing nearby listening avidly. I inclined my head, silently requesting them to leave.

They shared curious looks with each other but did as I asked.

Once it was just Avery and me, while Charlotte continued to lay on the ground, still unconscious from the enchantment that Lex had used to expedite her healing, I shuffled closer to my mate.

The urge to touch her was so strong it nearly overwhelmed me. "Tell me more about the tall one. Did you see his face? Can you describe him? Did you see anything that would help us identify him?"

She took a breath, the sound deep and shuddering. "No, his face was covered by his hood, so I only saw his mouth." Her eyes widened. "His skin was a strange green color."

Green color? I eyed Bavar to see if he was listening. He was. The fairy commander pulled his tablet out, sending that extra tidbit of information off to Nicholas.

"But then everything happened so fast that I didn't pay much attention to it," Avery continued. "After you carried Charlotte outside and they surrounded us, it all kind of blurs together. But that man, the tall one, he seemed to know me, and they were there for *me*, I'm sure of it." Her wide luminous eyes flashed to mine. "But when they shot that spell at me, you jumped in without a second thought. You risked your life to save me."

She wrapped her arms protectively around her waist, and a snarl rose in my throat at the thought of them threatening her, but I swallowed it down. "Go on," I said gently.

Sparking power zapped softly on her skin. "The tall one ordered the others to take me. I thought you were dead, and that's when I felt it. The power in me *opened*, and then time stood still. Everything stopped, but it was like the tall one was still there with me. He was the only one who was still aware of what was going on."

My brows furrowed. "Can you describe that more?"

"Everything paused, went still, stood absolutely motionless." She recounted how everyone had frozen, some even stopping in midair. "But his eyes followed me. He wasn't as affected by it."

I took a deep, ragged breath. I'd never heard of power like that or someone who had a trace of immunity to it.

"What's wrong with me?" she whispered.

Before I could stop myself, I pulled Avery against my chest. Her scent flooded me, my nostrils flaring. "Nothing's wrong with you," I said gruffly.

Her body was stiff in my arms, so reluctantly I began to let her go, but then her arms grew softer, her body slowly melting against mine.

My heart ached—fucking *ached*—at the feel of my mate against me. Even though it'd only been a couple days since I'd last held her, it felt like eons.

"You would have died to save me," she said quietly against my chest. "You didn't even hesitate."

I ran my hand up and down her back, soaking up the feel of her like a man dying from thirst. "I would give my life for you."

At my raw declaration, Avery shook her head and began to pull back. It was agony to let her go.

"But why?" She peered up at me. "Why would you do that?"

Because I love you. You're my mate. I live and breathe for you.

But I knew she wasn't ready for that kind of brutal honesty. She didn't remember me, didn't know me. To her, I was a stranger.

Clenching my jaw, I replied, "You're someone who's very special to me. That's why."

Her gaze searched mine, as though if she looked hard enough she'd be able to see my memories, feel what I felt. Even though I detected her pent-up need to know what I did, she eventually shook her head.

"I wish I could remember."

"So do I, Avery. So do I."

CHARLOTTE ROUSED AN HOUR LATER, and we quickly mobilized. Avery stayed by her friend, helping her stand even though Charlotte acted like her typical self—tried to brush it off and act like she was fine.

But I still caught the slight tremor in her hands. As much as she was trying to pretend the attack hadn't affected her, it had. And for good reason. She'd nearly died.

I pulled her to the side as Lex waited patiently behind me with the sleeping draught. As much as I loathed to take it, I knew I needed to. It would take hours to get to the safe house, and sleep was a good way to pass that time.

But before I did, I needed to speak with my former new recruit.

"Morris, I owe you an apology. What I did back at the inn was unforgivable, but still, I ask for your forgiveness."

"Did you really leave me?"

Shame crept up my neck, so I locked my jaw. "I did. My focus was entirely on Avery. It shouldn't have been."

She crossed her arms. "She said she made you go back for me. Is that true, sir?"

"Yes and no. When I realized what I'd done, I was going to go back, but she also wasn't taking no for an answer."

Her brow furrowed, and she was silent for a moment. "She's your mate, isn't she?"

Her question was quiet, and didn't end in *sir*. I knew she was talking to me as a fellow wolf—one werewolf to another. "She is."

"Then I forgive you. I know you were acting on

instinct. I also know from what I've been told that you're sleep deprived and it's affecting your judgment, and while I don't know all of the details between you and Avery, I can see what's going on, and I've come to know you well enough during my training to realize that you normally wouldn't leave a fallen squad member behind." She slugged me lightly in the shoulder. "Just don't make a habit of it . . . sir."

I dipped my head. "I owe you, Morris, and I don't say that lightly. There aren't many supernaturals I owe a debt to, but to you, I do. You can call that chit in at any time."

The corner of her lips tugged up, and she dipped her head in return. "Noted. Having you in my back pocket almost makes my near death worth it."

I grimaced, and she sobered.

"In all seriousness, sir, I get it. I do. Since I'm a werewolf who grew up in a pack, I understand all too well what male wolves are like when they want a female. It doesn't mean that I'm not pissed at you at all. I am, but I also understand why you did what you did. But I'll still gladly take that chit."

I chuckled as relief filled me. "Something tells me you'd make a solid bargainer."

She shrugged. "Perhaps I missed my true calling."

Shaking my head, she and I joined the rest of the

group. Avery hung back, watching us, and smiled in relief when Charlotte approached her.

"Lex, that draft," Bavar said, nodding at the tall sorcerer.

As much as I hated not being alert for the ride to the safe house, I took the draft and downed it. The bitter taste was like eating grass.

"Jamison, you'll be on my carpet. Everyone else, stay close." Bavar directed the carpets into the formation he wanted.

Heidi, a witch in her early thirties who'd been with the SF for longer than me, mumbled an incantation under her breath and wove her magic through the air. It shimmered like twinkling stars and left a hazy dome around us.

To anyone looking at us from the outside, they would simply see the field and hear the distant crashing waves from the sea. An advanced sorcerer, or perhaps those robed men, would be able to see through her cloaking spell, but it wouldn't be completely obvious. They'd have to be close, within a hundred feet, to detect us.

We could only hope that there weren't more than the group who'd attacked us. For all I knew, they had spies stationed throughout this realm who would be watching and waiting.

Heaviness gripped my eyes as I stepped onto the enchanted carpet. Avery and Charlotte sat on the one in the middle, surrounded on all sides by Squad Three who had weapons drawn. I felt my mate's gaze on me when I settled back. A memory of the kiss I'd given her, along with her relief when she'd realized I was okay, clouded my mind as the sleeping draught took hold.

Bavar activated the carpets with a sharp command, and as my eyes closed and darkness claimed me, we were off.

CHAPTER EIGHT
AVERY

The fae countryside flew by as we zoomed over the land. Small villages, sprawling crops, and occasional estates dotted the hillsides. There were roads, too, but most were either single-lane cobblestone or simple dirt tracks that didn't hold any early-morning travelers.

Bavar had informed me that most fae flew on carpets, rode domals—fae-like horses—or transported to their destinations using magic.

Somewhere in my foggy mind, I knew that since there were no electric or engine-powered vehicles here that this realm was much quieter and more tranquil than earth. The picturesque landscape reminded me of an English manor that I assumed I'd seen on a TV show or perhaps once visited, but the manors here were more vibrant. The colors were brighter and more vivid, and an underlying scent of magic filled the air.

Unlike yesterday afternoon, the wind didn't slap my cheeks or sting my eyes as the carpets hummed over the lands. Heidi's protective cloaking spell warded off the elements, leaving us to travel comfortably.

We'd already been traveling for several hours when the sun began to rise. A few stars still shone above, but they were quickly disappearing.

I blinked, my eyes feeling gritty. Bone-deep fatigue pulled at me, but I couldn't sleep. Too much had happened, and every time I closed my eyes I saw the robed men and felt their clawing hands digging into me.

Despite my whirring mind, I would have enjoyed the carpet ride, especially the dips and sways over the hills, if Charlotte's complexion wasn't so pale. Even though she'd received blood, she still looked weak.

"How are you feeling?" I asked her when she finally roused from the heavy slumber she'd fallen into shortly after starting our journey.

Her lips curved up, but her smile was brittle. "Like a million bucks."

"You're not fooling me. I can see that you're in pain. Should I see if Lex has any opiates?"

Her smile turned wry. "You know what opiates are?"

My lips parted with a smart reply, but then I cocked my head. "Strangely, yeah, I do."

"No. I'm good. Human drugs just cloud my thoughts, although if he has a witch potion I'd be game."

I signaled Lex over, a tall man with shaggy blond hair. He hopped from his carpet to ours and handed Charlotte a potion.

"Thanks, bro," she said, then downed it in one swallow.

"Let me take a peek at that shoulder."

She angled her neck, and he peered under the bandage. "No fresh bleeding. That's good. We'll clean it again when we reach the safe house, and apply a fae salve so it'll heal faster, but you should be okay for now. Just avoid any jarring movements."

Once he was back on his carpet, Charlotte pushed up on her elbows to face me better. "This is kind of backwards, isn't it?"

"What do you mean?"

She waved at her injury, then me. "I'm the one injured, yet it wasn't from protecting you. It was from getting hit by one of those motherfuckers while Major Jamison was protecting you. I can't help but feel that I didn't do my job well."

My eyes bugged out. "You're kidding, right?"

A flash of guilt overtook her face. "No, I'm not. This

is just my really lame way of saying I'm sorry for not protecting you better."

I faced her squarely as I worked to control the buzzing energy growing inside me. "Charlotte, you were hurt because we left you in the inn with a group of crazy supernaturals that were there for *me*. The one who should be apologizing is me or Major Jamison. We shouldn't have left you on your own."

"Well, for what it's worth, Jamison already apologized."

"He did?"

"Yep, and he said he owes me." She grinned. "That'll come in handy one day, but still, I fucked up on my first week on the job. That's not cool, and I feel really shitty about it, so I wanted to say sorry."

I balled my hands into fists. I hated seeing her look this way. Even though I didn't really know her yet, I'd come to learn in the short hours we'd been acquainted that she took her job very seriously. And like she said, she was new to the job. It seemed like a lot had been asked of her in a very short amount of time, and that was hardly fair.

A shiver raced up my spine when I remembered the standoff Wyatt and I had after he'd left Charlotte in the inn. My insistence that he retrieve her had left me alone when that robed man—or whatever he was—had slithered toward me.

My gut tightened. "Well, I appreciate your apology even though it's entirely unnecessary, and I'm glad to hear that Wyatt apologized to you." Strangely, a warm feeling filled me that he'd done that. I imagined someone in his position may see others as simply being there to serve him, but he'd apparently done the right thing and had taken ownership of the blame for leaving her. The fact that he'd even apologized said a lot about the kind of person he was.

And realizing that made that damned fluttering motion begin in my stomach again.

"Wyatt, is it?" Charlotte's eyes, now wide open, danced with amusement. I could tell the potion was kicking in. "You're on a first-name basis now? Girl, now that I know what I know, you *totally* held out on me during training. You did hook up with him, didn't you?"

My cheeks flushed just as we dipped down a hill. I gave a little squeal from the unexpected free-fall sensation, but Charlotte was right. At some point this morning, I'd stopped thinking of him as Major Jamison and had started thinking of him as Wyatt.

But that didn't mean I'd hooked up with him. Truth be told, I had no idea if I ever had.

"I don't know," I replied once we reached the bottom of the hill and were gliding over fragrant wildflowers. A sea of petals that resembled crimson roses, blue bonnets, and vibrant marigolds brushed along the bottom of the carpet. Tall swaying stalks of fae-sage and long grasses were intermixed with the flowers. The scents were so heady that it made my head swim, but their potent fragrance was better than acknowledging what Charlotte was implying.

Because the curling motion in my stomach was now flipping with a vengeance. Had I hooked up with him?

Charlotte quirked an eyebrow, looking strangely smug. "It's all making sense now."

"Anyway!" I said loudly, desperately hoping we'd change the subject, but my loud exclamation only got a curious look from Bavar as Wyatt slumbered beside him.

I cleared my throat and hoped the fairy commander couldn't see my cheeks burning.

But instead of taking the hint—or maybe she was purposefully ignoring it—Charlotte laughed and said, "The next time you hook up with him, I want the details. Like, *all* the details."

"Charlotte," I hissed under my breath. "Stop!"

My hiss, of course, got another assessing glance from Bavar, but thank the Gods that Wyatt was still asleep.

Having him hear this exchange would have been mortifying.

Charlotte at last sobered, and we carried on for another thirty minutes in relative silence—thankfully.

As the carpets began climbing another hill, Charlotte angled her chin to peer around me at the commanders. "Looks like someone just woke up."

My entire body instantly tensed, and I slid a glance their way. Wyatt was sitting up and yawning. He'd probably gotten a good four hours in, and even though I knew he needed more sleep, he looked better.

Bavar handed him some food and drink, which he quickly consumed, and then the two men hunched together in conversation.

My heart skipped, and my stomach made that somersaulting sensation again when I studied him. With his back to me, Wyatt's sinewy shoulder muscles created ridges visible through his shirt, and he sat cross-legged, awarding me an ample view of his strong thighs.

"Those two are definitely a sight for sore eyes." Charlotte nudged me.

I elbowed her since she still wasn't keeping her voice down, but then immediately apologized when she grimaced. "Sorry. I forgot about your injury. Is it bleeding again?"

She studied the bandage as we crested the hill. At the

bottom of the hill lay another field, and after that, a huge forest.

"Nah, it's okay. I'll be right as rain in a few days."

"Good. I prefer that you stay living."

She chuckled. "I may be easier to kill than those two" —she nodded toward Wyatt and Bavar—"but I won't go down without a fight."

As we skimmed along the field, the forest grew closer. Early morning sun bathed the field in golden light. Above, the light-green sky grew brighter with every second.

A few minutes later we reached the woods' edge. The second we entered the trees a wall of magic washed over me.

"What was that?" Goosebumps sprouted on my skin, and a tingle raced down my spine when we dipped into the trees' shadows.

"*That* was the enchanting magic of the Shroud Forest," Bavar replied from his carpet. He and Wyatt glided closer to us, the fringe of their carpet brushing ours.

The carpets had slowed to maneuver carefully around the trees' thick trunks.

Since Wyatt was awake now, I kept my attention ahead as we flew deeper into the trees even though I felt him watching me now that he and Bavar were done discussing whatever they'd been talking about.

"Is this the forest we're staying in?" I asked no one in particular.

"Indeed it is. There's a safe house deep in these trees." Bavar withdrew his dagger. "My family has owned it for centuries. However, we allow the SF to use it when needed. It's heavily warded with ancient magic, and that, along with this forest's natural debilitating enchantments, makes for a very secure home."

The more the trees surrounded us, the more I understood what Bavar meant about the enchantments. Things felt different here—like up could be down, and left could be right. And the forest was so thick that it cut out most natural light. If the bizarre sensations of these woods weren't enough to put one off, I imagined the darkness would.

The forest grew thicker as we traveled farther into it. The carpets had to separate at times to move around trees before coming back together.

Squad Three, which consisted of five individuals apart from Bavar and Charlotte, all tensed, and their gazes constantly assessed our surroundings. Weapons were firmly gripped in their hands.

Heidi, the witch who'd been controlling the cloaking

spell, waved her hand and whispered a spell. The dome around us disappeared. "The forest will hide us now."

Cool wind caressed my cheeks as I took in the pulsing energy growing in the group.

"Why's everybody so tense?" I asked Charlotte.

She shrugged. "I don't know. Honestly, I haven't spent much time in this realm outside of the capital so I'm as unfamiliar with it as you are."

"It's because it's not only the enchantments that keep most fairies out of this forest." Wyatt's deep voice jolted through me. "This forest is also filled with creatures that will happily eat you for breakfast, and flora that will choke the life out of you." He stood on the carpet next to Bavar. Both of them had their feet planted steadily, as if the shifting and swaying vessel beneath their soles was motionless.

Someone's nap had done him good.

"This is a deadly forest?" I eyed the thick canopy with unease. "So *why* are we staying here?"

"We're hoping it will deter the men that are after you, or at the very least, hide you for a few days until we can learn more." Wyatt abruptly raised his weapon and fired. A vine—that I hadn't even realized had been following us—had begun slithering across Wyatt's carpet toward his feet. His shot blew it into a dozen pieces, and a shrill squeal immediately followed.

So the plants can scream. I shivered as the high-pitch sound died.

But that vine wasn't the only thing pursuing us. The other squad members began firing. Vines and tangled weeds were creeping toward us at an alarming speed as if excited by the fresh meat that had arrived in their midst.

The carpets sped up, under Bavar's command, and we were soon whizzing through the woods, dodging trees so quickly that at times I feared I'd fall off.

"Keep steady!" Bavar yelled. "And don't let your guard down. She's angry with us, that's for sure."

"She?" I asked Charlotte in confusion.

Before she could reply, a great rumble rose all around us. It sounded as if it came from everywhere and nowhere all at once, like the realm had muttered her displeasure.

I wrapped my arms around myself, suddenly glad that Charlotte and I were in the center of the group, despite the heady power thrumming through my veins. I knew I had immense magic, but that didn't mean I knew how to use it. I was more likely to blow up my friends than hit any creatures or nefarious plant life.

A shriek came from my right, and I darted a look there just as a tiny creature yelped and scurried up a tree trunk. A male SF member shot at it.

Another deep rumble came from the soil and trees.

"What *is* that?" I asked. "It almost sounds like *growling*."

"That was the forest." Bavar scanned the trees. "She wasn't expecting us, and she's a bit put out that we're firing at her children. We'll have to tread carefully." He stood straighter, turning on the carpet to face everybody as we continued moving at a dizzying pace. "Squad Three, only fire if directly threatened. The last thing we need is the Shroud Forest as an enemy."

The other members all dipped their heads just as a steady pounding of what sounded like stampeding animals came from behind us.

"Be ready!" Bavar yelled. "We have incoming."

My eyes widened when I took in the rustle and movement on the forest floor. Charlotte and I both gaped at one another. Something was moving beneath the fallen leaves and tangled roots.

A head popped up, then another. My jaw dropped when hundreds of monkey-like creatures emerged from the soil and began running behind us. They stood no more than two feet tall and ran on spindly hind legs, but their razor-sharp teeth, impressive speed, and wicked-looking claws told me they weren't to be written off.

"What are those?" I gaped.

"Forest sprites. Damn. I've only read about them but

have never seen one. Shit. They're going to need my help with this." Despite her injuries, she reached for her weapon and pushed to a stand. A dot of blood appeared through her bandage when she raised her bow and nocked an arrow.

All around us, the sprites began jumping and trying to land on the carpets. They came from everywhere. The vicious little creatures clawed out of tree trunks, emerged from the forest floor, and fell from the canopy above.

One managed to leap onto the carpet beside us, but a swift kick from one of the women had the sprite sailing through the air. Its enraged scream made my ears hurt.

"How much farther?" one of the men standing on the carpet ahead of us called. Another sprite landed by his side and he fired a shot. It flew off the carpet.

"At least a half a mile!" Bavar shouted. "We'll need to keep them off the carpets. We won't be protected from them until we reach the wards!"

The sprites continued to grow in numbers and despite trying to keep on the defense, Squad Three was quickly outnumbered and had no choice but to engage in all-out war.

Shots rang out. Arrows flew. Screams and high-pitched shrills echoed through the trees. I got caught up in the chaos, kicking at least half a dozen sprites back to the forest floor.

The carpets moved even faster, their tumbling, dipping movements making it hard to stay upright. Most of Squad Three was kneeling, although Bavar and Wyatt stayed standing.

"Behind you!" I yelled to Charlotte.

She spun and let her arrow fly in the same maneuver. It struck a sprite straight through the chest, its eyes rolling back in its head before it landed with a thud behind us.

Another one managed to jump onto our carpet, but I swiped out my arm when it leaped for Charlotte. It squealed in fury at my unexpected attack.

"Keep fighting but only when necessary!" Bavar commanded.

"There's so many!" Lex yelled as he shot two sprites at once, casting spells from both hands.

"We're almost th—"

A swell of magic rose from the forest floor, cutting Bavar off. The carpets buckled beneath us, sending most of us to our bellies or rolling toward the edge.

"Dammit, she's really fucking angry," Bavar seethed.

"We're losing one!" Wyatt yelled.

Before I could blink, Wyatt catapulted off his carpet, somersaulting through the air over me and Charlotte, to land on the carpet to our right. He grabbed a hold of one of the women just as she was about to fly off.

Hauling her back up, Wyatt pushed the dazed squad member behind him and punched a sprite square in the face when it tried to latch on to his arm.

"Are you hurt, Marnee?" Wyatt asked the woman.

Blood trailed down Marnee's leg, seeping through her pants. With wide eyes, I realized she'd been bitten.

"I'll live." Her cobalt-blue eyes flashed. She pushed back to kneeling, her weapon ready.

Wyatt nodded curtly then leaped off the carpet, in between two branches, before landing next to Bavar.

Bavar smirked. "Show-off."

Wyatt grinned and swung when another sprite flew from the trees. His punch shot it to the ground behind us, its indignant hiss following.

Someone's nap had *definitely* done him good. My heart pounded from the sheer power that Wyatt channeled as screams from the descending sprites rose higher and higher.

"How are there so many?" The energy strumming in me vibrated and swelled, as if sensing my fear of the erupting chaos. If only I knew how to wield it, then I could shoot the sprites as they came for us.

"They come from tunnels underground," Bavar called out as he kicked two off his carpet at once. "They live in intricate channels beneath the forest floor, but also have pathways up through the trees' trunks. They can literally come from anywhere, which is why they're so dangerous."

"Charlotte!" I yelled just as another sprite leaped off a tree branch toward her.

But she didn't turn in time. It landed on her shoulder, its ragged claws digging into her injury. She screamed in pain, and fire burned inside me.

"Get off my friend!" I yelled and then power burst from my chest, completely out of my control.

The wave of magic shot out of me in a circular blast and everyone ducked. The crackling electric power zapped through the forest, obliterating everything in its path. Trees fell. Sprites screamed.

My eyes widened in horror even though Squad Three had reacted fast enough to avoid it.

But the sprites hadn't been so lucky.

Hundreds of cries rose from the creatures. Those it hit were dead, their legs twitching and their bodies convulsing as their eyes rolled back in their heads.

"Well, that's pretty wicked," the woman with red hair said on the carpet beside us. "Why didn't you do that sooner?"

The others all grinned as my power gave everyone a moment's reprieve.

But before I could congratulate myself for not killing anyone in the squad and only harming the nasty creatures, the sprites that had managed to avoid my fury-laden blast, all turned their eyes on me. They hissed and bared their teeth as they raced through the trees, keeping up with the flying carpets.

"Oh, shit," I whispered, realizing I'd just made myself a direct target.

CHAPTER NINE
AVERY

The power inside me hummed. Electrical snaps zoomed down my arms, but I was just as likely to kill those around me as I was the forest sprites. *Shit on a brick.*

"Avery, watch out!" Wyatt called.

I spun around just as two dozen sprites launched toward me from the trees. They struck from all angles, descending like locusts.

My hands rose automatically to shield myself, and a part of me hoped the dome would form automatically again, but since I didn't know if it would, I clenched my eyes shut and waited for the creatures' razor-sharp teeth to tear into my skin.

But only a grunt followed, then the pummel of fists on flesh.

I opened my eyes to see Wyatt standing in front of me, his eyes glowing gold as alpha power radiated from him.

Several of the squad members winced when Wyatt's energy hit them, but he quickly sucked it back inside.

Behind us, two dozen sprites lay dazed on the forest floor—the two dozen that had tried to attack me all at once.

Wyatt rapidly assessed me, wind ruffling his hair as his attention shifted up and down my frame, but I was completely unharmed. None of them had touched me.

"I'm fine. Don't worry about me," I said.

His nostrils flared, then he jumped back to his carpet to help Bavar with seven sprites that had landed around Squad Three's commander. They were all trying to latch on to his legs, but Wyatt once again turned into a blur of action making it impossible to follow his movements.

"Look!" Marnee yelled. "We're almost there!"

I twirled around, searching for a cottage hidden amidst the trees, but what greeted us made my jaw drop.

A castle glittered ahead. It rose two stories from the ground, its beige exterior and stone roof blending into the forest. It was built in the shape of a star. Five thin wings extended from the castle's center.

Trees grew around the entire perimeter of the five points, their canopies extending over the long wings, hiding the roof and dwelling, which would also keep the castle hidden from anyone flying above the Shroud Forest.

A solid stone wall surrounded its perimeter, glimmering with magical wards. At the wall's center, a large set of black towering gates waited.

Squad Three continued to battle the never-ending sprites as the carpets zoomed toward the castle.

"This is gonna hurt!" Bavar warned. He yelled a command, and the gates swung open just as we barreled into the wards.

A flash of pain zapped my nerve endings since we hit the wards going so fast. Charlotte groaned as the wards tugged and pulled, the ancient magic assessing if we were allowed to enter.

Finally, it released us and we ground to a halt on the other side of the wall. The wards shimmered in a deadly glow behind us.

I breathed deeply, my chest heaving. On the other side of the wall and behind the gates, hundreds of sprites lay on the ground either dead or dazed from hitting the wards. Hundreds more chattered around them.

The ones still alive jumped up and down, squawking, hissing, and growling at us, but when they approached the wall and tried to jump over its impressive height or attempt to enter through the gates, they squealed in pain when the wards flared and repelled them.

"Is that how your family trips always go here, Major?" One of the men stood, breathing heavily as he brushed himself off. Blood oozed from his forearm where a sprite had bitten him, but already his skin was healing, the wound closing.

He must be a werewolf. But then I frowned as I realized that knowledge had come from some deep-dwelling memories that I had but couldn't readily access.

"Usually not." Bavar dusted himself off. His uniform was surprisingly clean. "But that's only because we usually give the Shroud Forest fair warning when we plan to venture here. Given that I didn't have time today to appeal to her delicate sensibilities, I'm not surprised that she let her displeasure be known."

"Did she ever." Marnee twisted her blue-black hair back into a ponytail since most of the strands had come loose.

Wyatt hopped off his carpet, his eyes on me.

The fluttering began in my stomach again as he strode purposefully toward me. I jumped off the carpet and rushed toward Lex.

"I think you better take a look at Charlotte. One of the sprites attacked her, and her injury is bleeding again."

Lex gave a curt nod and set off to tend to Charlotte, which left me an easy target for my incoming commander.

Crap.

Wyatt's energy barreled into my back just as the two women that had been fighting beside Lex hopped to the ground.

"I'm Terry," one of the women said. She had long red hair and held some kind of crossbow. She'd been the one who made the comment about my magic taking out the sprites. "And this is Marnee." She nodded toward the woman with the blue-black hair who was fixing her ponytail.

I took in Marnee's blacker than black hair, cobalt-blue eyes and translucent skin. With a start, I realized she was a siren. On the other carpet, Heidi and the werewolf were assessing each other for injuries. I still didn't know the werewolf's name.

"You got a few nice kicks in and shots back there." Terry placed her hands on her hips as her long red hair brushed around her shoulders.

I shrugged, having a hard time taking my eyes off Marnee. I wondered if I'd met many sirens before. "If I knew how to wield my power better I could have done more."

Marnee's expression remained impassive as she watched me, but Terry laughed.

Her laughter abruptly died, though, when Wyatt's energy continued barreling into me, letting me know the silent predator had arrived, and this time, I couldn't escape him.

"We better see what Bavar needs us to do." Terry dipped her head respectfully at Wyatt. "Major Jamison."

Marnee nodded, too, but her lips titled up, a sultry heat filling her eyes. "Major," she said in a low, husky voice, a soft sing-song tone carried in that one word.

My lips parted when her siren's magic washed through me. Then came the jolt that she was using her seductive song on Wyatt.

A flame raced up my spine, sending sparks of power tingling all the way to my hairline, but Wyatt's jaw merely tightened, and his gaze remained clear. A wave of alpha power pushed off him, and I realized his power had protected him from her song.

"Marnee." He frowned.

The hopeful look in her eyes dimmed, some of the sultriness evaporating from her full lips. She shot me a look—one I couldn't quite interpret—before she sauntered off to join Terry.

I watched her retreating form, taking in her full hips

and round ass. Like most sirens, her body begged for a man's attention.

But Wyatt didn't watch her. He watched me.

"You've been with her." The accusing words slipped from my lips before I could stop them.

He stilled, then placed his hands on his hips. A moment of silence passed between us before he said, "Yes. Once. It was years ago."

He continued to watch me, his expression giving away nothing.

I bit my lip, not understanding the rush of—*gah*—something that sped up my spine and made me want to pull my hair out. *What the hell's the matter with me?*

"Does that bother you?" A glow flickered in his eyes, the only hint at emotion on his face.

I dropped my chin and spun around, my breath suddenly coming too fast. "No. Why would it?" I said tartly over my shoulder.

The energy from Wyatt grew, and it heated my back again. His magic warmed my skin and made my nerves electrify, but when I finally swung back around to face him, his power abruptly disappeared, as if he'd sucked it back inside him.

He stared down at me as his assessing gaze moved up and down my frame. "You look unhurt."

Breathing a sigh of relief that we were no longer

talking about *that* subject, I replied, "I'm fine. I think being in the middle gave me an advantage. That and Charlotte took most of the hits." Guilt stole over me when I caught Lex tending to her shoulder again. More blood had seeped through the bandage, soaking through in parts.

"She was doing her job, as she was trained to do. Don't feel guilty about that."

"Do you feel guilty about leaving her in the inn?" My question came from out of nowhere, but I had to know if he dismissed my friend that easily. I didn't think he did since he'd already apologized to Charlotte, but what he just said . . . maybe she was just a lackey to him.

The glow in his eyes intensified. "Yes, I do feel guilty about leaving her. It was wrong to do that. I shouldn't have, and if I'd been in my right frame of mind and not so sleep deprived, I wouldn't have. If any harm had come to her because of my actions—" His lips tightened. "Thankfully that isn't the case, but that doesn't mean this job is without danger. We all know and understand that, and right now, our assignment is about guarding you and solving the mystery that afflicts you. That's what I meant when I said you shouldn't feel guilty about Charlotte fighting to keep you safe."

A wave of relief washed through me that he did value her, which brought an entirely new array of sensations ripping through me. *Ugh.* Sensations I still didn't understand.

Shuffling my feet, I tried to ignore those feelings. "And are you in your right frame of mind now? You didn't sleep long."

He raked a hand through his hair. "Not quite. Those few hours of sleep helped, but I've been ordered to rest while we're here. Bavar is taking over, and Squad Three will be guarding this castle while those not on patrol duty confer with the SF library and database to learn what we can about the men who attacked us."

A breeze shifted the wind, and his oak and pine scent flowed through my senses. He continued to loom over me, which made the power inside me spark, and a zap of electricity raced along my skin. I tried to quieten my reaction, but something about this man made everything inside me come alive. Like how I'd wanted to claw Marnee's eyes out when she tried to use her song on him.

I crossed my arms, as if I could protect myself from these foreign feelings racing through me. "So when those sprites attacked me, and you jumped in front of me, was that you just doing your job?" My eyes bugged out. *Um, why did I just ask that?*

"Would it bother you if I only did it because duty called for it?"

"Did you?" I challenged. *Seriously, why do I need to know this?*

He drew closer to me, coming within an inch of my chest. Gold rimmed his eyes, and once again alpha power shimmered off him.

My breathing kicked up, and my breasts tightened, feeling like two heavy orbs that throbbed for his touch.

His nostrils flared, the glow in his eyes intensifying.

Just the feel of him so close to me made my insides twist, but I held my ground, not backing away or showing submission.

"Do you really think I only protected you because you're the subject of my assignment?" he said softly, his voice as smooth as velvet.

A deep ache curled in my lower belly. I opened my mouth to reply, but then caught the sight of blood on his shirt.

Frowning, I looked at the rest of his clothing. Tiny claw marks and puncture wounds riddled the sides of his shirt.

"You're hurt." I rapidly assessed the rest of him. Dried blood was everywhere.

"That's what happens when two dozen sprites attack you at once."

My lips parted. "You need the medic!" My hands came up of their own accord to probe his injuries.

The second I touched him, his breath sucked in.

Heat tingled my hands, racing up my arms as the rock-hard feel of him made a flush creep up my neck. He still stood so close. *Too* close.

I made a move to step back, but he abruptly reached up and covered my hand with his, holding my palm to his chest.

His muscles tightened beneath my fingertips, and my breathing grew so fast that I wondered if I'd pass out.

"I'm not hurt."

"But they bit you." *So many* bite marks littered his clothing.

"I'm already healed." With his free hand, he lifted his shirt, awarding me with a view of some very impressive abs, honey-hued skin, and a slight trail of hair that dipped in the middle of his stomach to trail tantalizingly lower to something else that waited in his pants.

My mouth went dry.

"See? I'm not hurt. Even sleep deprived, I still heal immediately."

Swallowing, I couldn't reply. Dried blood caked most areas of his skin, but there weren't any visible claw or bite marks. The only evidence of the attack lay on his shirt, which was entirely ruined thanks to the sprites.

"I'm a werewolf. We heal fast. You probably already noticed that with Bishop." He nodded toward the other wolf who was standing with Squad Three as Bavar outlined the plan for the next few days.

Wyatt let his shirt fall back down.

I nearly whined at the sight of his perfect body disappearing from view but managed to clamp my mouth shut.

An amused smile tilted his lips, and he finally released my hand.

My arm fell to my side, but my heart still pattered too fast.

Leaning down, Wyatt's warm breath washed against my ear when he whispered, "Were you worried about me?"

Goosebumps rose on my skin at the feel of him so close. *Oh my Gods.* Were these feelings what Charlotte had been talking about? Was my reaction related to Wyatt wanting to claim me? Maybe he was weaving some kind of magic over me. Maybe *that* was why I felt this way.

Before I could respond, he placed a feather-light kiss beneath my earlobe, and a million volts of lightning rushed across my skin.

Sucking in a breath, I gazed up at him wide-eyed when he straightened.

He didn't smile or say anything further, but his

nostrils flared when he inhaled, and I could practically feel the male satisfaction pouring from him.

He'd affected me, and he *knew* it.

Embarrassment flamed my cheeks just as someone behind Wyatt cleared their throat.

"If you two are finished, we would like to head inside." Bavar had his hands clasped behind his back as amusement danced in his eyes.

Shit. Bavar also knew that Wyatt wanted to claim me. Was there anyone who didn't know?

My cheeks had to be as bright as a tomato by now.

Wyatt faced his friend, blocking me from the fairy commander's view. "We'll be there in a minute. Don't wait for us."

"As you wish." Bavar's retreating footsteps carried away, and I sighed in relief that the fairy commander and the rest of Squad Three couldn't see me right now as I desperately tried to compose myself.

It wasn't working though. With Wyatt's back so close to me, his scent flooded me again, and the oak and pine fragrance stirred something deep inside me.

I wasn't sure if it was a memory or something else. Regardless, I gasped, reaching and stretching for whatever it was that his scent elicited, but nothing came.

"Dammit," I whispered, my eyes closing.

"What's wrong?"

The feel of his finger lifting my chin made my eyes open. Any earlier amusement or satisfaction in his expression was gone, concern taking its place.

"I keep trying to remember things, but nothing comes."

"Can I ask what you were trying to remember?"

I inhaled, relishing his intoxicating scent as a shiver danced over my skin. "It was about you."

A veil descended over his face. He watched me, waiting.

My lips parted. "But it didn't come. I no more remember you than I do Bavar."

Disappointment flared in his eyes, but in a blink, it was gone. "That's okay. Right now, it doesn't matter. You're safe and healthy. At the end of the day, that's what's most important."

Yet his comment left unspoken words hanging between us. At the moment it didn't matter, but what about tomorrow, or next week, or a month from now? What if I still didn't remember him? What then?

He abruptly turned, his shoulders like an unyielding wall. "We should join the others."

Ahead of us, Bavar was leading Squad Three across a small bridge that arched over a creek. On the other side, a wide cobblestone path led to the castle's interior doors at the center of the five spindly wings in the castle's strange pentacle design. At least a dozen fae servants stood to attention, waiting for their employer.

As Wyatt and I walked toward them, I couldn't help but admire the colorful flowerbeds that dotted the carefully manicured lawns under the trees' thick canopy. Couple that with the sound of trickling water coming from a large fountain halfway around the estate, and one couldn't help but be affected by the serene living environment. I almost snorted at the irony. The journey to get here was anything but tranquil.

"How do you suppose the grass and flowers stay alive when such little sunlight reaches them?" Similar to the forest, the large trees that ringed the oddly shaped castle kept most sunlight out.

"Magic," Wyatt replied. "Can't you smell it?"

I sniffed and a potent tang of metal filled my nose. "I thought that was the wards."

"The warded magic is there, too—it's strongest—but underneath that are the varying layers of fairy magic that imbue these lands with life."

I huffed in amusement. "I don't think my sense of smell is that good."

He gave me a sly grin. "Well, if it was, you would detect the sweet mint scent mixed with a sharp hint of balsam wood. Both of those scents often accompany garden-preserving magic."

"What's it like to be able to scent all of that?"

He shrugged. "Now, it's normal, but when my wolf first emerged and his senses became my senses, it was a bit overwhelming."

My brow furrowed. "Is that something I used to know about you?"

"Yes. We were friends, long ago when we were younger, but since then you've—" He ran a hand through his hair. "You've gotten to know me on a deeper level."

Bavar and the rest of Squad Three waited for us at the top of the pathway to the front doors. I dipped my head, hurrying my pace. I knew Wyatt hadn't meant to alarm me, but knowing that we used to be more than friends made me ache in a way that bordered on painful. Is that why he wanted to claim me? He wanted what we once had?

Damn, this was too much. Between the crazy night and now this, I was starting to get a headache.

"Avery and Wyatt." Bavar waved a hand toward a group of fae. "I was just introducing the squad to the staff here at Shrouding Estate."

A dozen servants waited for the introductions. Like most of the fae I'd seen, their hair and skin tones were various shades of color. They all bowed and waited for Bavar to continue.

"This is Meestry, head of the household. He'll make sure to tend to any of your needs while we're here."

Meestry bowed deeply, his face angular, as though cut from marble. Dark purple hair covered his head. "Lord Fieldstone, as always, it's a pleasure to serve you. We will happily attend to all of your guests."

Lord? With a start, I realized that Bavar wasn't just an average fae.

As if sensing my curiosity, or perhaps scenting it, Wyatt brushed closer to me, his warm breath near my ear. "Bavar is the king's nephew. He's a royal fae, which also means he's nearly immortal. The royal fae live longer than any other fae, and they control much of the lands on this continent, which also means they control the vastness of its wealth."

"Which explains the castle in a forest with a full set of staff," I whispered under my breath as Bavar introduced each member of his squad separately.

A twinkle lit Wyatt's eyes. "Exactly."

"That's rather lucky for the SF, that a royal fae works for your organization."

Wyatt chuckled. "Bavar's connections have come in handy once or twice."

I was about to reply, but my lips snapped shut when Bavar reached us.

He winked in my direction, then nodded at Wyatt.

"And this is Major Jamison, a fellow commander. We've recently joined his assignment, which means he's ultimately in charge of this job, but he's going to take a few days of rest to recuperate. Whatever he wishes for shall be given to him. Understood?"

All of the servants bobbed their heads or curtseyed.

"And at last, we have Avery Meyers, who is a very special guest. You are to treat her with the utmost respect and do anything she asks. If she's hungry, thirsty, tired"—He rattled off a bunch of various ailments, half of which I was certain I would never experience—"you are to wait on her immediately. Understood?"

As before, the staff either curtseyed or bowed, and the head servant, Meestry, lifted my hand to kiss the back of it.

His eggplant-purple hair glittered when a rare streak of sunlight hit it. "Ms. Meyers, it is our pleasure to serve you."

When he straightened, I slipped my hand back to my side, feeling entirely uncomfortable with anyone serving me, but since Bavar carried on as if such devotion was normal, I tried to smother my embarrassment.

"If you'll follow me." Bavar began gliding forward, his squad falling into line behind him.

They fell into rank, the highest rank following

directly behind Bavar, with the lowest bringing up the rear, which meant Charlotte was once again at my side.

"How's your injury?" I asked as the doors to the castle opened soundlessly.

"Those little fuckers really tore it up, but Lex got a fae salve from one of the servants. He said it should be healed in no time, but if I ever encounter another sprite, I'm going to wring its neck."

I laughed, but the sound died when we entered the castle.

If I thought the outside was beautiful, it didn't hold a candle to what lay inside.

CHAPTER TEN
WYATT

Even though I hadn't been to Bavar's estate before, I found myself watching my mate instead of admiring the lavishness of the fairy commander's country home as he gave us a tour of the castle's five wings.

Avery's eyes lit up as Bavar led us from one extravagant room to the next. I stayed at her side or just behind her the entire way. I ached to touch her but knew I shouldn't.

To keep myself from draping an arm possessively around her shoulders, I kept my hands stuffed into my pockets and my back rigid.

But her scent called to me, and the way she'd reacted to me outside only made my wolf yearn to claim her again.

She'd been aroused and flustered when we'd stood so near one another by the gates. Her scent had taken on that musky tint, interwoven with her signature lilac fragrance.

And when I'd kissed her beneath her ear, knowing I shouldn't but unable to help myself, her entire body had trembled.

She still responded to me as she had before the alignment. It only made me further convinced that somewhere, lurking amidst the powerful magic that now vibrated through her body, lay the Avery I knew and savagely loved.

"And here we have the music room." Bavar opened another set of doors.

We all stopped outside of it, everyone's eyes wide as we took in the rich blue and cream colors. Inside were over a dozen instruments, expertly crafted and beautifully polished as they waited near chairs and chaise lounges for one to pick up.

Twelve tall, narrow windows with light-blue curtains took up an entire wall of the room. A few rays of sunlight streamed in, and on the other side of the window panes, leaves from the ancient trees that grew around the estate's perimeter fluttered in the breeze.

Bavar arched an eyebrow. "My mother is the musically inclined in the family, so you'll have to forgive me for not entertaining you with a sonata tonight."

Bishop—the only other male werewolf in Squad Three—snickered. "Does that mean you won't be playing us bedtime lullabies either, commander?"

Bavar gave him a sly grin. "I'm very sorry to disappoint you, but no. However, if you need a warm cup of milk or would like a magical tincture to ensure a good night's rest, I'm sure the staff would be happy to oblige."

Avery muffled a laugh, although the rest of Squad Three didn't try to hide their amusement.

Bishop shook his head and grinned. "I haven't had a cup of warm milk before bed since I was a wee pup. So which staff member do I need to accost for one tonight?"

One of the staff stepped forward, obviously not picking up on Bishop's sarcasm. When Bishop saw Avery's pink cheeks, he winked in her direction which elicited a huff from Marnee.

My wolf's hackles rose, and it wasn't because I was still tired. I inched closer to my mate. I didn't like the jealous scent that had been coming from the siren. It had risen during the tour as Avery slowly blended in with the squad—something Marnee obviously didn't want.

But since Charlotte and Avery were already friends, and I'd been so attentive to Avery, I knew Marnee was coming to learn that Avery wasn't just any protectee in this assignment.

Unfortunately, I had a feeling the one-night stand I'd had with the siren three years ago was coming back to haunt me. Ever since that encounter, Marnee had been trying to bed me again. I'd caught her more than once tossing her hair over her shoulder and pouting seductively. She was bordering on desperate with how much she wanted to catch my attention, and that didn't bode well since Avery's trust in me was only just forming. The last thing I needed was a mistake from my past to come back and fuck everything up.

I shifted in front of Avery, subtly maneuvering her away from Marnee's heated stare. The siren's prickly energy tingled my back, letting me know that she was still watching me.

I gritted my teeth at the memory of her using her magic outside. She'd actually tried to manipulate me using her siren song. I'd have to report that to Wes. That would only piss Marnee off more, but protocol was protocol. Using her song was no different than a vamp compelling—both were illegal.

At least my alpha power was strong enough that I

was immune to her song, but three years ago, on one drunken night in the fae lands, in which my squad and Bavar's squad were out celebrating, I'd succumbed to her charms.

I still blamed the fairy wine on my poor decision. Sure, Marnee was attractive, but I'd never been interested in her beyond a working relationship. Although, my mate didn't know that.

Smug satisfaction filled me when I remembered the flare of jealousy in Avery's scent when she'd realized that Marnee desired me. Since the alignment, my mate had acted like she wanted nothing to do with me, but her scent couldn't lie. She felt more for me than she wanted to admit, even if she didn't understand what she was feeling.

"This tour is a bit long, don't you think?" Avery said under her breath. "Do we really need to know what's in every room? Not that I'm complaining, it's a beautiful home, but one would think Bavar is grandstanding his wealth."

I snorted, then choked down the sound when Marnee shot daggers our way. "Believe it or not, he's not giving us a tour to show off his home. He's doing this so Squad Three knows where each room is and any vulnerable points in them. I can guarantee that if you asked

Bishop, Heidi, Lex, Marnee, or Terry where a room is in any of the wings, they could immediately answer. It's their job to memorize details like that, and it's something I need to know, too, even if I'm stepping down for a few days."

Curiosity lit her eyes. "And Charlotte? Would she know?"

I shrugged. "She knows it's part of the job, but she's still new. It takes practice to master that kind of quick memorization. She probably couldn't accurately recall all of those details yet."

"And last, I shall be showing you to your chambers." Bavar's comment interrupted Avery's curious questions as he turned to his staff. "Please see to everyone's belongings. I'm sure we'll all want to freshen up before we reconvene."

The staff scurried off, and I was glad for the chance to clean up. After weeks of little to no sleep, enough hair had grown on my cheeks that I had a beard, which meant I needed a shave. And the tears in my clothes from those damned sprites, along with the dried blood all over me, meant a shower and change of clothes were exactly what I needed.

"The rest of you may follow me." Bavar clasped his hands behind his back and sauntered down the hall. "The sleeping chambers are in the Daphnis wing."

Bavar's bright orange hair flashed gold in the fairy lights twinkling above.

We were currently in the Titun wing. Each of the five wings of the house was called by the royal courts in the capital—which had been named after planets in the fae lands' solar system.

Our heels clicked on the marble floor, echoing down the vast area. The walls in each wing rose to at least thirty feet, decadent murals and tapestries adorning the walls and ceiling. Due to the estate's awkward design, the long halls proved lengthy to navigate, but Bavar had pointed out several internal portals that could be used to transfer from one wing of the castle to the next so one didn't have to walk the entire length.

"Bishop, you'll be here." Bavar opened the door to a suite with a fireplace, a king-sized bed, two couches, and an impressive wardrobe.

Bishop whistled. "Thanks, boss. I could get used to this."

Bavar smirked. "We'll reconvene again in an hour in the drawing room."

He led the rest of us to the next room. Everyone followed one by one, retiring to their chambers to wash off the dirt and blood from the sprites' attack.

When it was just me, Avery, Charlotte, and Marnee, Bavar paused. "There are only three chambers left in this hall. Major Jamison, where would you like to reside?"

I stepped closer to my mate. "I'll stay in Avery's chamber. Given what happened this morning, I'll be staying at her side for the remainder of this assignment."

Avery's lips parted. "Is that really necessary?"

I gazed down at her, keeping my hands in my pockets so I wouldn't brush the lock of hair off her cheek. "Yes. This estate may be secure for the time being, but that doesn't stop the fact that you're being hunted by a group that obviously has no qualms about killing others to get to you." My blood boiled just thinking about it.

Her cheeks flushed, making it appear that she was frightened, but her scent gave away her true emotion—apprehension at rooming with *me*. Apparently that was more daunting than a dozen men trying to abduct her.

Marnee's nostrils flared as Charlotte slid a sly grin Avery's way.

"Very well." Bavar bowed. "Marnee, you shall be here. Right this way."

The siren pushed past us, shouldering Avery in the process.

Avery jolted forward but righted herself before she fell. A low growl rose in my throat, but Marnee never uttered an apology.

"You're excused!" Charlotte called out after her, but Marnee didn't acknowledge that comment either. "Or not," Charlotte muttered. After Marnee slammed the door to her room, Charlotte cocked her head. "What's her problem?"

"Long story," I replied. "Don't ask."

Avery's nostrils flared. She inched away from me, and that jealous tint entered her scent again. With a brittle smile, she looped her arm through Charlotte's. "Since Charlotte is also an SF member, I don't see why I can't room with her instead of you."

Dammit. I would be thoroughly pissed if that one-night stand truly fucked this up.

Resisting the urge to pinch the bridge of my nose, I replied patiently, "I'm the commander in charge of your care. You'll be rooming with me."

"But if it's going to cause problems, with your . . ." She inclined her head toward Marnee's room.

"Charlotte?" Bavar interrupted, coming out of Marnee's room. "Your room is just over here."

Charlotte swung wide eyes between me and Avery, obviously reluctant to leave the lobbying battle between me and my mate.

"Corporal Morris?" Bavar said more sharply.

With a wistful sigh, Charlotte followed him to her chambers, which left me alone in the hall with my mate.

As soon as we had privacy, Avery crossed her arms, her eyes flashing. "Just because the SF has decided I need all of you around doesn't mean I'm a prisoner who has no choice in what happens here."

I bit back a smile as my blood heated. Damn, I loved her fire. It was one of the reasons I fell in love with her. She was a fighter, not one to back down even when an SF commander was looming over her.

"It's for your own safety," I replied calmly.

"If that's the case, why can't I room with Charlotte? She's perfectly capable of protecting me, and if you hadn't noticed, I'm not a weakling. *I'm* the one who saved the two of you during the middle of the night."

"True. You're not weak, far from it." I raised my hand when her mouth opened to argue again. "But the answer is still no because Charlotte's new to the job. She doesn't have enough experience to fully protect you."

She arched an eyebrow, the energy emanating from her still simmering. "And your girlfriend won't mind that you're sleeping in the same room with me?"

This time, I *did* smile. Taking a step closer to her, I leaned down and whispered in her ear, "Careful, I'm detecting some jealousy from you."

She tensed, and then shivered when my breath puffed against her skin. But as soon as that satisfying reaction occurred, she pulled her arm back and slugged me in the shoulder.

My eyebrows rose as a chuckle threatened to escape me. "Did you just hit me?"

Her jaw dropped, and horror filled her eyes. She quickly composed herself, snapping her mouth closed. She twirled around, her back to me so I couldn't see her face. "I . . . I don't know . . . I, uh . . . I don't know why I did that. I'm sorry."

I stepped closer until I knew she could feel my heat against her back. Once again, I leaned down and said softly into her ear, "Marnee means nothing to me. She's not my girlfriend and never was. You have nothing to be jealous of."

"I'm not jealous!"

"Well, if that's the case then you have no reason to hit me again."

She turned back to face me, but as soon as she realized how closely we stood, she took a huge step back. "Again, I'm sorry about that. I don't know what came over me."

I opened my mouth to tell her that I knew exactly what had come over her, but Bavar returned from Charlotte's room and waved toward the end of the hall. "Your chambers are right this way."

Avery rushed forward, staying close to the fairy's

side as I brought up the rear. Immense satisfaction rolled through me, making me want to grin. Avery may not have her memories back, but a part of her body remembered how she'd once felt for me, even if she wasn't consciously aware of it.

And that was all I needed to win her over.

CHAPTER ELEVEN
AVERY

Bavar showed us to the room that Wyatt and I would be sharing during our time at Shrouding Estate. My heart raced, thumping like a rabbit at the embarrassing way I'd just acted.

Seriously, what was wrong with me?

Bavar entered the room with us, and as soon as we stepped into the chambers, I used the impressive display to distract me. The room was so large that I imagined an entire family could live comfortably here.

On the far wall, a four-poster bed, bigger than any I'd ever seen before—well, as far as I was aware with my lack of memories—stood resolutely with thick wooden columns rising from each corner of the bed to support the canopy above.

Gauzy curtains hung from the top, pulled back and

secured to the posts with braided silk tassels. And the actual bed, while much bigger than I'd ever need, looked more comfortable than seemed necessary.

A mountain of pillows rested against the headboard, and I itched to feel the pale lavender fabric that looked as soft as silk yet made of the finest cotton. The top comforter looked so fluffy and comfy that I wanted to jump on it and see how far I would sink.

Of course, I didn't. I'd done enough to embarrass myself, but just as I was about to turn away, I paused and studied the bed. Something tickled the back of my mind.

Four-poster.

Canopy.

Mahogany wood.

"Is everything all right?" Wyatt shifted closer to my side, moving in that silent way of his.

"Yes. I mean, I think so. It's just that the bed . . . it seems familiar. Is that how my bed looks back home?"

He looked at the bed, then me, his expression impossible to read. "What about it looks familiar?"

"Its size, and the canopy with the curtains, and the large posts." I shook my head. "I don't know. I feel like I slept in a bed like that, but I can't tell what's real and what's not. It's like my mind's constantly playing tricks on me."

His fingers brushed mine when he stepped closer, but then he pulled back.

My heart snagged at the contact.

"There was a bed similar to this that you recently slept in." He was still watching me intently.

"There was?"

"Yes, only two nights ago you slept in a bed just like this."

I frowned, trying to remember, but just like before only blankness greeted me. I sighed heavily in frustration. "I'll have to take your word on that."

He continued regarding me, his sharp gaze making my stomach somersault.

I clasped my hands tightly in front of me, trying to control the erratic beating of my heart. Twirling away from him, I surveyed the rest of the room.

Lining one wall, two tall wooden wardrobes sat near a closed door that I assumed went to a bathroom. A small writing table stood next to it with parchment and feathers on its sturdy surface.

By the window, a small circular dining table with two chairs overlooked the fountain below. A pot of herbal tea rested on the table, steam wafting from the spout. A tiered tray filled with small sandwiches, tarts, miniature pies, fruit, and little cakes sat decoratively beside it.

I inhaled, my stomach growling, which I now knew meant I was hungry.

Beside the dining table waited a large fireplace with three couches and two chairs encircling it. If it were cold and snowy outside, one of those couches would be the perfect place to curl up with a book.

But as I finished surveying the extravagant chambers, I realized one large problem existed.

I twirled to Bavar. "There's only one bed."

"Indeed there is."

"But—" I sputtered. "I can't, um, I mean where will Major Jamison and I—" *Dammit.* I was sounding like a complete idiot, but there was *no way* I was sleeping in the same bed with Wyatt. Even if that bed was big enough to sleep five people.

"I'll sleep on the floor." Wyatt still watched me so intently that my breath caught.

Bavar casually placed his hands in his pockets. "I can have another bed brought to the room. I'll ask the servants to see to it after everyone's baggage is delivered."

"Baggage?" I cocked my head. "But we didn't travel with bags." And it was a good thing we hadn't. They would have tumbled right off the enchanted carpets given the crazy flying we'd done to escape the sprites.

Amusement filled the fairy commander's eyes. "Have

you not learned that everything has a way of being procured in the fae lands? With enough magic, anything is possible."

I frowned, not understanding.

"He'll have everyone's belongings transported from earth, or in our case, what's left of our belongings at the inn," Wyatt explained.

"Then why didn't magic transport us here? Why did we have to ride the carpets?"

Bavar tipped his head. "The magic used to transport non-living objects is much simpler than the spells needed for portal keys. It's much easier to move inanimate paraphernalia than live beings."

My lips parted. "Did any of our stuff survive the—" I swallowed, my mouth suddenly dry. "The attack?"

Wyatt took a step closer to me, his jaw locking. I knew the sudden sweep of fear I felt was written all over my face.

For a second, I thought he was going to reach for me, but then he stuffed his hands back into his pockets.

A fleeting sense of disappointment followed, and I inwardly scoffed. Why would I want him to touch me? Despite the obvious history he and I shared, he was still a stranger.

Yet, that lingering sense of longing remained.

"According to the report Bavar received, about a

third of the items you bought with Charlotte survived," Wyatt explained.

"Survived," I repeated, and a flood of memories slammed into me.

The rumbling building.

The robed men.

Screams.

Splintering wood.

Hands reaching for me.

I spun around, my breath suddenly coming too fast. On stiff legs, I walked to the window near the bathroom as the power inside me rumbled.

"I'll give you some time to freshen up," Bavar said quietly, then slipped from the room.

I made it to the window without electrocuting anything or stopping time again—thank the Gods—but I was too embarrassed to face Wyatt.

I was freaking out—like seriously freaking out—and it wasn't a state I wanted anyone to see me in.

But dammit, *so much* had happened in the past forty-eight hours. I'd awoken in a field with two strange men I'd never seen before hovering over me. Two people who were supposed to be my parents had desperately wanted me to remember them, but I could have sworn I'd never seen them before.

And then I'd been transported to a strange inn,

in a strange city, in a strange realm that oddly didn't feel like home even though I had no idea where home was because I had *no memories* of my experiences or travels. All I could remember were words and some random knowledge but nothing about *me*.

And if that wasn't bad enough, a group of men or supernaturals or whoever the hell they were had tried to abduct me. But why?

Fuck if I knew . . .

But most of all, what clenched at my heart and twisted my gut was knowing the man standing in the room behind me had once meant something to me. This werewolf commander from an elite organization, who hadn't pressured or forced me to try to remember him, had dug his metaphorical claws into me. Because the longer I was around him, the more I believed that he'd once meant the world to me.

An image of the large canopied bed again filled my mind.

Had we once shared a bed like that? Only two nights ago?

I wrapped my arms around myself because the feeling that evoked scared the shit out of me, because despite that innate feeling of familiarity, I still didn't know him or us.

Electricity sparked my nerves, and the immense power swirling inside me swelled.

I took deep breaths, doing my best to calm the rising panic and frustration inside me.

I closed my eyes. *Breathe. In and out. In and out.*

A set of hands softly clasped my upper arms, startling me, but then Wyatt's oak and pine scent clouded my senses.

He'd approached me from behind, completely silently. I was quickly coming to learn that when he wanted to move without detection, he was a master at it.

"Nobody can hurt you here." He rubbed his hands up and down my arms, the movement oddly comforting.

I expected the power inside me to zap him, since it was completely out of my control, but instead it calmed as though also soothed by his touch.

Without realizing what I was doing, I leaned back, my body pressing against his chest.

A low rumble from him vibrated into me, and his soft growl sounded strangely like *purring*.

"Are you hungry? Thirsty?" His lips feathered against my ear.

My breath stopped, then sped up when his lips brushed back and forth along my nape.

My chest heaved. Wyatt's hands were still on my

arms, his entire body melded to mine, and his warm breath puffed against my skin.

For some otherworldly reason, I wanted to tilt my chin and give him access to my neck so he could dot soft kisses along it.

That rumble again vibrated Wyatt's chest, and the sound cascaded through me. My core clenched, a flame of . . . of . . . *something* filled my belly. But what were these strange feelings?

Something hard pushed into my lower spine, and I spun around.

Gold lined Wyatt's pupils, the color so vibrant and alive.

"Yes," I said breathlessly.

The glow in his eyes intensified. "Yes, what?" he asked huskily.

I twisted my hands. "Yes, I'm hungry and thirsty."

With an abrupt push away from him, I hurried to the small table filled with refreshments. With shaking hands, I poured a cup of tea. Steam wafted up from the delicate china cup, and I cursed when my grip slipped and a large splash of tea poured onto the saucer.

Wyatt's sigh carried to me, and in that sound I heard the weight of the world. He still stood by the window, watching me, and the intensity of his stare made me . . . *ugh*. Made me what?

Dammit, why *can't I remember anything and* why *does all of this have to be so confusing?* I had no idea what the hell was going on between us, but it was as though my body remembered him even though my mind couldn't.

I brought the delicate cup to my lips and sipped, the hot brew slipping down my throat. With trembling fingers, I grabbed one of the little sandwiches from the tray and took a bite.

Flavors burst across my tongue, so rich and vibrant that a small moan escaped me.

Wyatt chuckled.

I blinked.

He was standing right beside me. "Fae food is always better than earth food."

I blinked again, completely ignoring his comment. "How did you do that?" I asked as my chewing stopped.

"Do what?"

"Move so fast. You were just by the window."

He shrugged and picked up one of the tarts off the tiered platter. He tossed it into his mouth, eating the entire thing in one bite. "Werewolves can move fast when we want to." He took another piece of food, this time one of the delicate meat pastries, his large thick fingers curling around the buttery concoction.

I tried not to stare at his hand, I really did, but for the love of all the Gods, even his fingers were attractive—

the skin smooth and tanned, his hands strong and wide, his fingers long and—

Another distant memory tugged at the back of my mind. I frowned.

His fingers . . .

I scrunched my face up, mentally pulling and clawing at the blip of knowledge that danced just beyond my cerebral fingertips.

Wyatt had done *something* to me with his fingers. Something that I had . . . liked.

But just as quickly as that memory teased me with that tickling sensation, it evaporated.

I huffed, the breath rushing out of me.

Wyatt peered down. "What is it?"

I shook my head. "I thought I was going to remember something."

"Something about the food?"

"No, something about you, but then it disappeared."

His eyebrows rose, and a fleeting hopeful expression washed over his features before he smoothed it. "Is that right?" He casually picked up a soft piece of what I assumed was fruit. It was circular and had a skinned exterior. When he bit into it, its inner red juicy flesh dripped with nectar. "Was it something I said that provoked the memory?"

I shook my head, dipping my eyes away from his

mouth. Even chewing made him appear . . . what was the word? Sexy? His jaw was so strong.

"No, it wasn't anything you said that provoked it." I fiddled with my teacup and took another sip. "It was your . . . fingers."

He took another bite of the fruit. "My fingers?" Amusement filled his tone. "Is that right? These fingers?" He held up his hand, wiggling the five digits. "Does this elicit anything?"

I laughed, unable to help it. I had the urge to slug him again, although in a playful way, not an angry way, and the laughter instantly died on my lips.

Once again, my body reacted to him, wanted to *play* with him even though I had no idea why.

I groaned. "Gods, this is so frustrating." I brought a hand to my forehead. "It's like everything is *there,* everything that used to be me. I can feel it, but it's just beyond my reach."

Wyatt dropped his hand back to his side. "I think that's a good sign. You're in there somewhere. You just don't remember."

"Exactly. I have yet to remember anything. I just have occasional feelings and tugging sensations in my mind."

"Which still sounds promising to me."

"Maybe." I shrugged.

A soft knock sounded on the door.

It cracked open, and one of the servants who'd greeted us when we entered the castle dipped her head. "I have your belongings. Is now an all right time to unpack them?"

Wyatt strode toward her, his hands extended for the bags. "We'll manage. I'm sure you have better things to do with your time."

She bobbed, her cheeks flushing when Wyatt took the bags from her before she hastily departed.

I eyed her retreating form, my head cocking. "You have that effect on women, don't you?"

He placed the bags on the ridiculously large bed then unzipped them. The contents spilled out. "What effect?"

I sidled closer to him but was careful to maintain my distance. "Women seem to notice you and want your attention."

He turned slowly toward me, and a waft of his alpha power rolled off him. "Is that what you think?"

I nodded hastily. "It's how Marnee acts around you, and Charlotte's made a comment or two, and then the servant who was just here—" I abruptly stopped and twisted my hands, my breath coming too fast again. *Did I really just say all of that? Why the hell am I pointing out that women find him attractive?*

But that strange feeling was swirling in the pit of my stomach again. That aching, gnawing feeling.

Wyatt sauntered toward me, one corner of his mouth kicking up. When he reached me, he didn't touch me, but his presence still washed over my senses and damn if I didn't respond to it.

My breasts ached, my belly sucked in.

He leaned down, his tongue darting out to lick his lips. "Again, you have nothing to be jealous of."

I frowned, peering up at him. "What makes you think I'm jealous?"

He smirked, then moved back to the bags as he began to pull everything out. "It's in your scent."

My brow furrowed as I studied the strange feelings inside me. "I'm jealous?"

He took an armload of clothes to one of the wardrobes before tucking them into the drawers inside it. "As far as I can tell, yes. Scents don't lie."

My cheeks flamed as hot as the sun. "You can *smell* my jealousy?"

"I've always been able to scent your emotions."

"Just mine?"

He shook his head. "No, everyone's. It's one of the perks of being a werewolf."

"Motherfucker," I whispered under my breath.

He laughed, then deposited the rest of my clothes in the wardrobe before stepping closer to me. "But again, you have nothing to worry about. Nobody has my eye except for one woman."

"And that woman is . . . me?"

He nodded.

"Even though I can't remember you?"

His nostrils flared. "Even though you can't remember me." He swallowed, his Adam's apple bobbing as that gold light flared in his eyes. "There was a time not too long ago when I had intended to wait years for you."

My stomach dipped for what felt like the twentieth time, and my voice was embarrassingly breathy when I replied, "You were? Why?"

His jaw clenched, the muscle ticking. "Because I fucked up. I hurt you and you pushed me away, but I was determined to make it right, even if that meant waiting years until I could make that happen."

I frowned, an uneasy feeling filling me. "You hurt me intentionally? Is that why I pushed you away?" I squeezed my hands together.

"No," he said gruffly. "I would never hurt you intentionally. It was just me being stupid and thinking I was doing what was best for us by pushing you away."

"But then something else happened?" I frowned. Again, I couldn't remember it, but something danced just off the precipice in my mind. Like a fleeting image in my peripheral vision, there and then gone before I could fully see it.

"Yeah, something else happened."

I crossed my arms. "Will you answer something truthfully for me?"

"Yes, anything."

"Before the alignment, and whatever the hell happened to me, were you and I in a good place?"

His eyes softened, a tender look filling them. He took a step closer to me, his hand coming up to cup my jaw as his forehead pressed against mine.

I stilled, breathing him in and feeling him pressed so intimately to me.

"Yes," he said quietly. "We were in a very good place, and it was a place that I was determined to keep us in forever."

My breath rushed out when he pulled back.

He grabbed some of his clothes from the wardrobe and a few toiletries. "I'm going to shower and clean up, unless you want to use the bathroom first?"

I shook my head. Any words I'd hoped to utter were locked in my chest.

When the bathroom door closed behind him, and the sound of running water came from the shower, I finally collapsed onto one of the couches near the fireplace.

We were in a good place. A very good place, according to Wyatt, one he was determined to keep us in.

But what did that mean? What had happened to us before that?

My lips pressed together in frustration as that twisty feeling started in my stomach again.

Even though I couldn't remember anything Wyatt spoke of, deep down, a part of me felt that he spoke the truth, and Gods help me if I wasn't already falling for him all over again.

CHAPTER TWELVE
WYATT

Warm water cascaded around me as I leaned against the shower wall. I squeezed my eyes shut, picturing the way Avery had gazed up at me with confusion, longing, and lust.

My wolf was pacing inside me again, urging me to push Avery more, demanding that I speed up the mating process. He wanted to claim her—now, *today*—even though she wasn't ready for that.

But the urge to claim her as ours overtook all reason with him. He desperately wanted me to sink my teeth into the smooth flesh of her neck until our magic again took root, marking her forever as ours.

But I couldn't do that. I'd pushed far enough today, maybe more than I should have, but when I'd scented her jealousy and seen how she'd responded to me physically, I hadn't been able to control myself.

Especially since her new skittishness around me was a far cry from how she'd been only two days ago. I knew she still didn't fully trust me, she had no reason to, but I also knew that I just needed to be patient.

I finally pushed away from the wall and washed my hair, then scrubbed the dried blood from my body, before I finishing with a much needed shave.

When done, I turned off the shower and closed my eyes, remembering the feel of Avery's round ass pressing against my groin and how her slim back had melded to my chest. When I'd been standing behind her, looking over her shoulder, I'd had a perfect view of her round breasts pressing against her shirt. Only two days ago, those luscious globes had been in my mouth as I sucked her tits raw.

My cocked throbbed.

Damn. Just . . . damn.

I STOOD by the window looking out at the fountain and the thick forest that surrounded Bavar's estate as Avery showered.

Even though I was technically on a rest day, there

were still a few things I wanted to do. I wanted to speak with Bavar, to see what his plan was should his estate fall under attack. I wanted to contact Nicholas, to learn if there had been any new findings at the Bulgarian libraries. The more Squad Three could learn about the men who'd tried to abduct Avery, the better.

And whether I liked it or not, I needed to write a report for Wes given there'd been an attack on fae lands' soil this morning—I also needed to tell him about Marnee using her siren song.

I bristled at that thought.

The door cracked to the bathroom, and the sound of Avery's shuffling feet drew my attention. She stood at the threshold, her hair freshly washed and dried. It curled around her shoulders, shorter strands framing her face as she wore one of the outfits that she and Charlotte had bought.

My breath sucked in as my gaze traveled up and down her frame. All thoughts of what I wanted to do fled.

She'd picked a simple pair of tight slacks and a cropped sweater. The sweater was a vibrant pink and made of a shiny material—both the color and material were often found in fae clothing. It made her breasts appear more prominent, and a hint of her taut abdomen flashed into view, teasing me mercilessly every time she fidgeted or stretched.

Fucking hell. How was I supposed to resist her when she looked like that?

She peered up at me uneasily, shifting her weight back and forth from foot to foot. "Does this look okay? I can't remember if this is what people normally wear or not?"

I swallowed, then nodded, unable to form a coherent response.

"I should change," she said in a rush, already closing the door. "Maybe I should ask Char—"

I had my hand on the door, stopping her from closing it before she could. My free arm shot out, encircling her around the waist before I thought better of it. My thumb rubbed against the bare skin on her back, just above her waistline where the taunting sweater revealed a peek of her gorgeous skin.

"You're beautiful," I whispered. "You just took me by surprise is all. No need to change. You're perfect as you are."

Her hands pressed against my chest—almost as if she were guarding herself against me—her palms warm through my shirt. A flash of violet light lit her eyes but died as quickly as it'd started.

I didn't know what to think of that hint of power which now swam in her veins, but if her pounding heart was anything to go by, my actions had taken her by surprise.

I could only hope it was a *good* surprise.

"You, um, really think so?" she asked uncertainly.

Since she wasn't pulling away from me, I kept my arm where it was. My wolf urged me on, begging me to lean down, inhale her scent and kiss her parted lips.

"Yes, I really think so," I replied huskily.

She bit the corner of her mouth, a musky tint coating her scent. A low grumble of satisfaction filled me, and I knew before I began dipping my head that I was going to follow my wolf's urgings.

Screw doing those list of things I'd thought about earlier. I was taking advantage of my rest day.

CHAPTER THIRTEEN

AVERY

My heart was going to explode. Wyatt's head was lowering toward mine, his cheeks were smooth and sculpted, and his firm lips were so ridiculously beautiful that I couldn't stop watching them.

And his *eyes*. His eyes were *glowing*.

My stomach turned into a jumbled mess of nerves, somersaults, and fireworks all at once. I squirmed, not knowing if I should pull back or pull him in.

But I did know that once again my belly was cramping and I had the urge to squeeze my thighs together.

Wyatt growled, the light in his eyes growing. "You smell delicious, Little Flower."

Little Flower? Another whisper of something brushed

against my mind, a gentle scrape, a questioning flicker. Was that the name he'd once called me?

Before I could question it, his lips were on mine, brushing against my mouth so slowly and gently that a soft moan escaped me.

My tongue flicked out, and a moment of embarrassment flowed through me that I'd done such a thing, but before I could pull it back, a deep possessive growl tore from Wyatt, the sound low in his belly. Then his lips were *devouring* mine, slanting over my mouth as he nipped at my lips and slid his tongue inside my depths.

Another breathy moan escaped me, the surprise of how good it felt to kiss him making me jolt. "Wyatt," I whispered.

"Yes, my love?"

He didn't stop, and the feel of his mouth felt so . . . what was the word? I didn't know.

Since I enjoyed this sensation, I closed my eyes and let myself get lost in his touch.

My fingers wandered up his chest as he trapped me in his embrace, plundering my mouth in a way that made my insides heat with internal fire and yearn for things I couldn't describe.

His other arm snaked around my waist, hauling me even closer until his hips pressed firmly against mine, and—*oh my*—his rigid length tried to spear my abdomen.

"Wyatt," I breathed again.

"Yes?" He tore his mouth free and pressed urgent kisses down my neck.

My eyes rolled back as his tongue darted out to taste and fondle the tender skin near my nape.

A delicious thrill ran through me, and I clamped my thighs together, the ache between them growing so strong.

"I can help with that," he said softly, whispering into my ear.

"Help with—" I panted, unable to continue. The man was a sorcerer with his mouth. He kept nipping, kissing, and tasting the most sensitive parts of my neck and below my ear. "Help with what?" I finally managed.

His hand wandered down and cupped me between my legs, rubbing the juncture of my thighs. "That," he breathed.

"Oh!" I cried out when his fingers ran over my pants, rubbing and tapping. One of his taps sent a bolt of pleasure skating along my nerves.

"Do you want me to help with that?" he asked softly, his mouth still on my neck, then on my lips again, sucking and tasting me.

He was driving me mad.

"What do you say, Little Flower? Do you want me to ease some of the tension you're feeling?" He tickled the area between my legs again, and a zing of fire coursed through me.

"You . . . you want to do that to me?"

He pulled back just enough for me to see the devilish smile curving his lips. "Oh yes, more than you could know."

Before I could respond further, a rush of air flowed around me, and then I was in Wyatt's arms and he was laying me down on the massive bed.

A breath of surprise escaped me as I sank into the soft covers. Wyatt hovered above me, his eyes like liquid gold.

"Your eyes change color," I breathed when he dipped his head to kiss the peek of flesh by my abdomen, that tiny sliver exposed by my short sweater. My stomach clenched when his lips met my skin. *Dear Gods, how does that feel so good?*

"They do."

"Why?" I managed before another breathy moan escaped me when he pushed my sweater up just enough to kiss more of my stomach. I could be wrong, but I felt for certain that his mouth was heading toward my breasts.

"Because you make me feel things. Werewolves' eyes

glow when we're overcome with strong emotions."

"I make you feel things?" I squeaked, then gasped when he nipped at my breast's peak. I was wearing a bra, but that didn't seem to deter him. If anything, he seemed to find the lacy black garment entirely fascinating.

"So beautiful," he whispered. He reached underneath me and flicked the clasp. The next thing I knew my breasts were spilling out of the material and he was rubbing one, his thumb brushing over my erect nipple.

The sensation made me buck.

Another growl rumbled his chest before he said, "Still so responsive, and yes, you make me feel things. Very, *very* strong things. But I think we've done enough talking for now. I believe I promised to help you with that achy feeling I can scent between your legs."

"Then why are you at my breasts?" I managed to say as he leaned down and pulled one nipple into his mouth. I gasped, my fingers automatically threading through his hair as he sucked and nipped while rolling that taut bud between his teeth.

"Because this is part of the process of relieving that ache." He sucked my tit more, then cupped my womanly mound again, delicately fingering me through my pants.

My hips bucked, completely out of my control, and I bit back another moan.

He chuckled. "I believe you're wearing too many clothes. Don't you agree?"

"Yes, I uh, yes." My mind became a fog. Sensations rolled through me, so vivid and strong that the ever-present electrical storm inside me, my internal power, waxed and waned. Good Gods, I had no idea he could elicit these kinds of feelings in me.

Wyatt unzipped my slacks, and in a blink, they were in a heap on the floor, and somehow he'd whisked my sweater over my head, tossing it along with my bra over his shoulder.

And then I was nearly naked on the bed, the only thing left the scrap of black lace covering my womanly area.

For a moment, Wyatt hovered above me, his chest heaving as his eyes turned to molten gold. "I will never tire of looking at you."

Hearing that I'd been like this with him before, so exposed and hot, made my natural inclination to cover myself disappear. In fact, looking at him as he gazed down at me with reverence glowing in his eyes, made a heady feeling of bold power flow through my limbs.

"You've seen me naked before?"

"Yes, but not nearly as many times as I would like."

"And you've touched me here?" I placed his hands between my legs. "Before?"

He groaned, and the emboldened feeling in me back-fired when his fingers curled against me, pushing my damp panties *into* me.

His fingers. A flash of memory scorched my mind, but before I could try to grasp it, he was on my tits again, licking and sucking them as he deftly flicked my panties to the side. His fingers rubbed against that bundle of nerves between my thighs. Except this time, with his fingers on my bare flesh, the pleasure ripping through me increased tenfold.

I cried out, arching off the bed just as one of his fingers sank into me. My inner walls clamped around that digit, tightening as a deep ache overcame me. He pumped into me again, slowly, his finger curving and scraping against something that felt—

"Oh!" I cried out when a meteor of sensations shot through me.

A rumble sounded from Wyatt's chest, that strange purring sound again, his movements never slowing. If anything, he quickened his pace, his fingers continuing their sweet torture as his mouth moved from my breasts to my lips.

I held on to him, entwining my fingers through his hair as waves of ecstasy began to build.

He kissed me and nipped, then sank a second finger inside me as his thumb continued to rub and play with that part of me that felt so alive I wanted to scream.

"Wyatt?" My breaths came so fast now I could barely suck enough air in to stay functioning.

"Yes, Little Flower?" he whispered.

His fingers increased their pace, stuffing me so full and scraping and rubbing against my inner parts—parts of me that I hadn't even known existed, yet were parts that felt as if they were made for him to do just this.

"Oh!" I cried out again when another ripple of pleasure overtook me, and the wave following continued to climb higher and higher with no end in sight. I clamped my eyes shut, the sensations coursing through me taking on a life of their own.

Wyatt moved again, his hard body drifting down mine, sucking, tasting, and kissing every inch of my skin. His fingers never stopped. He was a master of this torture, playing me like the finest violin, stroking and tweaking a torturous symphony from me which I was helpless to resist.

As his fingers continued their masterful onslaught, the waves rose again, except sharper this time, more acute.

"Wyatt!" I cried out, when a particularly charged wave rushed through me.

"Yes, Little Flower?" But his fingers didn't stop. They

kept pumping and rubbing, his thumb doing incessant swirls that were making me turn feral.

"Wyatt!" I snarled.

He chuckled. "I could get used to you screaming my name like that, but I think I've tormented you enough. Would you like release now, my love?"

"Yes!" I panted. "Please, yes!" My face screwed up in a painful need for . . . something. *Gah*, I hated that I couldn't remember doing this before.

A rush of warm breath washed over my sex, and my eyes snapped open to see Wyatt kneeling between my legs. "What are you doing?"

"This." His tongue slid out and licked that area where his thumb had been torturing me only a moment ago.

I screamed, bucking off the bed, and then . . .

It was like he became unleashed.

His fingers increased their relentless pumping, and his mouth *devoured* my sex. His tongue stroked, licked, nipped, and sucked that taut bud until I was a mindless tangle of limbs and need beneath his touch.

"Come for me, Little Flower. I want you to come on my face."

The wave in me rose higher again, his fingers pumping and pumping as his tongue—Gods, his *tongue* —wouldn't stop its relentless torture on my center.

"Yes," he breathed just as the mountain peak was reached. "That's it my love. Scream for me!"

I cried out when my insides came undone. The sensation ripped through me in a deliciously savage wave, commanding my body and slamming through my senses. Through it all, Wyatt's mouth continued his torture on my sex making the pleasure even more intense and prolonged.

And when I finally returned to the soft bed I lay on, the gauzy curtain above fluttering in an unseen breeze, I opened my eyes to see a very large and *very* satisfied male peering down at me.

"You look so happy," I murmured, barely able to keep my eyes open as sleepiness fogged my brain.

He grinned. "I am."

I cocked my head. "But why? You didn't seem to enjoy it like I did," I replied, referring to the fact that such a powerful feeling hadn't ripped his body into a million pieces.

"How wrong you are. I enjoyed that just as much, if not more, than you."

I tried to follow his logic, but that sleepy feeling again weighed on my senses. "I don't understand," I finally said.

"You still respond to me like you used to, Little Flower." He settled down beside me to haul me into his arms while running his hands lightly up and down my back. I shivered as zings of pleasure shot through me, eliciting goosebumps in their wake. If he kept that up, I'd be asleep in no time. "And knowing that I can still pleasure you like that makes me want to beat my chest in satisfaction."

I giggled. "Beat your chest? That seems rather—"

"Barbaric?" He grinned and then shrugged. "I think all wolves feel that way when they please their—"

I cracked an eye open again when the silence stretched between us. "Their what?"

That golden glow rimmed his irises, filling the emerald color with liquid gold. "Their mate," he said softly.

I lay silently, my heart pumping harder. "Charlotte said something about you wanting to claim me. Is that a mate thing? I don't really know what all of that means."

"All you need to know right now is that it means that I enjoy what I just did to you so incredibly much." He kissed my neck, his tongue darting out to taste me. "You look tired. Maybe we should sleep?" He kissed me again, this time softly on my lips.

I moaned at the taste and feel of him, and his *scent*. Gods. I inhaled. He had the most delicious oak and pine scent, but he was right. I was tired, incredibly tired, since I basically hadn't slept last night.

"Yes."

The last thing I remembered was the feel of the covers being draped over us and the hard feel of his chest on my back. I fell asleep with a smile on my face. Surely, this was what absolute bliss felt like.

I woke to the feel of my mate's warm body pressed against mine, my body naturally rising after another deep slumber. Lifting my head, I searched for a clock and found one on the desk. According to the ticking apparatus, it was mid-afternoon, which meant Avery and I had slept nearly six hours.

Damn. Ten hours of napping today. I couldn't remember the last time I'd done any napping at all.

But even though I still wasn't one hundred percent recovered from the exhausting past month, I was quickly getting there. My mind buzzed, my body becoming more alert. That and I was itching to know what was going on with Nicholas's findings and Bavar's defense plan, so I slipped quietly from the bed, careful not to wake my mate.

I gazed down at her as I tugged my pants back on, which I'd pulled off before our slumber as my wolf purred in pleasure. Because Avery had let me touch her, hold her, sleep beside her. My courtship with her was progressing well. Who knew, perhaps the next time we woke up beside one another, maybe just maybe, she'd be ready for me to pleasure her again. Only this time, perhaps she'd be open to that pleasure coming from my cock instead of my mouth.

Damn. So much for going slow with her, but fucking hell, I hadn't been able to resist her.

A groan escaped me when a rush of blood went south of my waistband. Ignoring the surge of lust, I silently slipped from the room and headed toward the stairs, but the thought of Avery sinking onto my shaft as she rode me with her tits bouncing in my face . . .

I groaned again. So much for trying to keep my erections under control.

Readjusting myself, I followed the sound of voices and approached a set of double doors just off the main entrance where the five wings converged.

Bavar and his squad sat in a drawing room, which appeared exclusively designed for entertaining. The room was large with a domed ceiling. At least a dozen couches and chairs were set up in three separate seating clusters.

The furniture in each cluster was arranged in a circle so everyone faced one another. That of course allowed for maximum discussion, which Bavar and his squad were in the midst of doing, so much so that they didn't notice my prowling presence at the door.

The colors of the room were done in rich purple, gray, pale green, and accents of cream. Velvet and thick brocades upholstered all of the furniture.

I treaded silently toward the group. The heavy, sweet scent of fairy magic filled the air—a scent that often accompanied magical cleaning. If not for that, I might have guessed the furniture had been newly purchased, even though given the ornate cut of the wood and elegant curve of the wingbacks, it was most likely bought when the estate was built. With fairy cleaning magic, items could look brand new for years.

Tall windows lined one wall of the room, allowing natural sunlight that penetrated the trees' canopy to fill the area. The leaves fluttering in the woods shimmered in the sunlight, but the Shroud Forest was so dense that even my superior eyesight didn't allow me to see more than a hundred yards into it.

That left me feeling uneasy, since it would be harder to see an attack coming, *if* an attack was to come.

"Ah," Bavar said when I rounded the back of his chair and took a seat on the opposite couch by Lex. "Looks like someone's decided to join us on his rest day."

Lex clapped me on the back, Charlotte snickered, and an amused and knowing smile came from Heidi.

I frowned. "Is there something going on that I'm unaware of?"

Bishop gave me a wink "Did you enjoy getting settled in? It, um . . . how do I put it? It *sounded* like you enjoyed it this morning."

Terry rolled her eyes. "I think we all know he *and* Ms. Meyers enjoyed it."

Charlotte snorted a laugh.

Fucking hell. They heard me pleasuring my mate. I shook my head when Charlotte gave me the thumbs up, but I couldn't stop my chuckle. *Damn, when did I become the butt of a joke from a newly graduated recruit?*

I grinned and shook my head again, then reminded myself to ask Heidi to cast a cloaking spell around the chamber Avery and I shared. The pleasure my mate had screamed this morning was only the first of many screams I planned to give her.

Yet that wasn't something Squad Three needed to hear.

Still, if nothing else, now everyone knew that Avery was *mine*.

That was something I figured Charlotte had already guessed given her knowing smirk and the fact that she and Avery had apparently been discussing werewolf mating.

I bit back another chuckle when Lex clapped me on the back again.

However, the jokes and elbow nudges weren't coming from everyone. Marnee sat near Terry, the siren's cobalt-blue eyes so sharp they could have cut glass. She wasn't even trying to hide her scowl.

My jaw tightened as the scent of bitter jealousy mixed with Marnee's salty tang—a scent that accompanied all sirens. It floated to me on a cloud of anger.

Ignoring her heated glare, I got down to business and turned to Bavar. "So what have we learned?"

"Well, as I was just telling the squad"—Bavar tilted forward in his seat—"We know that nearly all of the robed group at the inn were purebred sorcerers. The SF witches were able to unlock their cloaking spells, and then we called Squad Fourteen in."

I grunted in approval. Squad Fourteen was composed of all male werewolves. Their advanced sense of smell when they worked together made identifying criminals easier.

"They identified each sorcerer's scent so then we turned to the database. The latest database report from headquarters has found six sorcerers in the supernatural community capable of creating hexes that can penetrate an SF suit. Four have already been ruled out given their solid alibis and the fact that their scents don't match. The other two are being interviewed, but neither has ever had a run-in with the SF before, nor are they members of any anti-SF organizations. And if their scents also don't match—"

"Then they couldn't have been involved."

"Correct. As you know, we'll complete the investigation—on the off chance that either of them was able to mask their scent or change it—but neither fits the profile of a sorcerer gone rogue, nor has a motive been found for why they would have done it in the first place."

"What are their profiles?"

"The first is fifty-three. He's married, has two daughters—each half fae—who are attending university here. He lives with his wife, a full fae, in Culasberee, a medium-sized city three hours north of the capital. Stable employment. Pays his taxes. No previous criminal record."

I frowned. "And the other?"

"An elderly sorcerer who lives in Rostov, Russia. He lives with his wife who's his full-time caretaker. At his prime, he was the most powerful sorcerer in his region, but in the past decade he's mentally declined. Our latest report shows that he's no longer oriented to time or place. Given his advanced dementia, and the most recent update from his local community sorcerer chapter, he's been unable to wield spells for over five years."

"Because he can't remember them?"

"Exactly."

I grumbled. "So the conclusion we're reaching is that whoever attacked us at the inn isn't in our database."

"Precisely."

"How is that possible?"

Bavar's lips turned down. "That I don't know, but there's something else we've discovered that could be the key to this all. Avery said that the tallest one told her that he's been looking for her for thousands of years. If the sorcerers working with him are of equal age and have remained clever at hiding, that could explain why they've never been added to the database since they would have been born before it existed. But quite frankly, that doesn't add up, not unless they're vampiric sorcerers, which didn't match their scents. Their scents were that of pureblood sorcerers."

"Unless they had a cloaking spell over a cloaking spell, and the witches haven't unlocked that yet."

Bavar raised an eyebrow. "Possible, but not likely." He leaned forward more, his face a mask of concern.

"What we've discovered about the tall one is what has me worried. His scent doesn't fit any species that we can identify."

My brow furrowed. "What do you mean?"

"Meaning that despite Squad Fourteen being called in, they weren't able to scent what species that man is. They easily identified him as male, and they were able to rule out his species as sorcerer, fairy, werewolf, demon, half-demon, or vampire."

"And if he's male then he can't be a siren, psychic, or witch."

"Correct."

My wolf growled, pacing in my belly, not liking where this conversation was going. "Is it possible he's a mixed breed and that's why they couldn't scent his species?"

Bavar cocked his head as the rest of Squad Three continued to listen raptly. "Again, possible, but not likely. Each wolf in that squad came to the same conclusion. The male smelled pure, not of mixed descent, and his scent was stronger than the sorcerers, which means he's probably the most powerful. And that leaves us with an interesting conclusion—perhaps he's a species we're not familiar with."

I stilled. "That hasn't happened in years, not since we added angels to the database."

"Correct. And as you know, angels never leave their heavenly realm, so it does beg the question—is this man from a realm we're unfamiliar with, or is he a new species we haven't previously identified in the explored realms?"

I leaned back on the couch, unease slithering through me. To have someone out there hunting my mate who was of a species we weren't familiar with made my blood run cold. Unknown species carried unknown strengths and gifts.

And a species we didn't understand was also a species we didn't know how to fight.

CHAPTER FIFTEEN
WYATT

I sat in for the rest of the discussions. There was no way I wouldn't despite technically being off-duty. A group of powerful men were hunting my mate and they were proving more elusive and lethal by the minute.

The only positive aspect of the meeting was that despite Marnee's obvious displeasure at Avery being my mate, she maintained her professionalism. She contributed to the squad's brainstorming session on how to best protect Avery within these heavily warded walls, which meant her earlier actions were perhaps one less thing I had to worry about.

"How long do you think it'll be until they find us, sir?" Charlotte asked after swiping a drink from a tray one of the servants was passing around.

"It's hard to say." Bavar lifted his glass and took a sip. "Our journey here was cloaked, the enchantments around this forest make navigation and scrying spells difficult, but that doesn't mean it's impossible. Best bet is several weeks. Worst bet is a few days."

My balled hands tightened. A battle was coming. That was inevitable, but now the question was when. "And when they find us, will Shrouding Estate's ancient wards hold?"

A swath of pink and yellow clouds rolled across the sky, blocking out what little sun came into the room as Bavar finished his drink. "I'm fairly certain the wards will hold if we're attacked, but for added measure, we could move Avery to the safe room if an attack is imminent."

I cracked my knuckles. "How long would the wards hold under a serious siege?"

"At a minimum, a few hours, but possibly indefinitely. They would only fall *if* those robed men possess enough magic to break them. Many have tried and failed, so it's possible they'll never be able to breach them."

Bishop stretched his legs out. "Should we take Avery back to earth, sir, just in case they find us? Wouldn't she be safer at headquarters?"

"Yes, she would be safer at headquarters." I worked

my jaw. "But then we risk Avery's health failing again. We don't know if that would happen, but right now, that's not a chance I'm willing to take. So we keep her here at Shrouding Estate for as long as possible, only moving her if the wards fail and the safe room is compromised."

"My thoughts precisely," Bavar replied. "The safe room will hold as long as the walls stand. But if the wards fail and the walls fall, I'm afraid none of us are safe."

Most of this wasn't new information to me. Bavar had told me about the wards and the iron-clad safe room—the Whimsical Room—on our trip here after I'd woken from my slumber on the carpet.

He'd also mapped out the estate for me so I knew where all of the hidden exit points were. The combination of the estate's wards and the forest's magic—which could be less than welcoming to foreign visitors—was the entire reason Bavar had chosen this place as our safe house.

We'd already devised a strategy for how to best secure Avery's escape from the estate should it come to that, but it was good to bring the rest of the squad up to date with our plans.

If an attack did happen, we would need their help to

keep the robed sorcerers occupied while a group of us whisked Avery to safety.

"Squad Three, if you'll follow me." Bavar stood gracefully from his chair, the dagger strapped to his waist shining in the fairy lights which were magically suspended mid-air near the ceiling. "I'll reveal a few of this estate's secrets, namely the hidden exits and tunnels. Consider yourself privileged. Few outside of the Fieldstone family are privy to such information."

Since I already knew where the exits and tunnels were, I didn't join them. Instead I prowled back to the stairs, intent on seeing my mate.

I was halfway up the staircase when the scent of baking cookies drifted to me, and just underneath that was a trace of lilacs.

Reversing course, I retreated back down the stairs and to the Merimum wing where the west kitchen lay.

The cookie and lilac scent grew stronger the closer I got to the kitchen. Other, more distinct scents—sugar, chocolate, flour, and what smelled like vanilla but slightly different—mixed with it.

"These just need ten minutes in the oven, then they'll be ready." Avery's soft tone carried to me.

I rounded the corner and silently pushed through the massive swinging doors that led to the kitchen off the butler's nook.

Standing in the doorway, I stopped, taking in the scene. Inside the sprawling kitchen, dirty bowls sat on the large stone island in the center of the room. Several tin trays with evenly spaced out cookie dough balls were lined up on it. And flour coated every surface of the spacious countertop.

Avery was bent over, sliding one of the cookie trays into a large double oven. Several other trays were already inside it. Her ass faced me, so round and perfect that for a moment, all I could do was stare.

She straightened and turned to the fairy who was assisting her, a smile on her face. The fairy wiped her hands on her apron, but then her eyes suddenly grew wide, her back going rigid when she saw me. Avery followed the fairy's line of sight.

"Oh." An attractive flush filled my mate's cheeks. "I didn't realize you were there."

I stalked toward her, taking in her pink complexion, her eyes alight with happiness, and the messy bun on the top of her head. Like the fairy, she also wore an apron. Floury handprints stained it white. Beneath her apron were the same bright pink sweater and skintight fae slacks she'd worn before I'd peeled them off of her.

Damn, she looked fine.

When I reached her, her breath caught, and she tilted

her head back to meet my stare. I was fairly certain a predatory look stole over my face, as a hint of musk entered her scent.

But even though my wolf rumbled in pleasure at the effect our courtship was having on our mate, that wasn't what had hit my gut so hard that for a moment I couldn't breathe.

The feeling of absolute gratefulness overtook me. Down here, in this kitchen, coated in flour and dressed so cutely that I wanted to smack her ass playfully, Avery looked *alive* and healthy. It was a far cry from how she'd looked only a few days ago when the Safrinite comet had taken her life.

I swallowed the thick feeling in my throat and said gruffly, "Looks like you've been baking."

To hide how overwhelmed I felt, I pushed a stray lock of hair behind her ear. Tendrils framed her face, and a light sheen of sweat coated her forehead, but she looked happy. Content.

And fuck if that didn't make me the most elated wolf in this realm.

"Yeah, I, uh . . ." She cleared her throat, her gaze darting to the fairy assisting her. "I woke up and wandered into the hall. One of the servants told me that you were all deliberating in the drawing room, and I don't know, I just had this urge to bake something." She frowned, her forehead creasing. "I don't know why. I'm not sure if that's something I used to do or not?"

"You did. You *do*," I corrected, waving toward the trays. "You love baking. It was something you often did every time you moved to a new city when you were growing up. It would keep you busy when you were new to a place and didn't have many friends."

A curious glint entered her warm brown-flecked-with-gold eyes. "Did my parents tell you that?"

"No, you did." I took a step back since her heart was beating so quickly. I had a feeling my looming presence was to blame. "And I'm guessing you remember some-thing about baking, if you were able to create all of this?" I nodded toward the trays and dirty bowls.

"Yeah, I guess so." Avery frowned, and her gaze slid to the fairy again. The woman helping her stood quietly, her hands folded in front of her. "I don't remember exactly, but with Nessa's help, I was able to find the equivalent fae ingredients for what I thought I would need to bake cookies."

"Did Nessa help you with combining the ingredients or measuring them?"

Avery's frown deepened. "No, that's the weird thing. Once I had the measuring cups in my hands and the ingredients in front of me, it was like my body took over. I got lost in it. Not really thinking or worrying if I was doing it right." She shrugged. "I let my hands guide me, and I don't know"—she smiled, her lips curving in an expression of contentment—"doing it made me feel happy, and it calmed me."

"I'm glad to hear it." I curled my hands around the island's edge. Seeing her so at ease made me want to pull her into my embrace and nuzzle the smudge of flour just under her ear.

Gripping the edge tighter, my nostrils flared as I took in the subtle difference of the ingredients' scents. "Looks like you found the flour equivalent." I quirked an eyebrow at the powder coating her apron.

She laughed. "Yes, although Nessa said its texture is slightly different than the flour found on earth, although it bakes similarly so hopefully the cookies will turn out okay. Speaking of—" She sidestepped around me and grabbed the rest of the trays. The dough balls were warming, taking on a light sheen.

Nessa jumped into action, skillfully whisking away the trays Avery hadn't grabbed and loading them into the upper oven.

I stayed leaning against the island as I watched my mate work. It reminded me of our first night together under the stars, three months ago, when Avery had baked a sponge cake and I'd observed.

"Have you thought of attempting a sponge cake with jam and cream?"

She stilled. One of the trays she'd been holding sat on the edge of the oven, but she made no move to push it in.

Nessa took it from her, sliding it into place before closing the oven door. A twirl of her fingers and pulse of magic made the timer above the sink activate.

Turning toward me, still frowning, Avery bit her lip. "Sponge cake, jam, and cream."

"Do you remember anything?"

Her brow furrowed more, a confused expression overtaking her face. She closed her eyes, her face scrunching up into a knot of determination, but she groaned softly, then opened her eyes. "No."

I pushed away from the island, no longer able to be in the same room with her and not touching her. Before she could blink, my arms were curling softly around her waist and my head was dipping to inhale the sweet fragrance coating her skin.

She gasped when my lips brushed just below her ear. "It will come in time."

Her fluttering breaths grew shallower, her hands automatically steadying herself on my shoulders. My muscles tensed and hardened beneath her grip, and an urge to crush her to me was so overwhelming that I almost did.

But instead I pulled back, reminding myself that I needed to take it slow, not push her too fast or too hard regardless of what my wolf wanted.

She let go, and I took another step back until two feet of distance separated us.

"Are those biscuits I smell?" Bavar's voice carried to us, and a second later, he pushed through the double doors.

Nessa immediately lowered her head and sank into a deep curtsy. Avery merely blinked.

A brilliant smile lit the fairy commander's face when he spotted the closed ovens humming with heat. "Oh, it *is* biscuits." He rubbed his hands together. "How divine. That must mean your memory's returning?"

Avery shrugged and glanced at me again. "I don't know because I still can't remember anything concrete, but Wyatt said I liked to bake before . . ." Her eyes flashed violet for the merest second, and I knew she was once again thinking of waking up in the field by the capital, the otherworldly power strumming through her as she lay in terror.

"Indeed you did." Bavar sauntered to the island.

Avery cocked her head at Bavar. "Did I bake for you?"

He tilted his head back, rapture overtaking his features. "Did you ever. I may have persuaded you to make me an item or two. Your biscuits—or rather, cookies, as you refer to them—cakes, tarts, and pies were some of the best I've ever tasted, so imagine how relieved I am to see that such talent hasn't departed from you."

Avery laughed and then eyed the oven. The cookies had risen in the lower oven and were almost ready to come out. "Well, you haven't tried them yet. It's possible they'll taste like sawdust and will need to be thrown out."

Bavar quirked an eyebrow. "Doubtful."

A shimmer erupted over the sink, a melodic alarm sounding. Nessa silenced it and kicked into action.

She extracted the cookies, and when finished, a dozen trays sat on the island, so many steaming cookies waiting in front of us that I couldn't count them all. Their heavenly doughy scent filled the room.

"May I?" Bavar waved to the cookies.

I choked on a laugh when Nessa scrambled to scoop some cookies off the tray for him.

"I don't think I've ever seen a fairy so excited about cookies before," I remarked.

"Then you obviously haven't eaten enough of Ms. Meyers's biscuits." Bavar's eyes closed when he bit into the morsel. A moan of ecstasy parted his lips.

"I take it you like them?" Avery grinned as Nessa's cheeks flushed.

"Oh my. Oh yes." Bavar scooped another cookie from the tray, his first already gone. "Such pleasure I derive from your baked concoctions. Please tell me you'd like to switch professions and be employed as my personal baking chef."

Avery laughed again, and I rolled my eyes.

Bavar arched an eyebrow at me. "Taste this and then tell me you're not actually worried about every fairy in this realm trying to steal Ms. Meyers away from you, *commander.*"

Avery blushed, probably from how Bavar so casually referred to her as mine, either that or because he was so enamored with her cookies.

I obligingly took one of the morsels from his outstretched hand. The second I bit into it, a burst of flavors coated my tongue—rich chocolate, a doughy center, sweet sugar, and that fairy flavor that hinted at vanilla but was different—and I knew that my mate had missed her true calling. She shouldn't work at the Supernatural Ambassador Institute. She should open a bakery.

"Wow." I finished the cookie and reached for a second. "You may be right." I tossed another cookie into my mouth. "I may have to lock you up, babe, or risk another man trying to steal you from me."

Avery's cheeks flushed again, and I wondered if I'd embarrassed her by calling her *babe* in front of Bavar, but I didn't have time to ask because Bishop, Heidi, Terry, and Charlotte strode into the kitchen.

All of them looked tense. Given what we'd learned from the database and further findings at the library, I wasn't surprised. We didn't know when the sorcerers were coming but coming they were.

A fresh bandage covered Charlotte's shoulder, but she moved easily and didn't appear in pain. I wondered if Lex had done another healing treatment on her after their tour.

"I thought I smelled something baking." Bishop's gaze landed on the cookies. "Are those up for grabs?"

"Please eat as many as you want," Avery replied.

Bavar shook a finger. "Now, now. I wouldn't go that far."

I smothered a chuckle but felt grateful that the squad members not on patrol duty were getting a much needed break as they began devouring the sweets.

The disappearing cookies got a glower from my

fellow commander, but then Bavar shook his head, his expression light.

Underneath it, though, I saw the same feelings lurking in his eyes that I had.

Who were we fighting, and more importantly, what did they intend to do with my mate?

CHAPTER SIXTEEN

AVERY

S quad Three, minus Marnee and Lex who were on patrol duty, stood around the island gorging on cookies. I muffled several laughs when Bavar continually threatened his squad with extermination for eating all of his biscuits. He even pulled his dagger a time or two.

"You must be remembering stuff, eh, if you remembered how to bake these?" Charlotte sidled up to my side as she bit into another cookie. "That's a good sign, right?"

"I didn't really remember, though. I just followed my instincts."

"Hmm." She made a face. "Well, that still seems like a good sign even if you don't have concrete memories."

"That's what Wyatt thinks too." I ducked my head

when I felt him regard me from across the room. He'd been doing that ever since he entered the kitchen, gold rimming his eyes during most of his heated stares.

A blush filled my cheeks when I remembered how he'd touched and kissed me.

A wry smile tilted his lips, his nostrils flaring.

Embarrassment flooded me when I remembered him saying he could scent my arousal. *Oh Gods!*

Charlotte gripped my hand. "Okay, spill it. What happened?" She slid a curious glance toward Wyatt, a knowing smirk tilting her lip.

"Char!" I hissed.

She pulled me away from the counter and dragged me toward the doors until we were through them and in the hallway.

My back tingled, the immense power inside me swirling, as I sensed Wyatt's gaze track my every movement.

It was only when the swinging doors closed behind us that Charlotte's eyes widened with excitement. "Okay, tell me everything." She held up a hand. "And before you try and act like nothing happened you might as well know that I'll never buy that. We all heard him fucking you."

My jaw dropped, my stomach bottoming out. *"What?"*

She laughed. "It's nothing to be embarrassed about. Wolves like sex. Female wolves do too, if you haven't already picked that up from me. So I'm not surprised you've already done the nasty with him. You know, all of us could hear him plowing you."

My jaw continued to hang open. I couldn't believe I was hearing these words come out of her mouth. I mean, not because her detailed rendition of what had happened between me and Wyatt was that far off base, but because of how colorfully and casually she'd just referred to Wyatt *fucking* me and *plowing* me. And she'd heard what we'd done! *Oh Gods.* Red bloomed on my cheeks.

Charlotte snickered.

I cleared my throat and hoped my blush was receding. "We didn't, you know . . . do it."

She raised an eyebrow. "Is that right? And you expect me to believe that? After I heard you screaming?"

Okay. Nope. My blush definitely isn't receding. "He . . ." I pulled her into a small alcove off the hall when a servant passed us. The alcove contained an urn on a pedestal and a mural of fairies dancing in a forest. Weirdly enough, I wondered if the urn contained somebody's ashes.

Clearing my throat again, I hoped the dead soul forgave me for speaking so vulgarly in their body's ashy presence. "He touched me and maybe kissed me in an area or two, but we didn't have sex."

"Now we're getting somewhere." Charlotte grinned and crossed her arms. She leaned against the wall, obviously settling in for a good chat. "Where did he touch you? And please tell me the man is as good with his mouth as he is with his sword."

"I'm assuming you mean an actual sword and not a figurative sword?"

For a moment, she just stared at me, and then she threw back her head and laughed. "Oh, Avery, you wicked little she-devil. I love it. Now tell me *everything*." She pushed away from the wall and slung an arm over my shoulders. "Come on. Let's go back to my room. I want to hear all the juicy details."

CHARLOTTE DID INDEED DRAG me to her room. Okay, not drag, I went willingly. But once she'd sequestered me in her chambers, I ruined her anticipated fun by not revealing any further details. Well, not many further details.

She groaned. "Seriously. You're no fun. If I slept with Bavar, Lex, or Bishop, I'd give you all the juicy bits, including the length of their cocks, the noises they make when they come, if they get all wolfy or fairy-glowing or start shooting magic when they ejaculate, and I would definitely tell you if they did anything kinky."

I slapped a hand over my mouth but couldn't stop my laugh. Once I regained control again, I lowered my hand but was still shaking with mirth. "Yeah, but that's only because you don't actually like any of them. They'd just be an afternoon of fun for you."

She sighed. "True, very true." She leaned back on the couch, still looking contemplative. "But does that mean Wyatt is more than a casual afternoon for you, since you don't want to tell me about it?"

I immediately sobered, her question striking a chord with me. *Was he?*

"I don't know," I finally answered truthfully. "I'm incredibly attracted to him, and I know we share a history, but I can't remember our past so he's still a stranger to me."

"A stranger who will happily fuck you fifty shades till Sunday."

I laughed, then rolled my eyes. "Yeah, perhaps."

"Not perhaps. I know he would. The man is obsessed with you. I told you, didn't I? Back at the inn? He wants to claim you, and he thinks you're his mate. He told me."

Scarlet heat bloomed over my cheeks again. Charlotte may be right, but Wyatt was still new to me even though I wasn't to him. I wasn't ready for that kind of commitment yet. I'd only just met him as far as my limited memories were concerned.

"But anyway, back to kissing and telling . . ." I said in an attempt to change the subject.

She sat up straighter. "Now if any of the dudes here actually knows how to properly use his cock, and he's feeling horny, I'd be down for an afternoon or two of mindless fucking."

I groaned. "So descriptive."

She laughed. "You always gave me a hard time about that, but if you were more than a quarter wolf you'd probably be the same."

I joined in her laughter just as a forgotten memory brushed my mind like butterfly wings. *A quarter wolf. Was that what I was?*

Sobering, I pointed at the bandage on her shoulder. "Say, how's your shoulder doing anyway? You seem to be moving well and don't seem to be in any pain."

"Oh, right, you don't know." She pulled the bandage back to reveal her wound.

My breath sucked in. "It's nearly healed!"

She nodded and let the bandage fall back into place. "I'm telling you, Major Fieldstone's servants are the bomb. They have all sorts of potions and fairy concoctions in one of those rooms downstairs. When we got situated here, after you and Wyatt were, you know, *not fucking*"—she waggled her eyebrows—"Major Field-stone came and got me and Lex and took us to that room. Two of his servants poured their fairy stuff on my injury while Lex watched, and even though it hurt like a bitch, it was totally worth it. Their potions expedite healing way faster than anything the witches on earth can do."

"Nice, that's handy."

"No shit. Now if those assholes come back and try to take you again, I'll be in top fighting form, so I'll be able to nail those suckers with my arrows."

My throat tightened when I remembered that our little trip here wasn't for reconnecting with Wyatt or laughing with my best friend. It was really to keep me safe and protected from the group of men who'd tried to abduct me.

My blood chilled when I remembered the tall man's gaze. He'd followed my movements, even when my unleashed power had stopped time. What the hell kind of supernatural could do that?

Nobody good. That was for sure.

"Char? I have a request, and I'm hoping you can help. You know this magic inside me? It's powerful, sure, but if I don't know how to use it, what the hell good is it to me?"

Her eyes brightened. "Meaning you want to learn to wield it."

I lifted my hands. "It's not like I have anything else to do here, and who knows how long we'll stay. But the only thing is, I don't really know how to train."

She rubbed her hands together, a grin splitting across her face. "Lucky for you, I do, and I'm not on patrol duty until tomorrow morning since I'm technically still injured, so I just happen to be free for the rest of the day."

"So you'll help me?"

"Damn straight." She shot to standing, excitement dancing in her eyes. "Let's go. There's a place out back we can use which Major Fieldstone showed us. The wards are stronger there since it's a training area, so we won't have to worry about you blowing any shit up."

CHAPTER SEVENTEEN

WYATT

I left the kitchen not long after Charlotte and my mate disappeared so that I could find them. Given that laughter rang out from Charlotte's room when I passed it, I didn't stop.

Instead, I carried on to the chamber Avery and I shared, figuring I could check in with Nicholas and write my report to Wes.

I knew I could sleep, but if I kept up with these daytime naps, I'd inevitably get my days and nights mixed up, which would be problematic, so more sleep would have to wait until tonight.

At least Heidi had placed a cloaking spell at our chamber's threshold, meaning Squad Three wouldn't hear any further pleasuring I gave Avery. Thinking about that made my lips curve up when I stepped into the room.

A wash of magic flowed over me, the cloaking spell sturdy and strong. In the privacy of our room, the scent of Avery's sex still saturated the air. It wasn't nearly as potent as it'd been when I'd left her sleeping a few hours ago, but it was strong enough to make my cock twitch.

Damn. I needed to fuck her. *Really* needed to fuck her. I knew I wouldn't feel satisfied until I did, and my wolf wouldn't feel calm until I'd claimed her again.

But a claiming right now was out of the question. She'd probably freak out if I descended on her neck with elongated canines while my eyes glowed wildly. She'd only just learned that glowing eyes meant I felt strongly about something.

Sighing, I cupped the back of my neck. *All in good time.*

I sat at the small writing desk, the chair groaning in protest when it took my full weight, then pulled out my tablet. I began dictating my report into it, making sure to include Marnee's reprehensible behavior. Even though it felt a bit like tattling, protocol was protocol. None of us were above SF law.

After that, I recounted the events starting with Avery waking up in the field, then progressed through the attack at the inn, adding the holographs to the report when needed by extracting them from my memories using magic the SF witches had programmed into our devices.

Once complete, I had a detailed six-page report with real-life graphics which accurately recorded the events since we'd entered the fae lands.

An image of Avery under the magical dome in the field outside the capital was the first holograph to pop up. I studied her face, the miniature rendition glowing above my tablet. It accurately reflected her fear and distrust since the magic had pulled it straight from my memories.

My stomach twisted to see my mate like that again, but then I reminded myself that she'd come a long way in only a few days since she no longer looked at me like I might eat her.

I smirked. Well, there was certainly one part of her I was more than happy to taste again. I sent the report off to Wes and then sent a message to Nicholas.

Any new findings?

His response dinged a minute later, and my stomach tightened when I read it.

> Yes. I was just about to message you. Urgent findings to report. Attaching translated documents and one image now.

I sat forward, my spine snapping into place as I waited for his attachment.

It didn't come.

> Did you send it? No sign of it.

Impatience made my knee bounce, so I placed a video call to him in the Bulgarian libraries to discuss what he'd found, but a faint alarm buzzed from my tablet, then an error message appeared.

Frowning, I tried placing the call again only to have the same message appear.

"What the hell," I whispered.

The error message was a general one, saying that calls to the Bulgarian libraries were unable to be completed at this time, so I settled for typing another message since messages seemed to go through.

> No attachment from you has arrived. I just tried to call, but that didn't go through either.

My tablet dinged.

> Having technical difficulties on my end. I've just been informed that the sorcerers are doing monthly maintenance on the libraries' wards. Calls and attachments won't work until they're done. Only messages are getting through right now.

I growled. *Dammit.*

> When will they finish?

> Late tomorrow night.

My stomach sank. If he truly had something urgent to show us, that meant either me or someone in Squad Three would have to return to the Bulgarian libraries to retrieve it. And considering I wasn't a member of Squad Three, and I technically wasn't on active duty, it only made sense to send me on the errand.

I strode from the room in search of Bavar. This hiccup was the last thing I wanted to deal with right now, but I'd have to.

The scent of cookies still clung to the air on the main floor, although roasting meat now accompanied it.

Not surprisingly, I found Bavar in the kitchen, sitting at a table near the window, away from the commotion. Beside Bavar sat a plate of cookies. He took a bite of one while he read something on his tablet.

Meestry was ordering the servants about and they scurried to follow his directions. Supper was likely only hours away.

"Funny finding you here." I pulled out the chair across from him.

Streaks of the late afternoon fae sun streamed through the windows. Its warmth hit my cheeks, and I had to admit that the Shrouding Estate got one thing right with its strange pentacle design—the natural sunlight that graced each room. Given how narrow each wing was, the multitude of windows allowed for cross light, which brightened each room considerably. I imagined that design had been done on purpose, since such little light was able to penetrate the trees' canopy.

Bavar popped the last cookie into his mouth, then dusted off his fingers. A rush of magic shimmered on his skin, and the remaining buttery smudges disappeared. "Such delicious biscuits. I do say I have a genuine fear of growing fat with Ms. Meyers around."

"You've been the same weight since you hit adulthood."

"True, but even my constitution is no match for such sugary, buttery delights." He pushed his empty plate to the side. "Now, given the energy pulsing from you, I'm guessing something urgent has presented itself?"

"It has." I showed him the messages between

Nicholas and me, and then told him what happened when we tried to place calls or send attachments.

Bavar leaned back, frowning. "In that case, one of us may need to venture to Bulgaria."

I grumbled. "Exactly, but a trip to the Bulgarian libraries is not what I had in mind right now."

"Nor I. Even though nothing amiss has been reported by Lex and Marnee—the two on patrol duty right now—that doesn't mean we won't be attacked at any moment. The more of us here to defend Avery, the better."

"Agreed. So what options do we have? Invite Nicholas here? Or should I go to him using a portal key and hope that the time difference doesn't mean I'm gone for days?"

The time inconsistencies between the two realms often proved problematic with assignments. This certainly wasn't the first time I'd run into a similar obstacle.

Bavar cocked his head. "I would hate to lose you if an attack is imminent. Perhaps inviting Mr. Fitzpatrick for a visit is the best option."

I leaned back in my chair, stroking my chin. While the thought of seeing Nicholas didn't make me smile, a rage-induced glower didn't twist my features either. Nicholas had proven kind and useful during the past few days. Perhaps he was right and I should let the past go. Let bygones be bygones.

I pictured my little sister's face.

The age-old rage burned in my gut, but I pushed it down.

That was a long time ago.

"I'll extend the invitation, and if he's unable to come here, I'll have no choice but to leave and visit the libraries." I made a move to pull out my tablet.

Bavar raised a hand. "Before you do that, I'm hoping to discuss your rest days a bit further. I'm guessing that you've been doing a bit of work today if you've been conversing with Nicholas. Does that also mean you sent your report to Wes?"

"I did, not long before coming to find you actually."

Bavar sighed. "I suppose I should count it lucky you've slept at all today. How are you feeling?"

"Better. More like myself. I'm still a little tired, but not like I was."

"Excellent. Consider it fortunate that you're a wolf. Many species wouldn't recover as quickly as you."

I scratched my chin. "Speaking of my report to Wes, I had to include an incident with Marnee."

Bavar cocked his head. "Oh? Pray tell."

I described how Marnee had tried to use her song on me and her jealous reactions I'd scented on several occasions. With every sentence I uttered, Bavar's expression grew darker and darker.

"You have a history with her, if I recall correctly?"

I nodded curtly, still hating that I'd allowed myself to succumb to her all those years ago. "Once. Three years ago."

"And she's carried a torch for you ever since."

"Unfortunately."

"I knew something was amiss with her. This confirms that the other warning signs I've seen aren't to be taken lightly. I fear she's been gone from the sea too long." He shook his head, an orange strand of hair curling across his forehead. "She's supposed to be there now as she was due a six-month soak, but as you know, with this incident regarding Avery, many of the squads were shuffled around or called back from leave."

I leaned forward in my chair, a scowl brewing. "Has she done anything else worrisome?"

Bavar frowned. "Nothing concrete, but she's been slower to respond to orders and less social with the squad. I've sensed restlessness in her during the past few months, which isn't surprising given her extended time on land. It was also the reason she was due for a soak."

"How long has it been now, since her last leave to the sea?"

"Two years."

I winced. "That's pushing it." Sirens, like werewolves, had an inherent need for their natural worlds. If a wolf stayed alone for too long, away from his pack or other wolves, he turned rogue—becoming a bloodthirsty psychotic wolf no longer in control of his mind.

It was the same for sirens. Away from the sea for too long, a siren could change mentally, becoming too salt deprived to function normally. In severe cases, entire personality changes occurred. But unlike wolves, returning to the sea—for soaks as we called them in the SF—could reverse the process for a siren. She would become healthy again, returning to her former self.

Not so for a rogue wolf. Once a wolf went rogue, he stayed rogue.

"She'll need a sabbatical the minute this assignment is over," Bavar said, more to himself than me. "And I'll need to keep a closer eye on her, as well as touch base with Wes. Let me know if you witness further concerning behavior from her."

I dipped my head. "I will."

"Now." Bavar sat straighter. "Back to the matter at hand. You shall be inviting Nicholas to Shrouding Estate?"

I pulled out my tablet. "Yes, I'll do it now." I typed in a message, keeping it short and concise.

> Are you able to bring copies of what you've found to us? The SF can provide a portal key.

A few minutes passed before Nicholas's reply came.

> I will speak with the library governor and request temporary leave to conduct SF business. I will be in touch to let you know if it's approved.

"Sounds like he'll try to come to us. He'll let us know."

"Wonderful. Please keep me abreast of all developments."

The two of us left the kitchen. In the hall, Bavar clasped his hands behind his back. "I've arranged for an additional bed to be brought to your chambers after the supper meal." He gave me a side-eye.

I quirked an eyebrow. "And?"

He feigned an innocent look. "And what?"

"I've known you long enough to know you're fishing for information."

"Whatever do you mean?"

"Just ask, Bavar. You know you want to."

He sighed as we reached the end of the wing and the great central room soared forty feet to a domed ceiling. Railings from the second floor halls overlooked us, as the wide staircase waited to the left. But nobody was traipsing around upstairs, so we still had relative privacy.

"Oh, all right," he finally conceded. "I can't help but wonder if you still need the second bed. We did all hear the rather"—he cleared his throat, a devilish glint in his eye—"*impressive* performance you gave this morning. Surely, Ms. Meyers is welcoming you into her bed now."

I shook my head, irritation washing through me that everyone had heard my mate's screams, but also amusement at the roundabout way Bavar always asked things.

"She hasn't accepted me as her mate if that's what you're wondering."

"Who said I was wondering?" But an interested curve of his lips told me that my mate status with Avery was exactly what he'd wanted to know. He fiddled with his dagger, the jeweled hilt flashing in the sun. "Did she, um, accept you as her mate prior to the event which led to her resurrection and unfortunate memory loss?"

"She did." I bit back a smile that he'd actually asked the question outright. "And I expect with time that she'll do so again."

"In which case the second bed won't be needed tonight?"

I crossed my arms. "You still better send it. I'd hate to have made progress with my mate today only to have us backtrack if she thinks I now have free access to her bed whenever I please."

Bavar laughed, but then quickly sobered. "You're right, best to play it safe. Otherwise she might not allow you to have any more of her biscuits, and we all know *that* would be a tragedy."

I took in his very aghast expression and barked out a laugh.

CHAPTER EIGHTEEN

AVERY

Charlotte and I called it quits on my magical practicing around eight. Supper was being served, and I was mentally spent. In the past few hours, what I'd learned was that trying to harness the power roiling around inside me was as complicated as astrophysics.

Without an external environmental trigger that provoked an automatic response, the power was an intricate web of layered smoldering magic which couldn't be utilized by simply snapping my fingers. Essentially, I had no idea how to access it properly or wield it.

And since I felt safe and content at Shrouding Estate with Wyatt and Squad Three around me, the strange power inside didn't want to come out to play. I hadn't been able to stop time again or blast anything to bits. Not once.

"So much for being a quick learner," I grumbled.

Charlotte slung an arm around my shoulders. "Don't beat yourself up. You have no memories, you have no idea where this power came from, and you've only had it for two days. The fact that you've been able to use it at all is impressive."

I made a face when I thought about how I'd created the dome, stopped time at the inn, and then shot the sprites. "But that's the problem. I *didn't* really use it. It erupted on its own as a reaction to something frightening and stressful that was happening around me. I was barely able to dismantle that dome I'd created around myself. It was only by thinking about happy things and feeling safe that did it. It wasn't because I'd directly ordered it to disappear."

She cocked her head as we crossed the arched bridge to the estate's front doors. "Maybe I need to scare you or stress you out more. I'm sure something can be arranged." She waggled her eyebrows.

I laughed, just imagining the schemes she would come up with. "Don't you dare. I'd probably accidentally raze this castle if you pulled some terrifying prank."

She dropped her arm from around my shoulders when we entered the castle. "You're probably right, but don't worry. We'll try again tomorrow and will come up with a plan B. Whatever plan B is."

We joined everyone in the dining room. After a supper of braised meats, rich wine, soft bread rolls, and a plethora of cooked fae vegetables, everyone stood to leave the impressive dining room with its dropdown chandeliers, a table that could seat thirty, and strategically arranged bouquets of beautiful fae flowers.

Meestry bowed deeply to all of us as we left the room. I could tell the head of Bavar's staff was very pleased that all the guests had enjoyed the evening meal so much.

Everyone headed toward the main stairs which led to the second floor—well, all except for Heidi and Bishop. They were on patrol duty tonight.

Twice I caught Marnee watching me as the rest of us sidled down the hall. Her expression was indecipherable, but both times she looked away when we made eye contact. I tried to brush it off, but something about her put me on edge.

When we reached the second floor, Wyatt prowled behind me. My skin tingled at the feel of him. We hadn't spent time alone together since our nap earlier, and my stomach was somersaulting with a vengeance at the thought of sleeping in the same room with him.

One by one, everybody retreated to their chambers,

which meant that once again I was alone with the SF commander.

Moonlight bathed our room in silver when we stepped inside it, and the wash of *something* prickled my skin when I crossed the threshold.

"What was that?" I shivered as the feel of it slowly died away.

"The cloaking spell that guards our room." Wyatt's eyes glowed dimly. "It'll keep all . . . sounds . . . contained to this room."

A flush burned my cheeks when I realized exactly what *sounds* he was referring to.

He stood by the door, watching me intently. I'd felt his gaze repeatedly on me during dinner, and a flipping sensation had set me on edge ever since.

"I see that we have a second bed." I waved toward it, anything to take that heated look off me.

The second bed, which the servants must have brought to our room during the meal, was tiny compared to the colossal four-poster that dominated an entire corner of the room.

"We do." His gaze on me didn't waver.

I squeezed my hands together, suddenly feeling incredibly unsure. I knew we'd slept in the same bed earlier today, but now we had two beds . . .

"You must still be tired. You should take the bigger

bed. I'll sleep in the smaller one."

His jaw clicked when he snapped it shut. "I'll take the smaller bed."

"But you're bigger than me. You should take the larger one."

"The larger one looks more comfortable. You take it."

I rolled my eyes. *Oh for fuck's sake. Were we seriously arguing about a bed?* "I'm just being logical."

"Fine." He stalked past me, and I suddenly wondered if I'd done something to upset him.

I balled my hands into fists as a flare of anger rose in me. Surely he wasn't mad because I wouldn't share the same bed with him?

Even though Wyatt and I had a rather passionate encounter this morning, I was still getting to know him. And even though he and I obviously had a shared history—a history that I still annoyingly couldn't remember—everything about *us* was still new to me. What was so wrong with not wanting to jump into an intimate relationship right away?

Surely, he understood that just because he could play my body like a symphony, it didn't mean that we were a couple who shared a bed together. Sleeping nightly beside one another was much more intimate than a make-out session and a daytime nap.

Energy emanated from Wyatt. Without a word, he

stalked over to his wardrobe and pulled out a pair of basketball shorts.

That was all he pulled out.

His chin angled in my direction, his nostrils flaring.

I hastily looked away and hurried over to the opposite wardrobe which contained my clothes. That curling feeling began in my stomach again, and I knew that if I didn't get a hold of myself I would do something embarrassing—like throw myself at him, or salivate when I fantasized about what his shorts concealed.

"I'm going to wash up unless you need the bathroom first?"

"No," I squeaked. Seriously, what was it about this guy? It was like simply being in the same room with him made my body come alive and caused tingles to shoot along my nerves. It was such an extreme reaction. Surely that wasn't normal?

When he retreated to the bathroom, I slipped into a pair of cotton shorts and a tank top. Since the clothing that had been retrieved from the inn was minimal, I didn't have dedicated sleeping attire. This would have to do.

The door to the bathroom cracked open just as I finished dressing, and I dove under the sheets in the smaller bed. I still had to pee and brush my teeth, but that could wait. Once Wyatt was asleep, I would get settled.

He came out and clicked the light off, plunging the room into darkness. The only light sources offering some kind of illumination were from the three moons in the sky outside. I glanced out the window, the glowing orbs barely visible through the trees' canopy.

But something about those orbs felt . . . familiar.

"What is it?" Wyatt asked as he pulled back the covers to the larger bed.

I shook my head, the spell breaking. "The moons. I feel like I've seen them before."

He settled back on his bed, making a loud *thump* when his head hit the pillow. "You have. This isn't your first time in the fae lands."

I rearranged myself, not feeling overly tired given our long nap earlier, but I knew I needed to sleep. "Except I don't think it's that. There's something about the sky and the light from them that—" I shook my head again. "I don't know. Never mind. Once again, I don't even know my own mind."

For a long moment he didn't say anything, and I wondered if he'd fallen asleep, but then he murmured quietly, "You died under a night sky like this."

Shivers raced along my arms and legs.

"It was the worst night of my life. It's one that will haunt me for the rest of my days."

A thick feeling clogged my throat. "I was somebody very special to you, wasn't I?"

"You say that in past tense."

I shrugged. "Because it's different now, isn't it? I'm not the same person I was when you knew me before. Surely the way you feel for me now isn't the same?"

His eyes glowed when he looked at me, then he said fiercely, "I will *always* feel the same for you—now, back then, and in the future. That will never change."

My lips parted at the boldness of his declaration, but my breath felt so trapped that I didn't reply.

He settled back on his bed, and eventually I did the same. I turned on my side to look at the three moons. A few more minutes passed, and Wyatt's breathing fell into a steady rise and fall. I knew he was sleeping and that I should try to do the same.

Huffing, I threw off the covers and got up to use the bathroom and brush my teeth. I still didn't entirely understand what had passed between Wyatt and me tonight. He seemed upset that I wouldn't share a bed with him, and then grouchy when I brought up how things were different now.

That niggling sense that there was so much about Wyatt that I didn't fully understand still clung to me.

What had he and I once been?

A LARGE FIRE rose from a pit in the earth. A group of men stood around it, their hands joined. Robes draped from their shoulders, the hems swaying softly as they chanted and swayed.

But it was the tallest one whose presence demanded my attention. He stood completely still, yet his power washed over me.

He joined the other men in the chanting, his voice low and deep. Lyrical words drifted from his mouth making my body rise and flow.

No!

But his magic had ensnared my soul, forcing me to glide higher and higher above them.

In my spectral form, I hovered above the ground, their power all-consuming, owning me. It was the end. I knew it was. I couldn't fight them, not like this.

I screamed again, kicking and clawing and fighting as mightily as I could against their power, but they were too strong—he was too strong.

He tilted his head up, and I swear he could see me, actually see me. He chuckled. "Ah, there you are. I knew I would find you. You can't hide from me."

A scream tore from my throat, and I bolted upright in bed. Sweat dripped down my temples, and my fingers dug into the sheets. He'd found me? That evil man had found me in my dream, here at Shrouding Estate?

I shook my head. No, that wasn't possible. It was just a dream. Nobody could find somebody in a *dream*.

Still, my power hummed and swelled, waves of purple energy flaring off me.

"Avery?" Wyatt knelt beside the bed, his eyes glowing as bright as the three moons outside. "Avery, it's okay. It was just a dream. You're okay." He dodged to the left when my power shot at him.

I sucked in a breath, only then realizing that the power inside me was erupting and shooting out. I still panted, barely able to gasp in breaths as I shuddered and heaved at the terror which clawed up my throat.

But it was just a dream.

It wasn't real.

Those robed men hadn't found me. That wasn't possible.

"Avery, it was a nightmare," Wyatt said soothingly. "You're safe."

I took a deep breath, trying to ease my panic. "I know. It just . . . it felt so real. And I think I've had these dreams before. They're of *them*."

Memories of the attack at the inn resurfaced making fresh terror slice through me.

In a flash, Wyatt was on the bed beside me, hauling me into his arms. He gritted his teeth as my power continued to swell and zap him.

I pushed him away. "No, I don't want to hurt you. I can't control it."

But he didn't budge. "I've dealt with worse. I'm fine." He flinched when a rush of magic singed his skin, but he still didn't let go.

I choked out a humorless laugh at his refusal to leave.

He continued holding me close, his soothing hands rubbing up and down my back. He had a way about him —his presence eased my panic, his looming bulk acted like a shield.

As the minutes ticked by, the power inside me calmed. Eventually, it stopped pulsing off me completely and retreated inside. Throughout it all, Wyatt never let go.

"Always so noble," I whispered tersely.

He stiffened. "Does that bother you?"

No. But for some reason I didn't say that out loud. But it was true, he *was* noble. He'd always been there for me, ever since I'd woken up. Waiting. Watching. Protecting. It seemed that no matter what I did, he was steadfast.

And while a part of me liked that, adored it even, the other part of me hated it. It made me feel unworthy. What had I done to deserve this kind of devotion from him? I had no idea of the woman I'd once been. But I'd obviously loved him, and he was expecting me to eventually love him in return. And even though my body ached for him, what if my mind never did?

His hand stilled from where he'd been rubbing up and down my back. "Care to share what you're thinking about?"

I knew he couldn't read my mind, but I could tell that he'd sensed my shift in emotions. I snorted inwardly. Of course he had. He could *scent* my emotions.

"Nothing," I lied. "It's just the aftereffects of the dream."

But I knew I wasn't fooling him. Still, he resumed his gentle touches, and my body once again betrayed me. That fluttery feeling began in my stomach, and that aching *need* clenched my core.

Without warning, he picked me up and carried me to the larger bed. My breath caught at how quickly and easily he did it.

"Relax," he said after laying me down. "I'm not forcing myself on you, but your bed is a mess of tangled sheets. Why don't you go back to sleep in this bed, and I'll take the smaller one after I fix it." His hands roamed over my back again. "I could give you a massage to help you get back to sleep if you like."

I tensed, waiting for his hands to dip lower than my waist.

But they stayed firmly north and only in safe areas. Well, as safe as any area on my body was around him.

Needing to gauge his expression, I turned in his arms. "Why are you always so nice to me?"

For a moment, he was silent, and then instead of answering my question he asked, "Would you rather I be mean to you?"

Yes. But I knew I didn't mean that. Of course, I didn't want him to be mean to me, although that would be easier to deal with. If he was an asshole, I would have no qualms about pushing him away and denying my attraction to him.

"Talk to me, Avery."

I covered my eyes. "I don't know. There's just so much I still don't know. Even though I've gotten a few niggling feelings about my past, I still don't remember the *experiences*. I don't remember being with you, and I don't remember loving you."

He continued massaging me. "Just give it time. It may come back."

"But what if it doesn't? What if this is how it stays? What if for the rest of my life I get glimpses and hints of the past, but it never fully returns? How would you deal with that?"

His body tightened, his hands pausing, but then he resumed his light touches. "Then I guess we would start over. We would have to get to know one another from this day forward."

"And if I never felt again what I once felt for you?"

He stiffened. Even his massages didn't resume. "Then I'd let you go, if that's what you wanted."

His quiet statement was filled with so much raw pain that it cut through my soul. I hung my head. "I don't deserve your devotion. Maybe I once did, but now? I don't think so."

He scoffed. "If anyone is undeserving here, it's me. *I'm* the one who fucked up a few months ago, not you. Perhaps this is my punishment. Perhaps you not remembering me is karma's way of paying me back for how I treated you."

Since our conversation had moved completely away from the terror I'd felt from the dream, I suddenly became more cognizant of how closely we lay beside one another. His warmth, his scent, and the feel of him pressed against me made my toes curl. I liked it. I liked it too much. "It scares me, the depth of what I think I once felt for you."

He swallowed, the sound audible. "The way I feel

about you scares the shit out of me if that makes you feel any better."

"Why does it scare you?"

"Because you have complete control over me, Avery." He brushed a lock of hair behind my ear. "There's nothing I wouldn't do for you. And do you know how vulnerable that makes me feel? Do you know how uneasy I feel on a regular basis that the possibility of you rejecting me and pushing me away still exists? I can try my damnedest to win you back, but ultimately, you're the one who gets to decide. I'm not going anywhere. I'll always be here wanting you, waiting for you, and hoping that you'll decide that I'm the one for you. But I can't make you want me. I can only hope that you do."

That dipping motion began roiling my stomach over and over again. "You do things to my insides," I whispered. "You have since the minute I woke up. I think that's why I was so distrustful of you when I came around in the field. I didn't understand the way you made me feel. I still don't."

"Who says you have to understand it? Since when has love been anything anybody can understand?"

Love. My heart clenched. I'd once loved this man. I could *feel* it. I could feel it to the depth of my bones that I'd once felt such a soul-searing love for him that it had all but consumed me.

But I also knew that love came from shared experiences and years of growth. It hadn't developed in two days. And right now, all I had with him was two days.

"Why don't you try to sleep? This is a rather heavy conversation for the middle of the night."

Since he'd probably scented the turmoil that had seeped into my being, I did as he said and rolled so my back was to him.

He shifted, and the mattress sank under his weight, but he was careful to keep his body from touching mine.

I closed my eyes when his warm hands began kneading my back. I relished the feel of his firm fingers rubbing my muscles and eliciting tingles of pleasure.

"You don't have to do this," I told him. "You need more sleep than I do."

He grunted. "I'm fine. Between the two naps yesterday and the additional five hours I just got, I'd be good to go if I had to get up and start working right now. I'm a werewolf, remember? We're stronger than most."

His fingers continued to ease and soothe, making my shoulders relax.

"Have you always been this . . . invincible?"

He chuckled, his fingers never stopping. "What makes you think I'm invincible? I'm far from it."

I shrugged. "It just seems like nothing fazes you. That you roll with whatever life throws at you."

"Maybe, but I wasn't born that way. I was trained to be this way. It's how all commanders are in the SF. We have to be able to deal with whatever our jobs throw at us. Now, enough talking. Go to sleep. It's still a few hours until sunrise."

I closed my eyes again and concentrated on the feel of his warm hands and sure fingers. But instead of his slow massages making me feel sleepy, that achy feeling began to pulse in my core again.

Wyatt sucked in a breath, and I could only imagine what scent I was giving off. But there was something *about* him, something that called my body to his.

I inched back on the mattress, little by little, scolding myself for doing so but unable to stop.

My ass brushed against Wyatt's thigh, then his groin. His stiff erection prodded my lower back.

In a gruff voice, he whispered, "Avery, what are you doing?"

I stopped, freezing my movements. "I don't know. I'm sorry. I just do things when I'm around you. It's like my body *wants* certain things."

I began to move away, but his hand clamped onto my hip, anchoring me against him. His chest brushed closer, and then I felt his hard length press entirely against my back as his mouth dipped. He nestled into the crook of my neck.

"I'm not complaining." His whispered words brushed my ear. "I like it."

"You do?"

"Oh yes, Little Flower. It's why I was so grumpy before bed. I'm *aching* for you in the worst way, and there's nothing I can do that will blow off this steam. Back at the SF, when I felt like this, I could distance myself from you, go to the gym, or let my wolf out and run through the forest. But I can't do that here. I'm stuck in close proximity to you with my balls throbbing."

My breath caught at the rawness of his words.

"But I'm not saying that to pressure you," he added quickly. "I just want you to understand. If I get moody sometimes, it's only because I want so desperately what I can't have. But if you're happy to lie with me like this, I'll happily keep you beside me, although I can't help the hard-on."

The tip of his erection brushed against me again, and I moaned, unable to help it. Gods, this *man*. I wanted him so much. Even though my mind was a mess, my body knew exactly what it wanted.

"Is this okay?" His breath made goosebumps sprout across my skin. "To lie beside you like this?"

"Yes," I breathed.

His erection prodded me again as his hand dipped around my hip, moving slowly toward the juncture of my thighs. "What about this?"

Another breathy moan escaped me when his fingers swept down to my core, between my legs and through the thin shorts. He began moving slowly, just teasing swirls and soft strokes.

I arched back, sensations already coursing through me at just a few mere touches.

"Do you want me to stop?" His fingers rubbed and dipped.

Fire grew inside me. "No."

He rumbled. "Good."

His fingers continued to play and tap, swirl and stroke. Within seconds, I was liquid heat beneath his touch.

When another gasp escaped me, he growled again. "So responsive. I will never tire of that." He kissed my neck, sucking on the skin below my ear while his hand continued its maddening assault.

"Stop!" I abruptly called out. I was already half lost, getting too far gone, but that wasn't how I wanted this to go.

He pulled his hand away, his body turning rigid. "I'm

sorry. I didn't mean to—" He sighed harshly. "I'll go back to the other bed."

But I rolled around and grabbed him before he could leave. "No, that's not what I meant. I just meant that I want to touch *you*. It seems unfair if you're the only one giving me . . . pleasure."

A deep glow lit his eyes, and his Adam's apple bobbed when he swallowed. "Okay. If that's what you want?"

"It is. Unless you object?"

"No," he said instantly. "No objections at all. Do with me as you please."

I giggled. His words were so desperate they were hoarse. "You can't judge me, though. I don't remember what you like."

His voice grew raspier, as if he struggled to catch his breath when I trailed a finger down his chest. "There's nothing you can do that I won't like."

"But do you have things you prefer?" I bent down and kissed his chest, just to the right of his nipple.

He sucked in a breath. "That's good."

"What about this?" I trailed my tongue to the ridge of his abdomen, kissing and sucking as I went.

"Uh-huh, that's good, too," he said in a strangled voice.

"And this?" I dipped my hand into his shorts. His

thick erection greeted me, and my breath caught. Gods, the man was *huge*.

"Oh yeah, I definitely like that."

I encircled his length and began stroking him as I kissed, touched, and fondled his chest, neck, and shoulders.

The heat off him grew with every passing second, and low groans and further strangled sounds regularly tore from his throat.

"Would you object to me tasting you?" I whispered, then nibbled his ear. "Here?" I squeezed his thick shaft.

His entire body shuddered. "Oh Gods, no. Definitely no objections to that."

I sat up, suddenly feeling entirely awake even though it was hours until sunrise. I slipped my tank top off, my bare breasts visible in the moonlight. My nipples were already peaked, the chill in the room setting them on edge.

Wyatt groaned as his erection speared his shorts, but I paused.

"What is it?" he asked as I stared at him with my tits only inches from his face. He leaned forward, his tongue darting out to taste one taut bud.

I sucked in a breath. "Your size," I managed. "I just wondered how I had sex with you. It doesn't look like you'll fit in me." A blush crept up my cheeks despite trying to stop it.

He chuckled. "Oh, don't worry, I fit." He lapped at my breasts again.

That throbbing clench began in my core at the feel of his tongue, his need, and his desire for *me*. Suddenly I wanted him, *needed* him.

"What if I want to do more than suck you?"

His hand gripped my waist, then trailed down to my thighs when I inched down. "Babe, you can do anything you want to me."

He hissed in a breath when I ripped his shorts off in one second and then encircled his pulsing erection in the next. The power in me strummed and flowed, infusing speed into me that I didn't realize I was capable of.

"Your eyes are glowing again," he said huskily when I looked up at him with the tip of his dick by my mouth.

"They are? My eyes glow too?"

"Only since the other day. I think it's the power in you. But we can talk about that another time." He tilted his hips up, inviting me to suck him.

With a curving smile, I lowered my head and allowed myself to taste him as desperately as I wanted to.

Wyatt's thighs grew harder and stiffer the more I licked and fondled him. Twice I almost made him come, but then I pulled back at the last minute until he'd retreated from the precipice.

His entire body was shaking with need, although mine was in a similar state. Seeing how much power I had over him, how I could make him shudder and groan with one hard suck or scrape of my teeth, made my core *throb*.

"Avery," he growled when I retreated to stroking him slowly again. "If your touch isn't enough to drive me mad, your scent will. I can smell the wetness between your thighs."

I released his erection, then crawled up his chest, my breasts trailing along his stomach.

"Fuck, woman." He reached down to cup them, kneading their flesh.

I slipped my shorts off, my breaths coming so fast and the need inside me so great. "I want more than just touching and sucking."

He stilled, his eyes whipping to mine. "So do I."

I straddled him, my naked sex sliding along his abdomen since I was so wet.

He groaned, the tendons in his neck jutting out.

"So you won't mind if I do this?" I straightened, just enough to reach between us and grip his erection. I shifted lower until his tip prodded my entrance.

"Fuck, no." His teeth clenched so tightly that his jaw muscles popped.

I tilted my head back, closing my eyes, and slowly, inch by inch, I lowered myself onto him until I'd sheathed him completely inside me.

I moaned in pleasure. The feel of him filling me and stretching me, Gods, it felt *so good.*

"Oh, Little Flower. You're as tight and sweet as I remember you." He moaned when I tilted my hips, his length still completely buried inside me.

"You're so big," I breathed, and then I began to move, his hard length sliding in and out of me as I set a tempo that rubbed that ache deep inside me. "Oh Gods!" I whispered. "You feel so good."

His hands locked onto my hips, lifting and moving me, slamming me back onto his cock as I fucked him harder and harder and rode him faster and faster.

The feel of him pulsing and rubbing inside me made my breath stop, and then he tilted his hips, hitting me deeper and harder and . . . Gods . . . *scraping* that area inside me.

"It's happening again," I moaned. Those sensations were starting again, the ones he'd done to me yesterday. How quickly I was coming to learn what these delicious feelings meant.

"Fuck. Me too, babe." He growled and gripped me

harder, his head arching back as I sank onto him again and again, moving faster with every bounce.

And when his erection rubbed on that deep spot again, I became undone.

I screamed when a flurry of stars and cresting waves pulsed through me. Wyatt's roar came next, his hips bucking and his hands clenching as the veins in his neck stood on end.

His dick throbbed and convulsed, my inner walls clamping around him as wave after wave of ecstasy rocked through me again and again.

Gods, this man. He gave me unending pleasure and a continual throbbing need. How could I ever escape that?

When I finally collapsed on Wyatt's chest, so spent and satiated that I couldn't move, a hint of moonlight revealed elongated canines in his mouth.

I blinked and his mouth closed, erasing what I'd thought I'd seen.

He gathered me in his arms as I used his shoulder as a pillow. A deep rumble of contentment came from him as his scent flowed around me and a warm feeling grew in my heart.

"That was amazing," I breathed just as my eyes drifted closed.

"Yes, my love." He pressed a soft kiss to my forehead. "It was."

CHAPTER NINETEEN
WYATT

Dim sunlight slipped past the curtains' seams. Avery's warm body pressed against my side, her soft puffs of breath even and deep.

I stared down at her as the night returned to me in vivid details.

Her gasps.

Her moans.

The feel of her stroking me, tasting me, *riding* me.

My dick was hard again. It had been since I'd woken up.

My wolf growled in contentment, and for the first time since I'd claimed her at the Bulgarian libraries, he wasn't itching and clawing at me to shift or to claim her again. He still wanted a claiming, but the fact that Avery continued to grow closer to us and wanted to be with us, physically at least, quieted his soul. For now.

But I knew that wouldn't last forever.

I lay on my side, propping myself up on my elbow and cupping my head so I could watch Avery sleep. I trailed a hand softly up her hip, marveling at the smooth feel of her skin, the curve of her waist, the swell of her breast.

Gods, she's beautiful.

She stirred a few moments later. I dipped down, kissing her softly on the neck. "Good morning, Little Flower."

She murmured something, still not fully awake, but she rolled onto her back, her breasts completely bare for me to admire. Her toned yet soft stomach called to me, and her womanly mound which was still concealed by the sheets taunted me.

Not being able to help myself, I ran my finger along the shape of her breast again.

She shivered, her lips parting before she murmured something sleepily.

I trailed my finger down her stomach. Goosebumps sprouted on her skin, and my cock was so hard now it pulsed.

She sighed, and her body stretched languidly.

I moved the sheets down more, little by little, until her womanly mound was exposed.

"Gods," I said in a hoarse whisper. Already I could scent her. Her sex was moistening, her lips swelling. My mate's body was readying for me again, even though she was still half asleep.

Mine. The savage possessive thought seared my thoughts. *My* mate.

And it was true. She was mine. The way her body responded to me proved that. Only a true mate could become so ready so easily with only a few touches. And even though she was half asleep, she still responded, which cemented what my wolf and I already knew. She was our mate. Our *true* mate.

"I want to touch you."

Her lips curved up in a sleepy smile. "Yes."

Her monosyllabic response was all the encouragement I needed. My hand dipped, my fingers gently parting her folds until I was playing and stroking her in a way that I knew drove her mad.

Within minutes, she was panting and writhing, becoming more awake by the second, yet she still seemed somewhat lethargic from the fucking we'd done during the night.

I rolled her so that she was on her side again, her ass

against me, then lifted her knee so her sex was easily exposed.

She gasped when my tip parted her lips from behind, then she arched her back to allow me to enter her inch by inch.

"Gods. So wet."

She moaned softly, arching more before wiggling to get me deeper inside her.

My breath hissed. She gripped me like a glove and already my cock was pulsing in anticipation.

When I was fully sheathed, I clamped a hand on the curve of her hip and began to move. Breathy gasps and little moans escaped my mate. Her sounds of pleasure only made me harder.

I moved deeper and rougher, rubbing her in the way I knew she loved.

"Wyatt," she whispered. Grasping the bed sheets, her fingers curled into them as the musky tint in her scent increased.

I inhaled, my nostrils flaring, then I nipped her earlobe and rocked my hips harder, increasing my tempo as I thrust into her.

Her channel grew slicker, gripping me even tighter as she arched again, moaning deeply.

I locked onto her hip, anchoring her in place, and her moans increased.

She gasped when my pace sped up even more, until I was slapping into her from behind, fucking her in every sense of the word.

"Don't stop!"

My hand slid around to play with her taut nub, and she shuddered and panted when I pinched and fondled that bundle of nerves.

"Wyatt!" she called out, and in that one word, I could sense she was close.

I tapped her, then lightly swirled, and it was enough to send her over the edge.

She screamed my name as her channel convulsed and tightened. With a guttural roar, I slammed into her one last time, and we climaxed together.

She moaned over and over as her orgasm refused to release its grip. The entire time I stayed buried inside her, letting her ride the waves on my dick and loving that I could pleasure her so intensely that her releases all but consumed her.

And when we both came down from our highs, she turned to me, my dick slipping out of her while she pushed hair from her face. A mischievous, sleepy smile tilted her lips, and that one look let me know that my mate had finally, fully accepted my courtship.

My wolf rumbled in pleasure.

Mine.

"Good morning," she said shyly.

I grinned, my smile lazy and content since she and I were in the place I'd always dreamed of—fucking and loving each other every day and multiple times per day. How long had I fantasized about this?

Leaning down, I kissed her softly. "Morning, mate."

Her cheeks blushed at that declaration, but I could tell from the happiness tingling her scent that she liked it.

I nipped her neck, my teeth grazing her skin. Every time I fucked her, my canines elongated, but I knew she wasn't ready for that yet. But in time she would be.

She stretched, her glorious body rubbing against me, and before I knew what was happening, I was hardening again, wanting her once more.

Except this time, unlike under the dome, she didn't show any hesitation or fear. If anything, excitement danced in her eyes, followed quickly by lust.

I rumbled in awe when my mate spread her legs, her womanly lips open and dripping, still wet from our fucking only a few minutes ago.

She giggled when I sank into her again, but when I began to move, all laughter died from her lips as her need became as great as mine.

"My mate," I whispered into her ear as I began to plunder her sex again.

She gasped and arched, tilting her hips to meet my thrusts. "Yes," she whispered.

I shuddered, my wolf purring in pleasure as our mating bond grew.

WE FELL ASLEEP AGAIN and didn't wake up until mid-morning. The fact that I didn't have to get up, that I could spend all day in bed with my mate since I was technically still on rest duty, made my wolf purr.

Avery pushed up onto her elbows and glanced toward the desk. "What's that?" Her long dark hair tumbled down her back, and her lips were swollen from all of my kisses.

I slid an arm possessively around her waist and followed her gaze. A flashing light came from my tablet.

"It means I have a message, but that can wait. I'm off duty, and I have no desire to get up when I have a vixen like you in my bed."

She giggled, trying to muffle her laugh behind her hand but to no avail. She playfully slugged my shoulder. "I'm not a vixen."

"Really? 'Cause from what I've seen, you're entirely a vixen. You suck my cock better than anything I've ever dreamed of, and you're insatiable even though I've already pleasured you three—"

"Wyatt!" she hissed, and slapped a hand over my mouth, but laughter danced in her eyes. "What if somebody hears you?"

I nipped at her palm, then slid my tongue along it. Her eyes darkened. Before she could utter another word, I rolled her beneath me and had her pinned to the sheets.

She gasped, her legs automatically parting.

My chest rumbled with pleasure at how readily she accepted me. I sank between her thighs and began kissing her neck. "Nobody can hear," I said between nips and kisses. "Cloaking spell, remember? You can scream as loud as you want."

She tilted her head to the side, giving me better access to the perfect curve just below her ear.

My tablet buzzed in quick succession. I froze.

"What was that?"

Dammit. "A high-priority message, which means I have to answer it." Sighing, I paused my downward journey.

Naked, I swung off the bed and swaggered to my tablet on the small writing desk. I knew my mate watched me. I could *feel* it. Just as I knew her gaze crawled up my legs, over my ass, and traveled the width of my shoulders.

The muskiness in her scent increased, and I felt like strutting around, giving her a full view of my body since her scent let me know how much she found my physical form appealing.

But, despite feeling like a cocky ass who wanted to puff around like a peacock, I didn't.

As always, duty called, and I'd never been one to hide from duty, even if my mate was naked in our bed with her sex ready for round four—as tempting as that was.

I picked up my tablet and saw who the message was from. Nicholas.

"What's it say?" Avery asked.

I glanced her way and immediately forgot what I was doing. She was toying with her hair and the sheet on our bed had fallen to her waist, giving me a full view of her bare breasts. Her nipples were peaked, those tempting buds taut and protruding.

For a moment, I simply held my tablet immobile as my attention fixated on those two perfect globes.

She curled another piece of hair around her finger. "Well? What does it say?"

Shaking myself out of my daze, I glanced down at my tablet and finally read Nicholas's message.

· · ·

PERMISSION GRANTED **to bring a copy of the documents to you. Departing now.**

"SHIT. He's traveling by portal key. He's probably already here."

She cocked her head. "Who?"

"Nicholas Fitzpatrick. He's coming here with documents from the Bulgarian libraries."

When she continued to look at me quizzically, I added, "Nicholas Fitzpatrick is the vampire who was with me when you woke up in the field."

"Oh, that blond guy."

"Yeah, that blond guy." With a regretful sigh, I eyed my mate's naked breasts one last time. "I need to shower and dress. Do you want to stay in here or come down with me?"

"I'll come down. I wouldn't mind hearing what he's found, and I'm hungry." She stood from the bed, and for the first time in my history at the SF, I actually considered saying fuck it to everything and throwing her over my shoulder and dragging her back to the mattress. We could have the servants bring us food in bed.

"Your eyes are glowing." She sauntered past me bare-assed, her perfect tits begging for my attention as her toned legs glided across the floor. "And your, *ahem*"—

She glanced down at my cock—"looks like it needs something."

Of course, I was rock-hard again. "Do you want to join me in the shower?" I practically stepped on her heels since I was in such a hurry to follow her into the bathroom.

She gave me a cheeky smile over her shoulder, a twinkle in her eyes. "I thought you'd never ask."

WE MADE it downstairs after a quickie in the shower. While we'd been occupied, one of the servants had brought our bags which we'd left in the Bulgarian libraries, so Avery was able to wear her own clothes from earth—jeans and a ribbed shirt that clung to her curves.

I guessed that Nicholas had not only brought a copy of the documents but our belongings too. A flare of gratitude slid through me. The vamp certainly seemed intent on making things right between us.

Squad Three was, of course, already up and probably had been for hours. Nobody commented on our late appearance, but Charlotte did muffle a cough when Avery strolled by her, and Marnee's gaze followed my every move.

I kept an eye on the siren, nostrils flaring, as I took in her scent. That coating of jealousy still lingered, but she didn't say anything, and she wasn't shooting daggers at my mate today.

Still, she needed to return to the sea. It was possible she'd even be pulled from this assignment to do so.

Charlotte hauled Avery to one of the couches, and my mate's cheeks flushed when Meestry ushered several servants forward who carried hot tea and scones.

She took a cup and a pastry, already falling into conversation with her friend.

When the servant passed me, I grabbed three scones. Famished, I wolfed them down. My high metabolism meant I ate a lot and often, but the buttery flavorful pastry only tasted so good.

Nicholas's vampire stench carried to me from down the hall along with his and Bavar's quiet conversation. I slipped out of the door, my footsteps silent as I prowled to one of the seating rooms off the Jeulic wing, about three doors down from where Squad Three lounged.

Nicholas's scent grew stronger the closer I got to the seating room. The door squeaked when I opened it, giving away my presence.

"Ah, there he is. Joining us at last." Bavar checked the time. "Hours at it this morning with his mate. Most impressive. You wolves really do have admirable stamina."

I snorted, knowing full well that fairy males who were enamored with a female were just as prolific in bed. As were vampires—rumor had it they could keep it up all night. My gaze slid to Nicholas.

He stood up gracefully from the wingback he'd been sitting on, his trousers perfectly pressed, his shirt open at the collar as the scent of an expensive cologne drifted my way. I inhaled. While the cologne was strong, it by no means covered up the vampire stench beneath it, which smelled of mothballs and rotting cabbage.

While vampires were perfectly preserved after they were changed, they were still dead—their skin forever holding a hint of aged flesh even though they never actually decayed.

As far as I knew, only male werewolves could detect that underlying odor since it was subtle. I even knew a few wolves who were mated to female vampires. I figured the mating bond made the stench obsolete.

A brief image of Avery dying in the field shot to the front of my mind and how Nicholas had offered to turn her. Thank the Gods he hadn't. Not because she also would have carried a vampire's odor, but because I'd never be free of Nicholas if he'd become Avery's maker.

My thoughts paused. Would that really have been so

bad? Nicholas was proving not to be the horrible creature I'd always thought he was.

But then my wolf growled. No, my wolf was right. It *would* be that bad. Neither of us wanted to share even a sliver of Avery with anyone.

"Major Jamison." Nicholas inclined his head.

I startled, realizing I'd been thinking about Nicholas for far too long. "Mr. Fitzpatrick." I moved to his side. "Thank you for coming. What have you found?"

He waved toward a piece of paper in a tube that leaned against the couch.

"Shall we?" Bavar waved toward a large table by the far wall. "I thought this room would be best so that Nicholas could roll the parchment out."

My eyebrows rose. "Only one document?"

"Only one photo." Nicholas picked up the tube. "The other information we've found is here." He tapped his pocket.

Photo?

The three of us went to the table, and my palms tingled in anticipation since Nicholas had deemed this an urgent finding.

In a flurry of vampire speed, Nicholas had the tube unscrewed and the paper spread out like butter.

"And there you have it." Nicholas waved toward the picture.

Bavar and I leaned forward, studying the drawing on the paper just as a shuffle of feet sounded behind us.

Avery's lilac scent danced toward me, along with Nicholas's sharp intake of breath before a slight hint of the vampire's arousal wafted my way.

A growl rumbled from my throat, my wolf's hackles rising just as Avery reached my side.

I was already reaching for her, ready to slide my arm possessively around her waist, in case the vampire needed a reminder that she was off-limits, but her sharp intake of breath and her sour scent of fear stopped me.

Frowning, I turned toward her, but she'd backed away, her eyes wide, violet light flashing in her irises.

Her gaze had glued to the drawing—to the picture of the elf that it held. He had olive-green skin, huge pointed ears that rose above his head, and a cold, terrifying smile.

She pointed at the picture, then backed up more. "Oh my gods, that's *him*. That's the man who tried to take me at the inn. He's the one in my dreams, the one who's been searching for me. *He* commands the Sacred Circle."

CHAPTER TWENTY
AVERY

Sacred Circle. That's what they call themselves. But how do I know that?

The backs of my knees bumped into a chair, as fear raged through my soul. I collapsed onto it. My hands automatically gripped the armrests, my fingers digging into the soft material.

The power inside me flared, electricity zapping along my limbs. That terrible well of magic simmered in my soul, threatening to unleash itself due to the terror swimming through my veins.

Deep breaths. In and out. In and out.

A dark scowl formed on Wyatt's face. "Who is he?"

"His name is Lord Nelifeum Godasara," Nicholas replied calmly. "He's an elf lord who lived two thousand years ago here in the fae lands. But he's no longer alive,

Avery. The elves are all dead, and the last elf lord was killed over a thousand years ago. I don't know how he could be the one you're speaking of, even though he meets your description and has an unusual history which also ties him to the Safrinite comet."

"I saw him!" I stated loudly, the horror still coiling inside my belly like a snake.

"But he's dead," Nicholas countered gently.

"No, he's not. That was him the other night. He's the one who attacked the inn, and he said he's been waiting for me for *thousands* of years."

Nicholas's eyebrows drew together. "But how is that possible? It's not, right?"

Wyatt's chest heaved as alpha magic rolled off him in tremendous waves. The power inside me responded, zapping and sparking along my nerves.

Both Nicholas and Bavar wore uncomfortable expressions when Wyatt's alpha magic barreled into them, but they stayed standing—a true testament to how strong each of them were.

"Those are very good questions," Bavar replied.

"Avery." Wyatt inched cautiously toward me. He moved slowly, as if afraid of startling me. When he finally reached me, he knelt at my side, his warm palm covering the back of my hand. "It's okay. You're safe."

I did my best to control my breathing, but the shock

of seeing the elf's face, of recognizing the supernatural, nearly undid me. He was the one who'd tried to abduct me at the inn. He was the one who commanded that circle of robed men. He was the one who *hunted* me in my dreams. Ice-cold dread slid through my veins and threatened to unleash the foreign power inside me.

"It's him. I don't know how that's possible, but I know I'm right. I swear it."

Wyatt's moss-green irises looked bottomless as a fierce flash of golden light rimmed the colorful orbs. "You recognize him? From the inn?"

"His mouth is the same. But it's not just from the inn. My dreams too."

Nicholas rolled the parchment back up after Bavar had taken multiple photos using his tablet. Both watched me now, Bavar's eyes concerned, and Nicholas's eyes kind yet . . . hungry.

I gripped Wyatt's hand. "He not only attacked the inn, but I've seen him before, or rather *felt* him in my dreams." The terror inside me increased when I remembered the horrifying nightmare I'd woken up from during the night. "That's what my nightmare was about last night. In the dream, he found me, and it felt so real, like he'd been looking for me and had *actually* found me."

Shock crept across Wyatt's face, then he stood and

faced Bavar and Nicolas. "Was Lord Godasara a projector?"

Nicholas pulled out the documents from his pocket, studied a few, then tapped one of them. "According to this, yes."

The concerned look on Bavar's face grew.

"You're absolutely certain that this elf is who's in your dreams?" Wyatt asked me. "And you're confident that he said he found you."

"Yes, completely. It's not the first dream I've had of him."

"How is this possible?" Bavar whispered. "A dead elf come back to life?"

Nicholas's attention swung between all of us, his confusion growing. "You're saying he's actually *alive?*"

Wyatt crouched back at my side, his tone turning urgent. "Avery, this is very important. Have you felt his presence at all today? Do you sense that he's near?"

I shook my head. "No, not since the dream, but I've only ever felt him when I'm asleep." More thoughts whirled through my mind. Not quite memories; rather, feelings and inklings of what had once been. Strangely, I wasn't sure if they were *my* feelings and thoughts or someone else's. I couldn't make sense of it. "I think"—I bit my lip, the realization only coming to me now—"I think he and I are tied somehow."

"And if he's alive and a projector, and he's locked onto her in a dream, then it's possible he *does* know that her location is here at Shrouding Estate." Wyatt growled so deeply that I knew it came from his wolf.

My eyes popped. "You mean he actually *did* find me in my dream?"

Nicholas swallowed, his Adam's apple bobbing. "*If* he's alive—and that's still a big *if*—and *if* these documents are correct in saying that he's truly a projector, then yes, it's possible he's found you."

"So our location has most likely been compromised." Bavar's gaze drifted to the windows and to the forest beyond, his hand going to his dagger. "Meestry?" He signaled to the servant. "Please get Squad Three."

I brought a hand to my forehead. "Will someone please explain to me what a projector is?"

"It's a very rare ability," Nicholas replied. "Not many can do it in today's world. It's like scrying but much more complicated. A projector is able to astral project himself to other areas in the realm. He can spiritually visit areas when he's seeking a source he's locked onto."

"Did I have these dreams about him before I woke up in the field?" I asked Wyatt.

Smoldering light filled his eyes. "I don't know, but prior to the alignment you were on earth. If you had dreams there about him, they were just dreams. Projectors can't cross realms."

"There's more that you need to be aware of." Nicholas stretched out another parchment, which was streaked with fresh ink just as Squad Three poured into the room. All of them were there: Bishop, Terry, Lex, Marnee, Heidi, and Charlotte. They all wore matching suits. In other words, weapons galore were strapped to their bodies.

In an instant, the seating area was overflowing with energy from a squad of supernaturals.

"Have we got movement?" Lex's blond hair was pulled back in a low ponytail.

"Not that we know of." Bavar's hand went to his dagger again. "But we may. The group after Avery possibly has a projector."

"It's not *possibly*," I corrected. "It's *him*, and he's been in my dreams."

Bavar dipped his head in apology as Marnee's lips thinned, her eyes narrowing.

Bishop put his hands on his hips. "Do we know where this definitely-probable-projector is now?"

"No, but we know what he looks like. Apparently, he's a dead elf come back to life." Bavar lifted his tablet. "I've sent you all a copy of his picture. According to Nicholas, he's been dead for two thousand years, yet according to Avery, he's the man who's in charge of the group that's pursuing her."

The entire room grew quiet.

"It makes sense though." Wyatt paced the room. "If this elf has returned, it would explain why Squad Fourteen couldn't identify his scent. Nobody's scented an elf in a thousand years." His feet stopped, planting into the thick rug. "So he's an elf working with sorcerers?"

Nicholas raised a finger. "Possibly, but I don't think they're sorcerers even though Squad Fourteen said all of the other men at the inn were."

Quiet again descended on the room as all eyes shifted to the vampire.

"Then what are they?" Lex asked.

"If they're truly working with Lord Nelifeum Godasara, then I would guess they're warlocks." Nicholas pulled out another sheet of parchment from his stack. "The texts we've uncovered about him all hinted at the trouble he found himself in near the end of his life—the trouble that spoke of the comet and prophecies and his obsession with ensnaring the power of a god. Lord Godasara turned to dark, powerful magic near the end of his life, as his ambition grew to gain more control of the fae lands. He used warlocks to strengthen that dark magic."

Heidi brought a hand to her throat. "That explains

why Squad Fourteen identified them as sorcerers, since that's what they inherently are. But shit, that's super creepy. Warlocks are bad news. Even a group of three or four can be hard to deal with, but a dozen?"

I scrambled to remember what I knew of warlocks. Of course, nothing came. "What's so bad about warlocks?"

"Warlocks are sorcerers who practice dark magic," Heidi replied. "That practice is illegal now, so if any are caught they face punishment in the courts. We don't get many assignments that deal with them, since dark magic is harder and harder to procure. That was one of the first things the SF dealt with when our organization was formed several hundred years ago, but the times that I've had run-ins with warlocks have been bad. We've never returned with a full squad."

My stomach sank like a stone.

A red strand of hair came loose from Terry's bun. "Okay, so a dozen warlocks and an elf lord. I should have called in sick today."

Bishop chuckled even though nobody else was smiling.

Terry shook her head. "But this still doesn't make sense. Nobody has seen or heard of an elf being alive in a thousand years. Not since the last one was hunted to extinction at the battle of Serfenivee."

Heidi nodded. "Exactly. I thought they were extinct too. I thought we'd *made* them extinct."

Nicholas smoothed the papers more. "Until today, so did I, but now that Avery's insistent he's alive, some of these findings actually make more sense." He waved at the papers. "These are the translations of other documents we found. Once the Bulgarian gargoyles realized Lord Godasara was interested in the comet, they began looking into him. According to the scrolls, he was obsessed with harnessing the power of the gods. Lord Godasara conducted many rituals and sacrificed many lives in attempts to lure one of the gods to our realm. And in some of the scrolls it says he succeeded."

The energy coming off Wyatt soared, his power vibrating through me, and I knew he'd reached the same conclusion as me.

Lord Godasara was obsessed with harnessing the power of the gods. The power currently inside me was strong enough to come from a god.

"He succeeded?" A skeptical expression formed on Bavar's face. "But none of the gods have walked on this soil in thousands of years."

Nicholas raised a finger. "One may have." He shuffled the parchments, then whipped one out. "Verasellee, the Goddess of Time, was rumored to have touched down in this realm where she was captured and enslaved by a circle of supernaturals, and was then forced into a dormant state."

Wyatt went completely still.

"*I* stopped time," I whispered. "And in my dream, the men are always in a circle—The Sacred Circle."

Nicholas eyed me, then continued. "However, before she fell into that state it says that she fought back and cursed the lord trying to take her power. What that curse was exactly, we don't know as the records get fuzzy. Some say her curse killed him, others say it only weakened him, but if Lord Godasara is the one who did this, and he's truly walking and breathing now—two thousand years after his life supposedly ended—then perhaps he fell into a state similar to hers. He could have been dormant and only just recently awoken."

"And if he's truly working with warlocks, that makes sense because casting someone into a dormant state takes dark magic," Lex chimed in. "That's a warlock's specialty."

Heidi crossed her arms. "So if he's been dormant for all of these years, why did he wake now?"

"Me." A chill rushed through me. I didn't know how I knew that it was because of me, but I did. Once again, it was as if foreign memories brushed my mind, just like the foreign power that swirled through my veins. The power that controlled *time*. "Whatever happened to me with the comet and alignment, I think it's tied to them—the Sacred Circle. And I think this elf lord has been waiting for thousands of years to awaken for *me*."

Wyatt snarled, and all of Squad Three shared uneasy looks, Charlotte giving me a brief fleeting smile which didn't reach her eyes.

I tried to shake the icy feeling off. "So what does being dormant mean and how would the warlocks do it?"

Nicholas flipped through the parchments again. "Dormancy means that your body goes into a deep coma and you're preserved in that state. Think of it like cryogenic freezing, except it requires immense and illegal dark magic, which is why so few dare to try it, but it could explain what's happening here if an elf lord is truly walking again."

"Well, shit." Bishop whistled. "So all of this could be true." He gave me an apologetic look when he caught my glower. "Not that I ever doubted you, Ms. Meyers."

Wyatt flanked my side, the energy off him now coming in tumultuous waves. Everyone else was doing their best to avoid his surges, stepping out of the way or behind furniture when necessary.

"There's something else I wanted to show you, commander," Nicholas said to Wyatt. He pulled out another sheet and pointed at a few lines of text. "One tome Master Godric found says that before Verasellee fell into a deep sleep, she released her power into the heavens for it to be given one day to a worthy heir."

Wyatt's jaw dropped. "An heir?"

Nicholas nodded.

"That matches what we found before the alignment."

"And that would be what?" Heidi asked.

Wyatt's gaze drifted to Marnee, who'd been strangely quiet during the entire exchange, before he brought his hands to his hips and addressed Squad Three. "The gargoyles made a few discoveries before Avery"—he swallowed, as if the next words pained him—"died. One of the tomes they found said, 'For on the night of the heir's conception, the great prophecy will begin. The stars will amass to twice their size, and the magic will be born in the fated starlight couple. And only when the Safrinite comet returns will the true prophecy occur. The magic will erupt in the heir destined to forge our path, creating the path for the gods to be born. Only then will we rise.'"

"So more than one document has spoken of an heir," Charlotte concluded.

Wyatt nodded. "We knew Avery was the heir after her parents visited the Bulgarian libraries, and now we know who was destined to rise. It's the elf lord and the

Sacred Circle. They're the ones who have risen. It's all making sense now."

The blood drained from my face. "So, Verasellee, the Goddess of Time, touched down in this realm, Lord Godasara enslaved her, but before he managed to do that, she released her power to be given to a worthy heir, and I'm that heir. So that's what's inside me? The power of a *goddess*."

Wyatt dipped his head, his hands coming to rest on my shoulders. I was thankful I was still sitting down. If I hadn't been, I probably would have collapsed.

"Well, shit," Bishop said again.

"Well, shit indeed." Charlotte drifted closer to my side and placed a hand on my forearm as Wyatt continued to loom over me.

The breath rushed out of me, but I was grateful for their presence. It wasn't every day that one learned she had the power of a goddess. *A freakin' goddess.* No wonder I couldn't control it. Nobody would know how to control power that strong.

"What's the latest perimeter report?" Wyatt asked Bavar.

Bavar whipped out his tablet, his fingers flashing over it. "According to the wards, all is still quiet, as it has been since we arrived yesterday. There's been no sign of foreign visitors or malevolent magic, and there's definitely not a once-dormant-come-back-to-life elf lord prowling the perimeter, but it's only a matter of time until he's here. If he's waited two thousand years for a goddess's power, and he now knows that Avery has it, something tells me he's not going to waste any time."

The energy off Wyatt soared. "We need to tell Wes. We're going to need more squads here."

"I'll message my uncle now, telling him we need clearance. Squad Three, prepare for an imminent attack."

Everyone whipped into action as a niggling sensation brushed the back of my mind. The feeling that hinted at a memory that wasn't my memory. Like how I'd known what the Sacred Circle was.

Could it be the Goddess of Time's memory?

I shook that thought off and tried to focus on what was happening around me.

Everyone had their weapons out, except for Wyatt and Bishop. As werewolves, their power lay in their wolves.

Bishop was holding it together, but hairs had sprouted on the backs of Wyatt's hands, only to retreat again. Some part of me understood what was happening.

Wyatt was very close to losing control. I was his mate. He felt my safety was in peril.

And he would die to defend me.

Or kill anyone that threatened me.

"Wyatt?" I stood and rounded the back of my chair. "It's okay. Bavar's right. He's not here yet. Nobody is trying to hurt me right now."

His arms closed around me. "But he *knows* you're here." His words came out guttural and inhuman, as if his vocal cords had become half man and half wolf.

I threaded my fingers through the soft hair at his nape, the texture like silk.

Waves of turbulent energy washed off of him like a raging river down a mountain. He hauled me closer and buried his nose in my neck. His entire body trembled. "I need to keep you safe." His voice was still altered, his arms like steel. "I can't lose you again."

"You won't."

Wyatt lifted his head. "Are we clear on the escape plan, Bavar?"

Bavar strapped a sword to his back. "Yes, she'll stay in the Whimsical Room, only escaping to headquarters via a portal key if the castle falls. We'll deal with health repercussions then if they come."

I scrunched my face up in confusion. I knew they were talking about me, but the apparent *escape plan* was news I hadn't been privy to.

But I didn't have time to ask about it. Bavar shouted, "Meestry!"

A shuffle of feet came, and then the servant entered the room. "Yes, my lord?"

"Please prepare the castle. I'm activating Mission Red."

CHAPTER TWENTY-ONE
AVERY

Mission Red?

Meestry's eyes widened for the merest second before he gave a shaky bow. "Of course, my lord." He scurried from the room, his face pale.

"Holy shit, Mission Red?" Excited energy danced in Charlotte's eyes.

My stomach dropped. If Charlotte looked that way, then Mission Red was bad news.

Wyatt's arms tightened around me more. "Avery's going in the safe room now."

"Already on it," Bavar replied.

My heart felt like it was thudding a thousand times a minute. Squad Three was acting like the elf lord could be here in seconds. "Care to fill me in? What's Mission Red, and what's the safe room?"

Wyatt took a deep breath. "Mission Red is a code word we use in safe houses when shit's getting bad. It's to ensure the safety of bystanders and civilians."

The blood drained from my face. "But nothing's bad yet. Nothing's happened!"

"But if Lord Godasara knows where you are, things can go south fast. For all we know, he's already here in the Shroud Forest, just waiting to pounce."

"But I thought the forest would deter him?"

"It would if he wasn't an elf lord." Wyatt's mouth flattened into a tight line. "The ancient elf lords were able to commune with forests."

"Seriously?"

"It's true." Bavar sidled closer to us, strapping more swords, daggers, and other sharp pointy things to his body. "If Lord Godasara has truly risen and has located you in your dream, then being surrounded by the Shroud Forest can actually work against us, an absolute first."

"We need to get you in the Whimsical Room." Wyatt tugged me toward the door, but I dug my heels in.

"Wyatt, I can't go to the safe room. I can't hide while all of you fight. *I* can fight him, remember? I saved you and Charlotte the last time he attacked."

A deadly scowl formed on his face. "Can you call upon that power now? Right this instant and make time stop again?"

I flinched. He knew I couldn't do that. I'd had this power for two days not years. I had no idea how to wield it. "Not exactly."

Wyatt cupped my cheeks, his expression softening. "Exactly, which is why you're not going to fight. The Whimsical Room will keep you *safe*, Little Flower, just like it was designed to do, and it will allow us to do our jobs without worrying about you."

Movement in my peripheral vision made my gaze shift. Marnee watched Wyatt and me, but the second I turned my head in the siren's direction, she resumed checking her weapons.

"So I'm being sent where?" I huffed.

"You and Nicholas will both go to the Whimsical Room. It's impenetrable. As long as this castle stands, nobody can reach you in there."

"Nicholas too?"

"He's a consultant, not a squad member. He's not trained to fight. You'll both be safe there."

"If it's really that safe then why don't we *all* go in there?" Fear coated my insides, and the power inside me rumbled.

The golden glow encircling Wyatt's green eyes intensified. "Then we wouldn't be doing our job. The SF is the one who stands against threats to peace. We don't hide."

Nausea made my stomach roil when Heidi's earlier comments returned. *"We've never returned with a full squad."*

I dug my feet in more. "But what if I *can* stop time again? What if I use this new power inside me to—"

"No!" Wyatt's one word, uttered with such ferocity and growly determination, made me pause. "You're *not* an SF member, Avery. And I know you're strong. I know you can fight—you were trained to fight at the SF even if you don't remember—but you're not a squad member. The training you received isn't what Charlotte received, and you still don't know how to control the power inside you. To the SF, you're a civilian. I can't allow you out there with us." The golden light around his irises swelled, and his expression turned pleading.

And in that look I saw it. He wouldn't make me do anything, but he was begging me to do as he asked.

"Please, Little Flower," he whispered. "If they're coming for you, then you're who we need to protect."

"But what if someone in this room dies because of me? What if you die? Or Charlotte dies? Or Bavar dies?"

His gaze hardened. "Then we die with honor, protecting who we all vowed to keep safe."

My breath stopped, and it felt as if my heart shattered. "But if all Lord Godasara wants is me, and I'm stronger now and can fight him—"

"NO!" he bellowed. He took a deep breath, and his hands dropped to his side. Hairs sprouted on the backs of them as his chest heaved. "He *can't* have you." Raw pain filled his eyes. "Please, Avery. *Please*. I can't lose you. Not again."

The stark terror in his words cut my heart into jagged pieces. But I could fight. I *knew* I could. Maybe I didn't have absolute control of the power inside me, but I'd saved him and Charlotte when the elf lord last attacked. If I was afraid enough, the goddess's power would come out. I knew it would.

"Please don't ask this of me," I whispered.

His expression hardened, his jaw tightening.

I opened my mouth to tell him that I wouldn't be a liability, that I truly could *help*, but a great rumble rattled the windows. My head whipped to them. "What was that?"

Bavar's mouth thinned, the starkness of his cheekbones looking ready to cut through his skin. My lips parted as I took in the deadly glint in his eyes.

"That, Ms. Meyers, were the wards. They're being tested. Squad Three, Wyatt, Nicholas, I fear they've arrived."

Terry scowled. "And backup isn't here."

"I've alerted the Fae Guard while we wait for SF backup." Bavar checked his remaining straps. "We won't be in this battle alone."

"But the Fae Guard aren't here yet either," Bishop said.

"Regardless, if the wards fall, we will fight." Bavar slammed his last sword into place, then began issuing orders. "Lex, on the roof above the potions nook in Eucaladas wing. Charlotte, the balcony off the sewing room in Titun's wing. Heidi—"

When Bavar had finished, everyone turned into a blur. In a blink, Squad Three was out of the room, kicking into action, which left me momentarily alone with Wyatt as Nicholas waited in the hallway.

"Avery, I need you safe." His expression turned to stone, a cold mask descending over his features. Gone was the tender, loving wolf from my bed this morning. Gone was the man who'd nipped my skin and playfully kissed my neck. In his place, an alpha warrior had been born, and murder shone in his eyes.

My shoulders fell, a deep feeling of resignation tightening my insides. No matter what I said, no matter what I did, no matter how strong the power was flowing inside me, he would never see me as strong enough to fight.

And we were out of time for arguing.

I eyed Nicholas, who watched us from the door, before I sighed in defeat. "Fine, I'll go to the room."

CHAPTER TWENTY-TWO

AVERY

The Whimsical Room was small, cramped, and filled with such heavy magical wards that it made my head spin. Not to mention there was nothing whimsical about it. It was more like a prison cell since it was bare stone with no windows, and the only furnishing was a lone narrow bed that couldn't be more than two feet wide.

I figured the name was intentional. Its poetic title promised fluffy pillows, endless candlelight, and fragrant rosebuds. It was the perfect way to lure an unsuspecting individual into the room so they could be locked inside against their will.

How fitting.

"Charming, is it not?" Nicholas stood, lounging against the wall, his feet crossed at the ankles as I sat cross-legged on the bed. He wasn't more than two feet away from me since the room was so tiny.

When Wyatt had rushed me down the stairs, it'd been on the tip of my tongue to ask why the rest of the household staff wasn't also being taken to the Whimsical Room, but then I saw the room.

It was big enough for me and Nicholas but barely.

"I suppose it could be worse," I replied, albeit a tad bitterly. A hum of annoyance still flowed through me. "I'm still surprised they didn't let you fight, since you're an old and strong vampire."

"As an SF consultant, my business lies strictly in the libraries." He raised his hands. "Alas, I'm not allowed to fight as I'm not a trained SF member, much like you."

I huffed again and eyed the single fairy light, which hovered in the middle of the ceiling, illuminating the raw stone walls that looked cut from a mountain.

Nicholas sank to the ground, drawing his knees to his chest, but he still bumped into the bed.

"You can sit on here with me if you want." I waved to the end of the bed.

"Oh no." He shook his head. "If your commander found me on that bed with you, I fear that my time in this charming room would have been for naught, since he would no doubt murder me."

I laughed, thankful for the ease of tension as worry

continued to pull at me. Who knew how long we'd be in here.

Despite being angry with Wyatt for not letting me help, I would be lying if I said I wasn't also afraid. I had absolutely no idea what was going on at surface level. Even though the entire estate had vibrated each time the wards had been tested while Wyatt raced me down a long spiraling staircase cut deep into the earth, nothing down here moved. Absolutely nothing.

The wards and spells in this room were cloaked in so much magic, it was as though we were in our own realm.

Knowing my internal thoughts would drive me crazy, I switched subjects. "What happened between you and Wyatt? Why does he hate you so much?"

"You picked up on that, huh?" Nicholas sighed and leaned his head against the wall. His blond hair looked as soft as silk, the strands brushing the tips of his shoulders. "It's a rather long and boring story. I'm sure you don't care to hear it."

I lifted my hands. "Looks like we have nothing but time right now, and no other entertainment to speak of."

A sad smile lifted his lips. "Well, I suppose I could divulge a few details." His gaze dipped to the floor. "He hates me because of something that happened with his sister."

My lips parted. His sister. I narrowed my eyes, wracking my brain for what I knew of his family, but nothing came. Come to think of it, I knew nothing about Wyatt's family at all.

"Her name is Lassa," Nicholas continued. "Beautiful and *mischievous* Lassa." He *tsked*.

I cocked my head.

He sighed again. "Oh, all right. I'll tell you everything." He shifted on the floor as though settling in for a long chat. "I met Lassa a few years ago when I was at the SF, consulting again for the Bulgarian libraries. The first time I saw her, she was on the grounds and was unaccompanied. Naturally, I thought she was SF staff, especially since she so confidently maneuvered the walkways. I honestly had no idea she was Major Jamison's younger sister and that she was merely on the grounds because she was visiting him. And I had no idea just how young she was. As you know, or as you once knew before your memories left, in our community, a young face can be quite deceiving. I've met women who look like they're thirteen years of age, but in reality they're really six hundred years old."

I nodded in understanding. Even though I didn't remember experiences, I still remembered random *things*. "You mean like a vampire, or a fairy who cloaks their true appearance?"

"Yes, or a very talented witch who specializes in illusion spells."

"So you thought Lassa was older?"

"I did. I had no idea she was sixteen. She told me she was twenty, and I believed her."

I grimaced, already guessing where this was going.

He took in my expression. "Exactly. Suffice to say, I'll spare you all the flowery details, and only reveal that Wyatt found us in a rather compromising position. And when Lassa realized that her trip to see her big brother was about to land her in a world of trouble with her parents, she turned on me. She said I'd attacked her, compelled her, and she hadn't willingly complied to be with me."

My mouth dropped. "He thinks you *raped* his sister? But surely he can't still believe that. If you had actually done that, you'd be in prison, and you certainly wouldn't be a consultant for the SF."

Some part of my brain knew that if a vampire compelled a supernatural, they could be sent to prison if the compulsion was deemed evil enough.

Nicholas again sighed. "Yes, logic does deem that if I'm free now I didn't commit the crime, but I was initially arrested and detained. After investigating the matter, the SF eventually determined that I'd done nothing wrong. Lassa was found guilty of lying. If she

hadn't been a minor, she could have faced serious consequences. But as she was, she was banned from ever
visiting SF grounds again."

I shook my head. "I still don't understand. What's the
problem? You did nothing wrong."

Sadness entered Nicholas's eyes. "To this day, Wyatt
still believes I took advantage of his little sister. He no
longer believes that I raped her—I have a feeling I would
be dead if he did—but he doesn't feel I'm entirely innocent either. In his eyes, I seduced his baby sister and
took her virginity. And let me tell you, he is one protective older brother. I pity the man she eventually ends up
with."

I forced a smile, irritation washing through me
again. "Yes, I've experienced how protective he can be.
That's why I'm in here."

He laughed humorlessly. "Touché."

"So that's why he acts so growly around you?"

He nodded. "So, there you have it. As I tried to warn
you, it was a rather boring reason and nothing overly
interesting."

"But you bait him," I said, curiosity getting the better
of me. "I saw you goad him a few times in the field I
woke up in."

A mischievous smile lifted his lips. "Well, when it's so
easy to do, even I have a hard time resisting."

I laughed and shook my head. "Vampires."

"Yes, yes, I know. It's not the kindest behavior on my part, but you're correct, it's in my vampiric nature to poke the sleeping bear. It keeps life more interesting."

"Do you think you two will ever reach an understanding?"

He shrugged. "Truth be told, I would like to, and I'm even making efforts to be more gallant. Take you, for example. I've seen how he looks at you. I know that he considers you his mate, so despite my carnal interest in you, I've curbed my . . . appetite." He waved to how he sat on the floor and me on the bed.

My cheeks heated since a part of me knew that if he wanted to unleash his sexual energy I would undoubtedly succumb to it. "Thanks for that."

His lips parted, a flash of fang revealed. "Of course. Now, what should we talk about to keep ourselves occupied?"

CHAPTER TWENTY-THREE

WYATT

I prowled on the roof with Bavar at my side. Leaves from the giant trees that stretched over the pentacle design of the castle brushed the top of my head.

Shudders and shakes continually vibrated the building beneath my soles. The robed warlocks stood on the other side of the castle's wards, each strategically placed around the perimeter. They constantly cast spells that flared off the wards, but they were powerful. Their hits rumbled the ground and tested the ancient magic which protected this land.

Even though I didn't want to admit it, I couldn't help but wonder if the wards were weakening. These supernaturals were *extremely* powerful.

"They're certainly not afraid to attack in broad

daylight." Bavar stood beside me, his hands on his hips. His SF-issued suit gleamed like obsidian in the sunlight which streaked through the trees. On his wrist, his SF communication device glowed, updates from Squad Three constantly coming through.

"They're bold, that's for sure," I agreed. "And I don't know if that's from stupidity, arrogance, or because they know something we don't." I paced again. My wolf itched to run free, but unless they penetrated the wards, I would stay in my human form.

Bavar inclined his head. "True, which I have to say, is worrisome."

"Commander?" Lex's voice came through Bavar's wrist device. "I believe the ward near the south is thinning. Something they threw at it penetrated the dome before it sealed again."

Bavar's jaw locked. He tapped a button on his glowing wristband. "Stand firm. We don't move unless the wards truly fall."

"Copy that."

My skin heated, hairs sprouting on my arms. "How long until the Fae Guard arrives?"

"Any minute. Let's hope the wards hold until then."

Another flare lit the wards up, sending shooting sparks as beautiful as glistening stars over the entire dome.

I locked my gaze on the tall elf. He'd just cast a spell, his magic like nothing I'd seen before. One hit from him was like a rippling tsunami, the wards shuddering and groaning every time he cast.

He didn't try to conceal his form, but his hood hid his face. The robed warlocks were the same. They stood eerily still, only their arms moving and their lips whispering as they cast dark magic.

They worked in unison, their efforts coordinated and precise. My stomach churned, as it had been for the past two hours. I had a bad feeling about what was to come.

My wristband glowed, then Wes's voice barked through the device. "Squads Nineteen and Twenty-two are mobilizing. Five minutes out. ETA 1650."

Bavar nodded. "Good. We'll need them."

I hit a button, letting Wes know I'd received the message. Then I prowled along the roof again, the stone beneath my soles feeling like coarse rock. "If they make it through, and we start to lose, we move Avery."

"Agreed. If the castle falls, she's easy prey. That safe room is only solid if the walls stay standing. The second they start to crumble, the magic may fail."

A rustle of branches a mile out had me standing straighter. I tuned in to the area, filtering out the spells constantly thrown at the castle.

Voices carried to me, then the rumble of hooves and the clang of metal. "That sounds like the Fae Guard."

Bavar smiled. "And not a moment too soon—"

"We have incoming!" Terry's voice shouted through the commander's wristband.

Flashes of light had my head snapping up. My lips parted when a thousand bursts of tiny particles pelted the wards, like a giant had thrown a handful of burning embers onto the dome, millions of them striking at once from all angles. "What the—"

The wards shattered, an explosion of light and showering sparks that knocked me off my feet and flew Bavar onto his back.

"No!" I roared.

I leapt to my feet and shifted mid-air, my wolf landing on the roof in a rumble of snarling rage and hackled fur.

Below us, the robed men advanced, taking advantage of our momentary distraction and knocked state.

Lord Godasara tipped his head back, the hood of his robe falling from his face.

He looked exactly as the picture depicted him.

Large pointy ears curved from the sides of his head, twice the size of fairy ears. And his skin was darker, like ripe green olives, while his hair was the shade of snow.

"Good Gods," Bavar whispered, coming to his feet. "He truly is alive."

Shouts carried from below as Squad Three mobilized. Spells flew. Arrows whizzed.

And around the castle a giant rumble abruptly shook the earth.

My wolf snarled as my human mind observed the events happening around us.

Bavar's face paled as he unsheathed his weapons.

The Shroud Forest suddenly came alive, its branches and vines twisting and flowing together until they created a gridlock of tangled wood and bark.

"No," Bavar whispered. "He *is* an elf lord, one that controls the forests. It will take precious time for the Fae Guard to hack through that." He pointed his dagger toward the trees' branches that had all woven together. In his other hand, his sword gleamed in the sun, as sharp as a razor's blade.

A shimmer of magic materialized by the arching bridge over the creek. Twenty SF members appeared—Squads Nineteen and Twenty-two had arrived via portal keys.

"Thank the Gods. We'll need them." Bavar launched himself off the roof, his figure arcing to the ground as the robed men advanced and fought.

Lex, Terry, Marnee, Bishop, and Charlotte were

fending them off, fighting two at a time, but the arriving squads quickly jumped in, making it two SF members to each warlock until the Fae Guard joined us. Then we would outnumber them even more.

Lord Godasara's head tipped back, his gaze finding mine. His lips lifted in a knowing smile before he blasted a spell right at me.

Rage exploded in my chest as I blurred to the left, dodging the spell. I snarled and then leapt into the chaos below—heading right for the ancient elf that wanted to take my mate.

CHAPTER TWENTY-FOUR

AVERY

The minutes turned into hours. Nothing, absolutely *nothing* was happening in this tiny, heavily warded room. I had no sense of day or night. I would have had no sense of time either if it wasn't for the watch Nicholas wore.

When we reached hour four, I abruptly bolted upright on the bed.

"What if they're all dead?" The horrific thought made my skin pimple. I lay back down and turned on my side, peering over the edge at Nicholas. He lay on the floor beside me, as he had been for hours. My breathing grew rapid. "What if they lost to the elf lord and the warlocks, and that's why nobody's come down here?"

Nicholas swished his hand. "Not possible. Meestry assured me that if the estate falls, the door automatically opens. It's a safeguard measure so we're not trapped in here forever." He shuddered. "Can you imagine? A vampire locked forever underground with the only food source being you?"

I made a face. "I'd rather not imagine that, thanks." Vampires couldn't die even if they didn't have food. They'd simply turn into withered fleshy skeletons if enough time passed without drinking blood.

So while *I* would eventually die, Nicholas wouldn't. And I felt very certain that would only be after he'd drained me dry, his bloodlust getting the better of him.

"But have no fear," Nicholas said, probably scenting my terror. "That won't happen."

"Thank the Gods." My stomach stopped twisting with nerves. If the door hadn't opened, then the estate hadn't fallen, which meant Wyatt probably wasn't dead.

"Hungry?" Nicholas asked when my stomach gave another growl.

I slapped a hand over it. It was the second time in ten minutes it'd growled, but it felt wrong to be wishing for food when people I cared about were fighting at this very moment. "I'm fine."

He arched an eyebrow. "Clearly you're not. You're ravenous from the sounds of it, and truth be told, I'd rather not hear your stomach growling at me every two seconds."

I sighed. "Okay, okay, so I'm hungry, but what can I do about it? There's no food here."

"On the contrary, you may be delighted to hear that I have food and drink."

I cocked my head. "You do? Where?"

"Why, right here." He pulled a bag out from under the bed.

"How long has that been under there?"

"The entire time. One of the squad members gave it to me when they were frantically packing things. Something tells me they're used to seeing to all matters on short notice."

"Well, that was thoughtful." My stomach growled again when Nicholas pulled out a plate of haphazardly packed food and drink.

He handed it to me. "It's all yours."

"You don't want any?"

"Oh no, I fed yesterday. I'm most fine."

I took it tentatively. It still felt wrong to be eating at a time like this. Squad Three could be fighting for their lives right now, and I was about to enjoy a picnic.

"Avery, just eat," Nicholas said. "You can't stop what's happening out there, and it'll make you stronger if you do need to run or fight."

I sighed. He was right.

I peeled the cloth away from the top of the food and

stared in amazement at the selection of meats, cheeses, fresh fruit, and breads. Beside the platter was a thermos of some kind of drink.

Still feeling guilty, I pinched some meat, cheese, and bread together, making myself a mini-sandwich before I popped it in my mouth.

Flavors from the fairy food burst across my tongue, but I managed to control my moan. It was one thing to eat simply for hunger and another to actually enjoy it.

I ate quickly, only having enough to fill myself comfortably. When finished, I unscrewed the drink, sniffing first since I had no idea what it was. When the potent scent of ale or wine didn't greet me, I took a long swallow.

A sparkling feeling coated my tongue, like bubbles dancing across my skin, before a light aroma graced my senses.

"Interesting." I took another drink. "I've never had this fairy drink before."

"May I?" Nicholas held his hand out. "I've had most fairy drinks and foods. I can probably identify it for you."

I handed it over, and he took a long swallow. When he finished, he handed it back, his eyebrows slanting together. "Hmm, that is a strange one. I can't say I've had that drink before either."

I took another long swallow, something about the beverage making me want to drain it dry. "At least it tastes good." I gulped down another mouthful, and that strange feeling drifted through my senses.

"Right you are," Nicholas agreed, holding out his hand.

I handed the thermos back to him, and the minutes ticked by as we savored the fairy beverage. Since the ravenous hunger I'd been feeling had abated, I packed the rest of the food away.

"Feeling better?" Nicholas asked when I gave the platter back to him to store under the bed.

"Yes." A strange sensation washed through me. My nerves tingled, my stomach tightened. I shivered as a rush of awareness swam through my veins.

"You're looking quite flushed," Nicholas said as he placed the food and drink under the bed.

"I feel kind of—" I brought my hands to my cheeks. They felt warm. "Funny."

I lay back on the bed as a rush of dizziness swept over me.

"My, oh my." Nicholas also leaned back. "Is the room spinning?"

"Are you feeling weird, too?" I raised a hand to my head. A strange sensation crept over my mind, like a fog blanketing the ground.

"I am feeling quite . . . unusual," he admitted.

"What was in that drink?" My words were slurring. I placed my palm on my head again. The dizziness lessened, not fully disappearing, but in its place, something was uncoiling deep in my belly. A tightening. A thrumming. A *need*.

Nicholas inhaled sharply, then said in a breathy voice. "I don't know, but I have to say, you smell . . . delightful."

"Delightful?" I slurred.

Another flush swept over my system, and the tightening in my belly moved farther south. I moaned when a sharp sense of longing clenched my core. My breasts tingled. My nipples peaked, and my body . . . Gods, I felt on *fire*.

"Avery," Nicholas breathed. He sat up. His pupils were completely dilated. Stark need filled them. "Your scent . . . your scent is calling me."

My eyes rolled back in my head as I arched upward. Aching desire clenched my womanly area just as another feeling of dizziness swept through me.

"Oh Gods, I'm so horny," I whispered. Carnal hunger tightened my insides, my core swelling with desire. I felt so achy, so tight, and I *needed* to be touched. "What's happening?" I managed to ask, my voice breathy sounding.

Nicholas crawled up onto the bed beside me, his black eyes hungry. So hungry. "I fear we've been drugged," he said, also slurring.

"Drugged?" I replied sluggishly as my gaze fixated on his mouth. His perfect mouth. "Who gave you the food and drink?"

"The dark-haired one. The siren." He reached for me, groaning. "I shouldn't. I shouldn't do this, but the need . . ."

The world turned into a blur around me. My body was so hot that it rivaled the underworld, and a perfect and beautiful man was lying beside me. Exactly what I needed.

Wyatt.

An image of Wyatt slammed into the front of my mind. I scrambled away from Nicholas.

"Gods, what's happening?" I clung to that thought of Wyatt, that one coherent thought which reminded me that even though I didn't remember the history we shared, I still wanted *him*, not the vampire.

"Avery," Nicholas purred. "You have no idea how much I've desired this." His hand slid over my stomach, caressing my hip and *fuck me* if my entire body didn't buck from that simple touch.

"I can smell your arousal." Nicholas crept closer to

me, his long hard body pressing into my side. "You smell divine, like hot sex."

In a blur, he was on top of me, and my thighs parted automatically as I struggled to maintain control of my mind. The fog was creeping in, pressing down on me, weighing on the sliver of consciousness that was still *mine*.

No, no, no.

I struggled to maintain control of myself, but then an incessant need to have a cock—*any* cock—fill me, grew and grew.

What's happening?

The fire licked my insides. It consumed me. *Burned* me. Begged me for release as a deep-rooted throbbing took hold of my soul.

I would have begged any man to fuck me.

And then the fog descended, my mind swallowed whole.

The man on top of me nuzzled my neck. A sharp graze of teeth scraped my skin.

A moan left my lips. I needed a man inside me. I knew it was the only thing that would quench this painful desire that was trying to kill me.

"Yes," the man breathed. In a heartbeat, his shirt was off, his chest a portrait of smooth muscle, chiseled flesh, and pale skin.

"Wyatt," I breathed, the name tugging at the back of my mind, but for the life of me I didn't know who Wyatt was.

The man on top of me descended, his clothed hips grinding against me as his rigid length prodded my core.

But I still had pants on.

"Damn," he whispered. He tried again to spear me, but our pants stopped him, so he descended on my neck and a sharp pain cut my skin.

The man moaned and began taking long pulls. Something warm and liquid trickled down my skin, but the sensation that came with it—Gods—the feel of this man pulling from my neck was heavenly.

I moaned and arched, my back coming off the bed as the fire raged inside me. Good Gods, what was he doing to my neck? It felt *so good*.

I threaded my fingers through his hair, gripping him to me in ecstasy.

"Don't stop!" I cried.

And then the door opened.

CHAPTER TWENTY-FIVE

WYATT

Blood coated my naked chest. Bishop was in a similar state. The estate's walls shook around us. Fine plumes of dust came from the walls with each vibration. The entire Titun wing had just fallen even though Squads Nineteen, Twenty-two, and the Fae Guard still fought.

The Fae Guard had managed to hack through the trees and join the fight, but it hadn't come without a price. The trees had fought alongside the elf, the ancient elf lord bringing them to life to fight as living soldiers. The Shroud Forest had turned into a weapon of branches and massive weight impaling, knocking, and slinging fairies from the Fae Guard as if they were small children.

I'd thought for sure that once the Fae Guard arrived

it would be an easy win for us.

But such hadn't been the case. Not since the elf controlled the forest.

We were losing, the wards were long gone, and the castle was crumbling, which meant it was time to get Avery out.

"Hurry," I called to Bishop as we flew down the hall. "We don't have much time."

Bishop, also nearly naked, hurried behind me.

Simple shorts covered our lower halves, courtesy of the SF witches who stored the modest material in our wristbands. But we were barefoot, our feet slapping against the stone floors.

As soon as my mate was safe, we would join the battle again. Fear still filled me. I had no idea what her return to earth would bring, but we were out of options.

"Time until the evacuation team arrives?" Bishop asked when we rounded the corner at the bottom of the spiraling staircase.

Cold stone walls greeted us, along with the scent of the failing safe room wards. The sharpness of it stung my nose as we blurred to the Whimsical Room.

"Five minutes. Maybe less. We grab them and go. Understood?"

"Yes, sir."

We blurred to a stop at the door, my heart pounding

with adrenaline. I activated the ancient ward that surrounded the Whimsical Room with the key Bavar had given me. The ward shuddered and then groaned as the door cracked open.

Anticipation built in my stomach.

"Avery, we need to—" My words caught in my throat at the sight that presented itself.

Nicholas shirtless.

On top of my mate.

Grinding against her.

He sucked from her neck, *drinking* from her as he undulated against her in sexual waves.

She moaned from beneath him, her legs wrapped around his waist even though she still wore pants.

"Don't stop!" she cried, desire coating every word.

The vampire was trying to fuck my mate. He was trying to take what was *mine*.

"Oh shit," someone muttered beside me.

Time stopped.

My heart exploded.

A ferocious growl ripped from my chest.

Then all I saw was red.

A wave of power barreled into the room, but I barely noticed it as erotic sensations washed through me again and again. A mouth was attached to my neck, sucking and pulling, as fire raged through my veins. But it wasn't enough. I needed *more*.

A ferocious roar tore from someone's throat, bone-chilling rage coating that single guttural sound.

The mouth sucking my neck vanished. Cool air washed over my skin. The body that had been on top of me was gone. A chill settled upon me, and I whimpered in confusion.

The fog in my mind grew heavier and denser.

And the fire. Gods, the *fire* inside my core burned and burned. Fuck. I wanted to *fuck*.

Another roar filled my ears, a savage inhuman roar.

"Wyatt, no!" someone yelled.

The sound of limbs being pummeled.

The sickening sound of flesh being ripped.

A strangled cry before someone yelled, "Wyatt, you can't!"

Then a rush of air and hands were on me.

"Avery!" someone yelled. A hand tilted my neck, and a snarl followed. "He compelled her and *drank* from her!"

I opened my eyes, my brain so sluggish, but the need was *so great.*

Hands were touching me, and the scent that accompanied the hands—oak and pine. Gods, he smelled *good.*

Yes. Touch me!

I moaned and writhed, wrapping my legs around his hard body. I sought his cock, *needing* it in me.

Another angry growl. "Fucking hell, she's still in his thrall, and we need to get her out. *Now!*"

"Wyatt, I didn't . . . we weren't . . ." a sluggish voice called. "She gave us a drink that was—"

"Shut the fuck up!" the man holding me roared.

A kick thumped against flesh, and a pained groan followed.

Another man bent toward the one on the floor. "Wyatt, we still have to evacuate him! Even if he drank from her."

"No! Leave him. The bloodsucker dies! Compulsion on a wolf's mate is punishable by death!"

Then my body was off the bed. The hot, hard hands gripping me threw me over a shoulder.

"No," I moaned. My eyes drifted back in my head as the unrelenting rapture again consumed me. I rubbed my thighs together as I jostled on the shoulder.

I needed release. I needed to climax.

But we were moving. Running.

Oh Gods. *The fire inside me.* It was going to burn me alive. I needed to be filled. I *needed* a cock inside me. The cock that belonged to the man that smelled of oak and pine. Something about him called to me. I needed him.

But the world turned into a blur.

Air rushed past me as we flew up and around, up and around.

We were in a staircase, spiraling, going to the surface.

But the man wasn't fucking me, and I was going to die if he didn't fuck me!

"Please! Please!" I sobbed.

A guttural growl so loud and burning with so much rage was the only answer I got.

Why isn't he fucking me?

Then the sun was on my face.

A warm breeze on my cheeks as I was jostled on the man's shoulder.

Now we were running outside.

Shouts.

Vibrations.

Cries of pain.

Trees swirling through the sky.

Magic everywhere.

Is this a war?

"How could he? How could he?" someone growled over and over while the world was a blur of color, magic, and explosions as we raced as silently as a ghost. "I was finally starting to trust him."

We reached a clearing and stopped.

Sunlight bathed my face.

But the *need*. The need inside me was so great, and nobody was taking it away!

"We're ready for her," someone called.

I was heaved off the shoulder, placed back on the ground. My body swayed, air kissed my skin, and a vague part of me realized something was wrong with me.

Wait. No. I needed the man in front of me.

That's what was wrong.

I began to peel my shirt over my head, but his hands stopped me.

I snarled, anger consuming me. *Why was he stopping me?*

Moss-green eyes that bled to gold stared down at me. "You need to get out of here, Little Flower. I can only pray you stay safe on earth."

Little Flower?

Then someone gripped me from behind.

The man with moss-green eyes released me. He took a step back. Blood smeared his naked chest. "Take her to headquarters."

"Yes, sir," the person behind me replied. He gripped my arm and began to say words I couldn't understand. *"Open key for though I ask, I need a door for—"*

A flash of something whipped past me.

"NO!" The man with moss-green eyes lunged forward, a look of horror coating his face, but somebody else had grabbed me. Somebody extremely powerful and incredibly fast.

So *fast.*

"Avery!" the man coated in the scents of oak and pine yelled.

But I disappeared into the trees, and the trees *moved,* closing around us. The world turned into a dizzying blur as the person carrying me moved like the wind.

"Finally, I have you, and the goddess's power will be mine. Finally, it will be *mine.*"

A portal appeared in front of us, and the man's arms wrapped around me. Something poked my neck, and a rush of cold doused my veins as blackness started to descend on my vision.

A guttural roar came from the man with moss-green eyes. It was filled with so much fury and fear that the force of it threatened to consume me. He tore through the trees, desperation blazing in his eyes before he leaped.

The tall man holding me laughed, and then the portal winds swallowed us whole.

BOOK FOUR
SUPERNATURAL INSTITUTE

Avery

I fell into the clutches of those hunting me. Now, I'm enslaved in chains and at their mercy.

But I'm not the woman I used to be. My weaknesses have been stripped away, unveiling a strength and defiance I never knew myself capable of. And I'll be damned if I'm going down without a fight.
Because my mate is coming for me.

With him by my side, we will be unstoppable, and I am a storm cloud of rage ready to be unleashed.

Wyatt

I can't think. Can't breathe. Can't exist...without her.

I failed to protect Avery, and now she's imprisoned by them. Still, I won't give up. I will bite and claw my way to her, and when I do I will unleash my wolf on any who dared harm her.

Because failure isn't an option. Not when a realm is at stake and my mate's life is on the line.

I can only hope that I'm not too late.

ABOUT THE AUTHOR

Krista Street loves writing in multiple genres: fantasy, sci-fi, romance, and dystopian. Her books are cross-genre and often feature complex characters, plenty of supernatural twists, and romance in every story. She loves writing about coming-of-age characters who fight to find their place in this world while also finding their one true mate.

Krista Street is a Minnesota native but has lived throughout the U.S. and in another country or two. She loves to travel, read, and spend time in the great outdoors. When not writing, Krista is either chasing her children, spending time with her husband and friends, sipping a cup of tea, or enjoying the hidden gems of beauty that Minnesota has to offer.

THANK YOU

Thank you for reading *Hunted by Firelight*, book three in the *Supernatural Institute* series.

If you enjoy Krista Street's writing, make sure you visit her website to learn about her new release text alerts, newsletter, and other series.

www.kristastreet.com

Links to all of her social media sites are available on every page.

Last, if you enjoyed reading *Hunted by Firelight*, please consider logging onto the retailer you purchased this book from to post a review. Authors rely heavily on readers reviewing their work. Even one sentence helps a lot. Thank you so much if you do!

Made in United States
Troutdale, OR
11/27/2024

25372059R00222